WICKED MERCY

A WICKED LOVELY COLLECTION

MELISSA MARR

WICKED MERCY

QUALITY CONTROL:

This work has been professionally edited and proofread. However, if you encounter any typos or formatting issues, please contact

assist@melissamarrbooks.com .

Tales of Folk & Fey (2019)

Dark Court Faery Tales (2019)

This Fond Madness (2017)

Co-Edited with Kelley Armstrong (with HarperTeen)

Enthralled

Shards & Ashes

Co-Edited with Tim Pratt (with Little, Brown)

Rags & Bones

WINTER DREAMS

Set before *Wicked Lovely*

1990

The Summer King rarely missed his Mother's court. Keenan had been born as the child of Summer and Winter. He *chose* sunlight, that was the secret no one seemed to realize: He could have chosen ice.

Sometimes he thought he could have been happier in the Winter Court, but he had a duty to the leaderless Summer Court. Summer had needed him, and Keenan wanted to *matter*.

"Summer is dying," Tavish had whispered.

"You are so much like your father," Niall had said over and over.

"When you're of age, you'll save them," they both swore. "Better to rule a weakened court than be a servant to the Winter Queen."

But Keenan wasn't a mere child now, and his fantasy of rescuing *anyone* was barely a flicker of hope. He might not be a servant, but lately, he didn't feel like much of a king. The world was blanketed by snow more often than not. Crops died, and animals starved. His own faeries shivered under layers of furs and he was . . . useless.

And no one cared. No one noticed. No one seemed to realize he was on the verge of giving up. Somehow the Summer Court still believed in him, and his mother . . . the Winter Queen? She would gaze at him in fear, in hate, in shivering rage. They thought he was the kind of king he wasn't sure he could ever be.

Keenan doubted he'd ever be strong enough.

The curse meant that he was bound, unable to be at his true strength unless he found the one mortal in all the world who was carrying his sunlight. And he hunted for her, letting dreams guide him to this or that place. Somewhere out there a mortal was meant to be his, and the surety that every curse could be broken drove him when he wanted to surrender.

Today, he stood in a wooded area, and he clung to that truth. She was out there.

The trees, coniferous and towering, were dressed in ice and snow. The ground under his feet crunched as his boots came down on frozen grass and fallen needles. The air was chilled, reminding him that winter grew stronger and stronger. It was barely fall, and yet the earth looked like it was nearly Winter Solstice.

"I must find her," Keenan whispered.

The trouble was that finding his queen now carried a cost. He *had* found the one mortal in all the world, in all the centuries, who seemed perfectly suited to him. He loved her. Still.

Perhaps, he was doomed as his father once was—to love a woman who hated him. His own mother hated him enough to torment him because he reminded her of the man who betrayed her.

When Keenan was a child, he'd summon heat or spark life

in plants buried under thick layers of snow. And every time he did so, Beira, the Winter Queen, would rage. The more she raged, the more Keenan realized that his mother was kindling her hatred of his father—and in that icy rage she felt for the man who wronged her, she hated all things Summer.

She hated her son.

He looked too much like the last Summer King, and so he dressed in clothes that were mortal-made, a gesture to remind the approaching Winter Queen that he was, in fact, not the king she still hated.

"Sweetling," the Winter Queen greeted as she arrived for the test to determine his latest choice's fitness for the role of queen.

"Mother." Keenan let sunlight fill him, pulled on the strength of his court so he could face his opposition. He glimmered, casting sunlight that danced over the plants that Winter had frozen in her wake.

"Shall we dispense with this one?" Beira asked. She'd arrived alone, save for one other faery. The Winter Queen still enjoyed some measure of pageantry, and she swept toward him as if they were in a palace. As she moved over the ground, the length of a thick, black fur cloak trailed behind her. He thought, briefly, that it might be a grizzly bear's pelt, but he chose not to ask.

Keenan gestured toward the clearing. "Let us commence."

He'd like to pretend there was a chance that Tracey, the mortal girl he'd chosen, was his missing queen, but faeries can't lie, and even the Summer King was not above that law.

Winter walked away, preparing for another trial. As no one thought the outcome would be anything unexpected, Beira was almost pleasant.

The other faery, however, was not. Try as he might, Keenan could not stop the thrill that filled him as he looked at her. *Donia.* Although he smiled at her, the last woman who *had* loved him enough to risk the curse was now glaring at him.

"Another one who sees that you are not worth it," Donia said, voice no less musical than when she was a mortal. The ice that filled her only added richness to her words. "Tracey won't take the risk. She'll refuse."

"I know . . . and it's better that she doesn't." He paused, resisting the urge to touch her only because it would pain her if he did. His sunlight might be weak, but she was a creature of ice now.

"I still wish *you* were the one, Don," he whispered.

She looked away.

He still thought she was the most beautiful creature he'd ever seen. Her blond hair had faded to the white of a snow squall, and pallor made her lips seem blue, but she was still as beautiful as she had been before she'd taken over as the Winter Girl.

Together they walked over to the mortal he'd chosen, Tracey, for the ceremony that everyone knew wouldn't happen.

Tracey didn't love him, and he couldn't see her as the Summer Queen. He shouldn't have selected her. She was fragile in a way that he knew would make her an unlikely match, but she was lovely. He'd seen her dancing in patch of sunlight near him. He'd been *glamoured*, invisible to mortals. She was happy, dancing in the light, and he'd wanted her to live forever.

In that moment, that flicker of affection, he'd chosen her.

In truth, he hadn't truly encouraged her to risk the cold. He had, instead, spoken of a lifetime in the sunlight, knowing that she wasn't his destined queen and unable to bear the thought of her misery if she tried to accept the test. Lately, he wished none of the former mortals had to endure either of the curse's two options. If there was another way to break the curse without risking them, he'd do it.

"I wish you'd suffer the way I do," Donia whispered from his side.

"I do suffer, Don. I swear to you that I do." Keenan glanced at her, barely resisting the need to touch her. "You *know* I do."

"Tracey?" Donia said, louder now.

The latest in Keenan's long list of failed loves smiled at Donia and Keenan both. This part of the test was inevitable, the words unavoidable. Some traditions—and all curses--were as laws for faeries.

The Summer King knelt before Tracey. "Is this what you freely choose, to risk winter's chill?"

"Oh..." Tracey watched him—and he knew his skin glowed brighter as summer's flames flickered just under the surface. At such moments, he no longer looked anything like a mere mortal. For this moment, Keenan *was* Summer made flesh.

"Tracey?" he prompted, hoping she wasn't going to say 'yes.'

"It's not what I want," she said, sounding apologetic. "You're wonderful, Keenan, but . . . I don't want to be a queen. I'm not *her*. We both know that."

Curses were inflexible, though. Keenan had to say the words. Every single time, he said them. This was no different.

"If you agree to try and are not the one, you'll carry the Winter Queen's chill until the next mortal risks this." He paused, glancing at her, willing her to refuse. "Do you choose the test?"

Tracey shook her head. "I mean, I *understand*. . . and I'm sorry, but . . . I can't."

He whispered, "I know. . . ."

He beckoned to the Summer Court advisors, Niall and Tavish, who had arrived as soon as the test began. They gave Beira a wide berth, but both fey men watched her cautiously as they approached Keenan.

"Would you see Tracey home?" he asked.

Tracey hugged him. "You'll find her. I just know it."

Keenan wished silently that he still believed that.

Tracey giggled suddenly as the vines that wrapped every Summer Girl stretched and shivered over her skin. "They tickle."

"They *also* keep you alive and stronger," he told her.

"You saved me." Tracey smiled at him. "Someday, you'll find the person to save you."

Keenan nodded and looked at her, not sure what to say. She was a friend, but she was also his responsibility now. Every Summer Girl was. Like plants in need of sunlight, they stayed near him.

In a rare moment of kindness, Beira waited until Tracey left to behave in her usual way. "That was depressing," she said. "No one to *save* you . . ."

"Must we do this, Mother?" Keenan met the Winter Queen's gaze, seeking the remnants of the faery who had once loved him a little at least. Her love had always been capricious, but he remembered moments of it. Perhaps nothing of that maternal love was left under her bitterness and rage.

The Winter Queen's response was to exhale ice all around them, knowing the pain it caused him.

He stood in the sudden carpet of ice and snow, watching Donia's eyes fill with ice and her lips tint blue.

"Well, isn't that the way of life?" the Winter Queen said. "You're pitiful and alone, again."

Keenan, however, wasn't sure if he was intentionally selecting those who wouldn't be his missing queen—or if such a person simply didn't exist.

What if she'd died? What if the curse was worded in such a way that the one girl he needed had died centuries ago? Or what if the Winter Queen had sent her minions to kill the girl when she was found? *Could* they locate her? Were they as unaware as he was?

Donia, the current Winter Girl, was the last one who'd

attempted to be his queen and failed. That was almost half a century ago. Before her was Rika, who was currently living in the American desert, as far from the cold as she could be.

Keenan stared at Donia as he said, "My heart wasn't in it this time. It's already full."

Donia widened her eyes slightly. She stared at him, silent, but he knew she understood.

His mother, however, laughed in that horrible, chilling way of hers. "*Still?*" Beira asked. "After all these unfortunates, you're pining after *this* one?"

The Winter Queen stroked an icy hand over Donia's hair, leaving it glittering with snow crystals that, for a moment, seemed like diamonds. "Donia would've been a harsh queen once she realized how useless you are, Sweetling."

Keenan turned and walked away before Donia could answer. The truth was that he didn't deserve Donia. Fate had made that clear when she wasn't the keeper of the missing summerlight—but he loved her.

Still.

He feared that he always would, and the curse was so much more awful because of it.

When Keenan left, Donia felt the usual mix of longing and rage. As a mortal, her reaction to him had been far different. The mortals he romanced never knew *what* he was until they were near the point of changing. By then, it was too late. Their mortality was gone, and the only choices were risking the cold or being a part of his collection of vine-wrapped Summer Girls.

Donia wouldn't have turned back, even if she knew what he was. She wouldn't have surrendered the chance for eternity with him. That was the secret that she couldn't quite face. She couldn't entirely blame him—because she chose the risk. She chose love. She chose duty. And if she had to do it all again, Donia would still choose *him*.

Half a century ago, Donia had been young, poor, and dreaming of the sort of romance she read of in books. And there was Keenan, her own Prince Charming. He was everything. Handsome. Charismatic. And he listened to her, truly heard her ideas and thoughts. Of course, she thought he was *the one*.

He would arrive to see her, pulling up to her home driving a beautiful green Jaguar convertible or a deep red Triumph Roadster. To own *one* car was unfathomable to her, but to own two? He dressed smartly, took her on wonderful dates where they'd dance and laugh, and she imagined a life of such joy. She thought they'd grow old, have a family, and dance forever. She'd felt so lucky.

Donia had loved him wholly and that love had not faltered when she discovered that he wasn't human. He was, quite simply, a faery *and* still her fairy tale prince. Keenan was perfection to her.

So, when she faced the choice Tracey just had, Donia had accepted the challenge—and she'd been living with the pain of her failure for half a century now. She'd lost everything for loving him, and he'd lost nothing.

"Pack your things," the Winter Queen ordered, forcing Donia's gaze away from the weakened Summer King.

"Already done." Donia knew the pattern.

"Good. He'll move us now," Beira said, and then she was gone, too.

Save for guards that Keenan tasked with her safety, Donia was left alone in a clearing. Tracey was escorted away, cared for by the Summer Court advisors. The Summer Girls always were. Beira went off to gloat. No one cared about Donia's aching heart—not when she lifted the staff and was filled with ice, and not now when she watched another mortal lose everything for Keenan.

The Winter Girl was always in the unique position of being hated by both Summer and Winter Courts. The Winter Queen never forgave those who loved her son enough to attempt to break the curse, and the Summer King was always at odds with her. Her very function in life—as a result of the curse—was to convince chosen girl after chosen girl that she should resist Keenan's affections.

Donia, like the others foolish enough to risk everything for

Keenan, was cursed for loving him. Filled with ice as a reminder of her loss, each Winter Girl could only be freed if she *failed* and another foolish former mortal took the test.

"I don't need you," she muttered toward the Summer King's guards, who trailed behind her when she turned toward her current home. That home, too, was temporary. The Summer King never stayed long in the town where the last Summer Girl had been found. He'd follow some instinct or whim. Whatever the reason, he'd move his court, and Winter would follow.

For all that his power was bound, they were still beholden to his whims. The curse was placed about nine centuries ago, long before Donia was born, and the result was that the Summer King spent his life hampered, weakened by the binding of his power, ruling with half of his sunlight hidden away in a mortal. And he had to find *her*, one mortal in all the world.

Girl after girl had been romanced by the Summer King, given her heart to him and her mortality. He didn't *seduce* them physically. That was a particularly twisted bit. Those who truly loved him, who were willing to take the test to see if they held Summer, never knew him physically. Those who didn't love him, who refused the test, became Summer Girls. They knew him intimately—needed his touch to survive.

And Keenan knew they didn't love him.

In her calmer moments, Donia could admit that it was a cruel curse for everyone involved, but seeing the man she'd risked death for romancing other women year after year didn't leave her very calm. Feeling aches down to her very bones didn't make Donia feel forgiving.

Knowing Beira made Donia understand why the curse was so dark. The Winter Queen was a creature of rage and bitterness. Add that to all faeries' propensity for clever curses, and it was no wonder that the curse was awful.

Donia walked, invisible to mortal gazes, to her rented cabin.

She'd liked living here, surrounded by trees. This, too, she couldn't keep.

Because of him.

Who knew where they'd end up?

They'd live in the new place for a few years until the Summer King found the next potential queen. It was a horrible way to spend an eternity: she had forever to watch him woo woman after woman, knowing that he was telling them the words he'd once said to her, whispering their names, listening to their dreams.

Donia was almost to the cabin when Sasha, the wolf who was her companion animal, loped toward her. Sasha, like most sentient creatures, tried to avoid the Winter Queen. No one with sense wanted to be in Beira's presence for long.

A twinge of empathy for Keenan filled Donia as she thought about growing up under Beira's loving care, but the Winter Girl had no time for sympathy, especially for him.

She walked in quiet peace, silent as the path grew thicker with snow and the areas where mortals lived were far from sight. This part, the peace of nature, was her one true solace in her life of late.

He'd steal that, too. He always did. And Donia, for all that she wished otherwise, still loved him. Love was her curse, her flaw, her downfall over and over.

THE WARMTH at her back let her know Keenan was there. He sought her out after every failed test, as if she were a consolation prize.

"You know, I still wish you were the one," he said.

"Can we not?" Donia continued walking, not looking back.

"Don . . ." He caught up with her, so they were walking side by side.

"Every time, Keenan, every single time this happens you

come to me. What am I to do? Live an eternity with the scraps you have for me between your romances?" She glanced at him, hating the way her heart still reacted as he smiled. Fifty-some years had passed since she'd had the right to look at him with these feelings. Half a century of being the fallback prize stung.

"You know I—"

"No." Donia stopped and glared at him. "We talked about this. I will not hear those lies. Not again."

Keenan, as predictable as seasons once were, said, "We can't lie. You know that, Don."

Her breath was coming out in angry puffs that undoubtedly caused him pain, but instead of backing up, he reached out so his hand was near—but not touching—her cheek. "There is no one I *have* to romance today. So, why can't I be here with you?"

"Because there will be." Donia looked away from him, before she let herself give in. "I'm not her, Keenan. I will never, ever be the one you want."

"You will *always* be the one I want," he argued. "I want *you*, Donia. Now. Before. Later. That's not going to change."

"Fate disagrees," she pointed out.

"The curse not selecting you isn't about what I *want*." He moved so she was looking at him again. "I can't undo the curse, but if I find her, you and I will *both* be free. The Summer Girls will. The world will thrive again. I *have* to find my queen for all of us."

"When we met, you offered me everything, but look at my life . . ." She shook her head. "I understand why you do it. I do. I just don't want to be the second-choice, too."

"You're not!"

She exhaled a plume of frigid air. "The curse says otherwise."

"The curse is about the girl who has my sunlight. She's a vessel." Keenan ran his hands through his hair in frustration. "That's not *fated love*."

"It is fated matrimony," Donia snapped. "And you *always* love them. How can you say you won't with the one who will be your queen? Arranged or not, once you find her, you are forbidden to me. I will not be someone's mistress!"

Keenan took a breath, visibly restraining his temper and sunlight. "Have I found her?"

"No."

"Then I am free to romance you, am I not?" The Summer King gave her a smile that made logic and restraint vanish, and she hated him a little bit for it.

At the end of this, whether the next mortal or several mortals from now, he was going to be belong to another woman. How was she to let her heart begin to heal if Keenan wouldn't let her go?

"Don, please?" Keenan knelt in the snow and stared up at her. "Let me have more time with you."

"Give me peace for now," she half-ordered, half-asked. "Speak to me again when we are moved."

He smiled, hearing her acquiescence. Over and over, he broke her heart, and Donia had no idea why she couldn't resist.

One day, she swore, *I will refuse for good.*

IRIAL

Irial couldn't explain why he felt so drawn to this town. He walked around Huntsdale, Pennsylvania as if there was something that would jump out and answer the anxiety plaguing him.

The main street of this little town was a mix of buildings that hadn't seen better days in longer than even he could fathom. Humans were so peculiar. Why did they stay here? Why did they let poverty and disease eat them alive instead of moving somewhere with work? The simple idea of permanence in misery confused the Dark King—and he and his kind fed on the ugliest of emotions. If he could feed on humanity's misery instead of only fey pain, he might set up a home here.

He couldn't, though, so why did he feel like he wanted to stay here?

Irial summoned the Wild Hunt, sending his summons out of the bond he had with the leader of their nightmarish crew. *"Come to me."*

As he walked, invisible to mortal eyes, Irial studied facades that were presumably once attractive, but now bore telltale signs of age and decay. Stubborn weeds sprouted from cracked sidewalks and half-abandoned lots. It was a mundane town, steel tracks and abandoned train cars. There was nothing magical here. Sure, there was a portal to Faerie, but he was the Dark King. He could always find entry there.

The Summer King and Winter Queen had both relocated there, and as much as he tended to try to stay clear of their drama, this was one of the times he couldn't.

He was standing under a building, staring up at it, when Gabriel drove the Hunt through the streets of the steel town.

The Dark King inhaled the roil of terror and panic that accompanied their arrival before he turned to watch them. Cars, motorcycles, and beasts surged through the city. In Faerie, forever ago now, these steeds could wear whatever form they wanted all of the time. When invisible, they sometimes still did, but as centuries slipped away they became increasingly likely to take forms of machine over creature. A few skeletal horse-like steeds exhaled noxious clouds as they panted from whatever speed they'd used to reach him quickly.

Near the front of the mass of writhing, straining creatures and machines, stood the faery who was as close to a brother as Irial had in either world. Once he would've used that word for the long-dead Summer King, Miach, but he was centuries dead now. And while the Dark King wouldn't admit to Gabriel that he was always relieved to see the Hound uninjured, Irial still allowed himself a moment of thanks that his oldest living friend was here.

"Getting slower with age," Irial said in greeting.

The massive Hound snorted and swung a meaty fist toward Irial. The laughter it elicited in all of them eased the worst of Irial's anxiety. They were neither slow nor easily countered.

"Why am I called to you?" Gabriel grumbled.

Irial studied him. "Busy?"

"Later," Gabriel muttered, glancing back at his mate.

As Irial looked over the assembled group, he noticed the

increased presence of piercings. The toxic metal caused them pain, as it did all things fey other than royal or unusual exceptions. The Dark Court fey had developed a recent predilection for piercings that were popular among mortals, as if creating their own pain was pleasure. Admittedly, they tended toward silver, but Irial saw a few scattered Hounds with a steel ring or stud in his or her skin. They'd switch out, but Irial couldn't help but appreciate the pain-pleasure he drew from them.

"I will expect answers," Irial said.

"See Rabbit," Gabriel muttered in a low enough voice that Irial had to wonder what crisis that would lead to, but today was reserved for the uncomfortable need Irial had felt to find and guard the missing mortal girl.

He walked over to stare up at the unsightly iron-coated building, closer than most fey could go. From above him, he saw the curtain slide to the side and a woman stare down at him. She looked familiar, although he couldn't imagine why. As he stared at her yet again, his memory tickled. Could she be the child of a faery he wasn't recalling? There were reasons this mortal called out to him, eliciting protective instincts.

"Why do I care about *this* one?" Irial asked as Gabriel approached, a roll of fear accompanying his steps as if it was a tangible cloud.

"This one?" the Hound echoed.

"*She's* here," Irial said quietly. He didn't need to specify that he meant the one human in all the world who could change the shift of power between the faery courts. The girl the Summer King sought was here. As creator of the curse, Irial knew. He'd always known.

"Here?" Gabriel motioned out toward the dying city.

Irial caught his eye and then looked up at a window of the building. The curtain dropped closed, so it was simply a covered window, but she was in there. "No. *Here.*"

A look of worry came over the muscular Hound. "And what do you ask of the Hunt?"

"I want her protected, from all of them, from us," Irial scowled. "The mortal and her mother."

Gabriel scowled. "Protect . . . *mortals?*"

And despite not understanding why, Irial felt a tightening around his chest that made no sense whatsoever. It felt like a *geas.* What vow had he made, though? When he tried to understand, he felt an absence, a missing space in his mind that was only possible if the High Queen had been sinking her magic into his skin or if he had been cursed.

"Iri?"

The Dark King shook his head. "Keep them safe. I need to run an errand."

"Chela could do this," Gabriel offered. "I'll be at your side on the errand. If the other courts are here, you'll need to pay your respects to Beira."

Irial clasped his friend's arm. "I need to go to Faerie first."

At that, Gabriel stepped back. He wasn't eager to step foot back in the place where they'd been first formed. It might be the original home of the fey, and the Wild Hunt might be allowed free roam there, but the wild energy that the High Queen wielded was disquieting to the steeds that made up the Hunt. They preferred this side of the veil—and so the Hunt trusted that instinct.

"We shall guard them," Gabriel vowed. Ogham marks spiraled over his skin, confirming the Dark King's orders, and with that, Irial turned away from the window that had drawn his attention so strongly.

For reasons he couldn't explain, he paused and looked back. "She has the Sight. Moira Foy. She's Sighted, and she has . . . she has fey blood, Gabriel. Dark Court blood. I feel her, not just because of the curse on the Summer King. Her mother, too."

The entire Hunt had heard.

Irial met the gazes of the steeds and Hounds alike. "She might be *their* missing mortal, but she is of *our* court, somehow, too. Someone I know is parent to these mortals. No High Court fey may know of their heritage."

He thought of the fate of the Sighted. Eyes gouged out. Lives cut short. The fey were notoriously private, not liking their affairs to be the business of mortals. Those who saw them knew not to speak to them, not to spend time with them, not to be near to them at all if possible.

And as much as he needed answers from the High Queen, he decided not to share this detail. She collected the Sighted, but these mortals had Dark Court blood.

"Protect them," Irial stressed, sending the message out over the lines of connection he had with the entire Dark Court. "No Summer or Winter may harm them. Your lives for their safety if we must."

No one questioned his orders. They wouldn't when he was willing to unleash the Hunt to protect them, but he questioned it.

Why do these mortals matter?

When they arrived at the dingy town of Huntsdale a few weeks later, Donia thought she might have to seek out the Summer King and question his sanity. She had decided she wasn't agreeing to his request to court her, although she would have to see him soon to share that decision. Her heart missed Keenan, but her head wasn't seeing the point when the courting could lead to nothing.

Her heart objected.

And so she'd avoided any contact with him. Now, however, they settled in this new town, undoubtedly to find the next mortal girl.

The town was not thriving. She remembered the poverty she'd known and seen in her mortal years, but this wasn't much better. The town had a lot of alcoholism, despair, and a desperation to "get out." She'd seen that over the years, sometimes in the girls Keenan chose. She wouldn't admit it, but sometimes she thought he knew this or that girl wasn't the one he needed, but he still wanted to save them. In a few cases, Donia had wondered if the curse of eternity with the Summer Court was anything other than a *gift*.

Trust him to find ways to use a curse to help people.

Donia smiled to herself. He really did have a good heart and a drive to rescue those in need—which was why she was questioning why he'd brought them here to a city of steel and sorrow. Huntsdale was thick with steel-laden train yards and steel buildings, brick structures decorated in wrought-iron balconies.

The ground outside the city even had an unusual stink of iron in the soil itself. The majority of the fey who were seeking shelter here would find the town deadly. Donia was no exception.

"What are we doing here?" she whispered. Only the guards might hear, but the worst that could come of her question was a conversation after a guard reported her words to the Winter Queen or the Summer King.

"It's covered in steel," Donia continued.

Sasha, her wolf companion, joined her as Donia found them a cottage outside the iron-laden city. Her temporary home was in one of the few wooded areas in reach of Huntsdale. It was small and isolated, and she knew that both the Winter Queen and the Summer King would hate it. Beira was fond of old elegant homes and servants. Keenan had never moved beyond the need to live with a crowd.

Donia couldn't blame him entirely. The Summer Girls depended on him the way plants relied on the sun and soil. Having his advisors there was another matter altogether. For centuries, they'd shared homes, and to be truthful, she found it peculiar. Keenan argued that families lived together, but it wasn't the same. Sasha was all the company Donia needed—and Sasha was out roaming as often as possible.

The way Keenan filled whatever home he had with caged wildlife was another confusion point for her. Birds weren't meant to be indoors; she was certain of it. Admittedly, however, the reptiles Keenan collected likely benefitted from the Summer King's presence. Many living creatures did. He was the sun, warm and nourishing. He evoked joy and passion. His temper might be fierce and destructive, but rage was rare. Mostly, the Summer King was a pleasure to be near.

I would benefit in his presence, she thought. The Winter Girl reminded herself of that often. Keenan had chosen her, and now she was in daily pain. His love was bad for her.

Even though it felt so natural and right.

Feelings weren't always enough. Relationships—especially with a king—were not easy. Keenan was a cursed faery king,

He's not mine.

Donia felt a bit like an old woman sometimes, and lately, she'd realize that she'd been in this world as long as many a grandmother. And she'd been alone for most of it. No child. No spouse. She'd spent years as if in stasis. Her body, however, was not changed from when she'd been a girl. Loving Keenan had led to immortality, and as time passed, she started to think that eternity, at least, might have been a gift.

She was as strong as when she was mortal. Her health was unchanged—aside from the weakened state that iron caused and the constant chill of winter inside her body. Unless she was murdered, Donia had eternity in front of her. Sometimes she thought about the future, but in her imagination Keenan was still there. What foolishness it had been to fall in love with a faery!

I can resist him.

She thought about Rika, who had no love left for Keenan but whose heart was as surely walled up as if it had been made stone. Suffering under a curse did terrible things to a woman's ability to trust—and worse still, the only ones she could love were faeries. Mortals aged and died. So, Donia was caught in an in-between, nurturing her mistrust for faeries because of the curse, yet somehow still loving Keenan.

In truth, she was lonely.

She always thought—*hoped*—that eventually the fey could have their revelries among the trees near where she would make her home. In every city, she thought of it, hoped for it, but they never did. They wouldn't. No one got too close to her, as if Keenan still had a claim—or maybe they were simply afraid to draw the attention of the Winter Queen.

Beira was the worst of winter. She seemed to have forgotten the beauty of the first snow after a hot summer, or the gentle breeze that swirled snow into ephemeral images. Beira had become rage, blizzards, and pain. And many faeries were terrified of her.

Sometimes Donia was, too.

The rush of warm air outside the door heralded his appearance. There was no way to avoid the Summer King.

Before he could knock, Donia opened her door and stepped back. "Come in."

He smiled, beautiful and tempting, wicked and lovely, and her heart broke a little more. "You said when we arrived at the next place."

"It usually takes longer," she pointed out, stalling on telling him that she couldn't let him court her.

He shrugged. "I wanted to see you."

"But *here*?" Donia motioned outside. "This city is not . . . normal for you. There's so much steel. A thriving railroad, and-
-"

"It's where a faery queen would hide," Keenan explained. "The steel would protect her. I'd felt summoned here before, but I'd resisted, thinking I was wrong. Now, I feel it again. We've never looked in such places, thinking she couldn't bear the stench of iron either. If she carries the sunlight, surely, she'll be like us in some ways . . . but what if that was wrong? I thought this was what we missed, and when I felt called."

"You felt called here, then?" Donia pressed. She wasn't

entirely sure how it worked. Why this girl but not that one? How did he know? Or was it completely random?

"She's mortal, Keenan. She doesn't know she should hide." Donia shook her head.

He shrugged. "Maybe I'm wrong, but if I am, you and I shall simply date longer while I wait to find the right possible mortal."

A small sliver of her heart thrummed at the realization that he'd rushed everything, endangered all of them, so he could romance her. Fey and mortals alike needed him to succeed—not avoid his quest.

Keenan loved her in his way, and as much as she hated the reality of what that meant, she still gloried that her feelings were returned.

"But do you really think she's *here*?"

He paused, guilt clouding his face, and then he said, "I can feel her here, Don. It's different this time."

Donia sighed. "You always think that. She's never where you look."

"I know."

Suddenly, Keenan looked so despondent that despite everything, she felt a rush of guilt this time. She hated the well of compassion that bubbled up inside her, and from the way he smiled at her then, he knew what she was feeling. He *always* knew. It wasn't magic, or faery gifts or something. It was simply him. No one had ever understood her as he did.

"I want to be with you," Keenan whispered. "Sometimes I'm afraid I'm not looking enough because I spend my time dreaming of you. I picture you as my bride. Consort. . . lover."

Although she was nowhere near a girl in years lived, Donia still blushed like one as he looked at her.

"I think of you like that," Keenan continued.

Donia shuddered, but forced a laugh. "We'd destroy everything. Ice and heat, Keenan. It hurts just to touch you."

"Is it worth it, though?" Keenan stepped so close that Donia's clothing felt like it would burn her.

She let out a small sigh, a soft cloud of icy air. Her decision burned up in the heat from his nearness, and without a word spoken between them, Keenan knew.

He saw the opening, her weakness, and asked, "Come out with me tonight? No one needs to know."

"Fine." Donia shrugged, as if it meant little. She stared at him and insisted, "It's not a date, Keenan. It's two friends who—"

"We're friends?" He sounded far too excited by that, as if it was a gift, an unexpected one at that.

"We aren't enemies," she allowed. There wasn't a word for what they were. They weren't simply acquaintances. "Lovers" was wrong, but so was "enemies." He looked so hopeful, as if her admission changed something. It didn't, but she still understood that hope. The Summer King was wrought of hope and joy. Believing impossibilities came naturally to him, despite everything.

Donia held his gaze. "We might as well be friends."

"I'm glad." He took her hands, squeezing them carefully.

And Donia tried to keep the ice inside her body controlled, much as he obviously was keeping the sunlight under control. His touch hurt, but it was worth the pain.

"I miss you when we are at odds, Don," he whispered. "I hate the way you dwell on my weaknesses, and I know you *must* because of the curse, but . . . I hate it. I hate you, of all people, thinking about all of my flaws month after year after decade."

"I am as bound by the curse as you are." Donia resisted, tugging away as he pulled her closer. They'd done this too many times, this apart-and-together dance. She wasn't his mistress, but sometimes *that* was the closest example she had to what they could be—and it wasn't enough.

"What would happen if I kissed you?" he asked.

"Don't." Donia pulled her hands away. "You break my heart over and over, Keenan. What would *you* do if I found a lover? What if I fell in love?"

Sunlight sparked in his skin, like a firestorm caught inside his body. His already glimmering hair looked like copper-strand left under a midday sun. Donia winced at the pain, the glare of it.

"You wouldn't," Keenan half-asked, half-ordered.

She gave him a sad smile. "The way you feel right now is the way I feel every single time you leave me. You'll make me believe in us again, and then you'll leave me. I can't do this. Every time it breaks my heart just a little more."

His sunlight blinked out. "Don . . . the curse . . ."

"It's not the ice, Keenan. It's *you*. You destroy me," she said, trying to impress the truth upon him. Glimmer of sunlight slid over him, making the frost falling around her glow and melt in tiny puffs of steam.

He kneeled before her as he had the day she accepted the test to be the Summer Queen. "Once more, please? Let me have one more chance to court you."

"*Why?*" She crossed her arms and stared at him. "You need a queen. I'm not her. I'll never be the Summer Queen, Keenan. You know it. I know it. Your advisors. Beira. Why can't you let me go?"

"Because I lo—"

"No." Icy tears clung to her eyelashes. "What would make you let go?"

"Give me the holidays?" Keenan took her hand. "Can we have that dream we once shared?" He paused and offered, "If you give me this, I'll stop pursuing you and focus on finding my queen."

When Donia dipped her head, giving the slightest of nods in agreement, Keenan let out a *whoop* of joy.

Summer was meant to be happy, to revel in the things that were a part of the season—merriment and dance, languid kisses and long nights. Keenan was never sure if it was the curse or his parentage that made him fall into fits of depression. Did it matter why though? It was who he was, and he had no idea how to undo it. All he could say for certain was that Donia was the cure to his worst moods. In her, he found solace and joy.

"You make me happy," he told her. It was the simplest, truest thing he could say. Loving her was hard, and he was well aware that they had no chance at eternity. Today, though, he could love her—and the Summer Court was very much about finding joy in the moment.

He wanted every moment, as if he'd starve without them.

Daring her temper, he leaned in and brushed a kiss over her lips, knowing that it would sting. The brief taste of her lips was better than magic. He felt like he could spark volcanos or scorch deserts. Donia, even now, made him feel invincible. *Love* made him feel that way, as if his every weakness was gone.

She pulled back, but he wrapped his arms around her and rested his face against her icy hair.

"It should have been you," he whispered against her ear. Then he stepped away. Too much touching was dangerous, and not just to his heart. She was ice, and he was sun. There was no way to touch safely, not as often and truly as he wanted.

Someday, when the curse ends, I will make love to her.

That dream was almost as much a drive as freeing his court from the pain they suffered because he was a bound king. In that sliver between freeing his court and reigning with his destined Summer Queen, he would steal a few moments with the one woman he'd truly loved. He would know that joy before he fulfilled his duties. It wasn't enough, but he would have it.

"You're absurd," Donia said, stepping away and giving him a look that he knew well.

He wondered what she'd say if she knew his thoughts. He grinned. "So, we can date until the next one is—"

"Fine." She turned and walked into her cottage. Her voice drifted back. "I expect true romance. Impress me."

She sounded like she was laughing, and he felt lighter at the sound.

"Tonight, then, when the sunlight is calmer," he called back.

Her hand waved behind her, a shower of ice and snow swirled in the air, and then she was inside—and he had a date to plan.

IRIAL

*I*rial reached out to touch the fabric that divided the two worlds, the veil that now separated the world of mortals for the home of his kind.

He pushed his fingers through the fabric and parted it. The material twisted around his hands, holding him captive for a moment. It had always done so, recognizing him as its own, as if it would pull him back to Faerie. In theory it wasn't sentient, but one of Irial's theories was that it was an extension of the High Queen's will.

Irial parted the veil and let himself fall into the world he was technically to co-rule. Balance was the proper system for all of the fey. Each court had a balance—Dark existed to balance the logic and order of the High Court, and Summer existed to keep the ice and cold rage of Winter in check. There were those outside the courts, solitary fey, and there were those that defied classification. The embodiment of War, Bananach, lingered in the Dark Court, but she wasn't truly *his*. Devlin, brother to the High Queen and War, stood at the High Queen's most trusted. And Niall . . . the faery who now stood as advisor to the Summer King had once been Irial's beloved, his

30

intended heir, and in his sorrow, Niall had sought haven here in the arms of the High Queen. He was solitary before all of it.

"You dream of your love," Sorcha said, lowering herself from a swing that seemed tethered to the sky, which for reasons Irial didn't ask, was currently nearly purple with thick clouds.

The weather here was often expression Sorcha's moods, so Irial was cautious, as he took another step closer.

"Push me," she ordered.

There were moments when Irial missed Faerie. This was one of them. He'd missed being around a faery queen who was capricious and lovely and not trying to skewer him with ice-wrought knives. The Summer King had no love or even tolerance for the Dark, and the Winter Queen seemed angry at all times. The High Queen, however, was the sort of mad that Irial enjoyed. Sorcha was both clever and intriguing. He'd spent enough hours and days with her to know that avoiding boredom mattered more than power.

No fey other than Lady War or Death could have more power than Sorcha. What the High Queen sought in their negotiations was something else entirely. She wanted joy and unpredictability. Irial made it a hobby to offer her exactly that.

"Do you have a secret to share with me, Sorch?" he invited, lowering his voice as he teased.

Sorcha cringed at his bastardization of her name, as she always did, even though Irial felt her spike of pleasure at the act. He tasted her emotion, all fey emotions, and it was the weapon he used to know best how to manipulate other regents. The beauty of dealing with the High Queen was that the tightly controlled emotions of the High Court slipped just a touch in his presence. It was, he thought, why she tolerated his visits.

Once he acquiesced to her demand and gave her swing a push—which obviously she could have achieved on her own—he asked, "What shall I convince you to tell me?"

Sorcha smiled. "I have nothing save for secrets. Which one shall I refuse to tell you?"

"Does it have to do with Niall?" Irial stopped the swing and stepped in front of her. He looked into her eyes. Theirs was an odd honesty, a bond they'd shared over centuries. And the Dark King was well aware that she wasn't this open with most faeries.

"Ask me no questions, Irial, about the things you have forgotten." Sorcha reached out and cupped his face in her hand. "There was a time you asked me to take this knowledge from you. I will not give it back."

"I *asked* to forget?"

Sorcha gave him a small smile. "Yes. You asked. It was your idea, your request to me."

"When?"

Sorcha stared at him, as if she had no idea how to answer that, and Irial was reminded that time was complicated for the High Queen. She saw the threads of the past, the now, and many varieties of the future.

So he tried another question, "Would the future be better or worse if I knew?"

"Worse."

Irial was stunned that she answered so quickly. It was typically a hard question, one that took weighing many lives and many potentials. Carefully, he tried, "Will my lack of knowledge create balance?"

"In some time," the High Queen said.

The Dark King had spent other days, sometimes many in a row, trying to glean truth from Sorcha. "Will she—"

"I cannot answer questions about these halflings," Sorcha said.

He startled. The High Queen rarely allowed such half-fey beings to live in the mortal world. Cautiously, he said, "The curse was that a mortal girl had the sunlight."

The High Queen stared at him and in a droll tone pronounced, "Someone chose to bed one of the mortals who would be Summer Queen."

"Who would dare?" Irial thought about it, the arrogance it must take to risk eternal winter for ruining the terms of the curse. No wonder he had chosen to forget. His rage at such a person must have been intense. He thought about the fey he knew within his own court who might be so bold. *Niall? Gabriel?* Niall claimed not to be Dark Court, but truth will out in time.

"I recognize the feel of Dark Court." He watched Sorcha, seeking verification.

She smiled, knowing full well what he was doing, and he felt the laughter she didn't let slip. After a moment, she confirmed, "No one but the Dark King will notice her ancestry."

The swing backed away from him, pulling the High Queen backward into the air by way of a pair of long tree branches that had grabbed the sides of the swing.

"Even I cannot lie directly, " she said. "I will speak plainly: you, Irial, asked me to take this knowledge from you. It was a curse, devised by you, and I placed it on you. You will forget *again* after this one either is chosen or is not. Your court will forget. The Hunt will forget."

Such a curse was extreme. What had prompted it? Why had someone been so foolish as to bed the mortal meant to be the Summer Queen?

"Did he love her?"

"Thelma?" Sorcha asked. "Yes, he loved her enough to remake the world. And I . . . cared for him enough to make it so."

It *had* to be Niall. Sorcha had always been fond of Irial's beloved *gancanagh.* Irial stared at the High Queen, thinking about the questions he could ask. As she hurtled back toward him, Irial let the shadows that were extensions of his court loose. They caught her and slowed her, so that she was perfectly still in front of him.

His shadows held her aloft there and he asked the only thing he could, "Why?"

The High Queen leaned in and covered his mouth with hers, stealing his question and offering a distraction.

The swing vanished, and Irial felt a willow tree behind the High Queen. The branches of the willow draped around them, creating a curtain of greenery that granted them privacy.

When he paused in their kisses, Sorcha was crying. "One day you will have your answers. Between the young king's choice of her and the future, you will forget again. You *must*. Do not ask me more, Irial. Do not try to find these answers. Death will come if you do."

And that was all she would say.

*B*ack at the house he was renting, the Summer King was greeted by the scowling expressions of his advisors. Tavish and Niall had been at Keenan's side his whole life. They'd advised his father—and when Keenan was a child, they were his only guests from the Summer Court.

They were his family, and like any family they had secrets and discord.

If not for the intercession of the eldest faeries, those who lived in Faerie, he'd have only known Winter until he reached his eighteenth year. Tavish and Niall had been the ones who started to counter the stories his mother told him. In time, they'd become treasured friends as well as advisors. After nine centuries, they knew him better than he knew himself.

Today, however, Keenan was not as grateful for their insights. He didn't miss the assessing looks they gave him.

"My king," Tavish started.

Keenan shook his head. "No."

"I understand that you have feelings for the Winter Girl." Tavish shoved the long silver plait over his shoulder in a telltale sign that he was agitated. He was very loyal to the court, and his tolerance of the Winter Court or Dark Court was minimal at best.

"Stop." Keenan had listened to more than enough lectures on duty. He knew his duty, and he'd see it through in time. When he'd told Donia he thought the girl was here, Keenan had been serious. He was drawn here, to her, and oddly, he'd been drawn to this area before. He met Tavish's patient gaze and said, "I will take my joy where I ch—"

"Take it with the Summer Girls," Tavish interrupted. "They require your time. *She* does not."

Nearby, Niall sighed and rubbed his head. The second Summer Court advisor was the more emotional of the two faeries—on every topic save duty. There, Niall was quiet where Tavish had been willing to take risks that Keenan wasn't sure he could accept.

Niall was not at ease with conflict. Still. He'd fight, and he'd sometimes allow himself pleasures that were beyond the typical court debauchery. He disliked quarrels, though.

"Are you sure you need this?" Niall asked, drawing their gazes. He rubbed his hair with both hands anxiously. His shorn wood-brown hair stood out at odd angles, and for a moment, Keenan had a thought that he might let it grow finally. It wasn't mere vanity to hope that for him, but a wish that his advisor might finally heal. His close-cropped hair was kept that way to make certain no one missed the long scar that ran from his temple to the corner of his mouth.

"Tavish," Keenan rebuked, glancing back at Niall.

"Joy matters," Niall said with a shrug. "You know that, Tavish." Then to Keenan, he added, "You should see her— unless it will make you hate yourself later."

Those were words Keenan had said more than once to Niall, referring to the Dark King, though. His advisor, for all that he was loyal to Summer, had been a creature of the Dark Court before Keenan's birth. And it took no genius to see that a part of the *gancanagh* still missed the other court. That was one of the many things Summer did not discuss.

The Summer Court was a place of frolic, of leisurely naps in the sun, and naked dancing in the rain. They were not so serious, and they had little time for regrets. In that they were more akin to the Dark than to the Winter Court or High Court.

At that thought, Keenan grinned. "Summer does as it wants, and I want Donia."

Niall laughed at Keenan's boisterous proclamation. He understood impulsivity better than most any fey thing. He'd gone from Solitary to Dark Court to Summer Court. In every iteration, Niall was driven by emotions and *need*. He'd joined the Dark for either love or lust, and he'd left out of rage and betrayal. He stayed with Summer out of some mix of those passions.

"Wanting Winter resulted in your father's death," Tavish said. "The curse we bear now—and for all of these centuries— is Winter's doing."

"And Irial's," Niall muttered.

Keenan couldn't argue, but there were perks to being king. Not as many as he'd like, what with being cursed his entire life, but one undeniable fact was that the king answered to no higher laws. He shrugged. "I do my duties, Tavish. I shall continue to do so. Sometimes, to enable me to do so, I need to remind myself why."

"For a mortal who is *not* your queen?"

"No," Keenan corrected. "She's a woman—a *faery* woman thanks to the curse—and one I love. Breaking the curse will free her and all of them"—he gestured into the house where Summer Girls were giggling and running—"and the world. Forgive me if I need a reminder of why I don't give up."

Tavish sighed and walked away, leaving Niall and Keenan in the room alone.

After several moments, Niall spoke, "I understand."

Keenan waited, knowing his friend well enough to know there was more to say. Finally, Niall met his gaze and added, "The past is the past, though. You can't live in memories."

"The past is why I am cursed and you are my advisor," Keenan said. "My father's past. *Your* past."

Niall said nothing for several moments. He was never at ease discussing his time with the Dark Court, as if ignoring it would erase it. Keenan didn't have that luxury. If he didn't break the curse—and stop Beira's ever-growing power—his court and then the mortals that populated the world would perish.

Logic and hope both said he would find the missing Summer Queen, curses were meant to be broken. The Winter Queen might think she was invincible, but Keenan had faith. Somewhere in the world was a mortal who would save them. He simply had to find her.

Tonight, though, he was going to absolve himself of kingly responsibilities and simply pretend he was a faery who had the joy of romancing the love of his life. He knew that he would lose her when he found his queen, but regrets were the stuff of other courts. He might be a bound king, but he was still the Summer King.

He would figure out how to romance Donia, and he would *also* meet his obligations. Keenan paused as he headed toward his room, snagging a few Summer Girls who spun by him.

"Niall?" Keenan waited until his advisor met his gaze. "Please inform the Dark King that we are here. I saw the Hunt, and I know they are near."

And Keenan pretended not to see the flash of shadows in Niall's eyes. He wasn't sure if his friend knew they were there, but Keenan saw it. The raw truth was that Niall would always have divided loyalties, one even he denied. Eventually, he would need to face whatever he felt for the Dark King. If not, Keenan would be forced to admit to Niall that the element that healed him was not, had *never* been, sunlight.

IRIAL

When Irial left Faerie, he was no more informed than when he arrived. He had once known these mortals—or at least known of them. Tonight, he stood staring up at their building. He was unsurprised when he felt the approach of the one being he'd ever loved. Was the mortal one he'd rescued from the *gancanagh*? Had he hidden them because the eldest one was addicted to his beloved Niall? Or was she the child of his beloved? Why had he asked Sorcha to curse him?

Did Niall know he'd had a child?

Gabriel was the only other faery Irial could imagine protecting, and the Hound had a child already. A half-ling son, and if Irial's suspicions were right, he had at least one more child who was half-mortal.

Niall's daughter.

Irial strolled away from the building until he found a park. Once he was situated, he sent messages over his connections to his fey. *"Bring me my gancanagh. Gently. Trick and whisper."*

The minutes ticked by as Irial found himself at a table at the edge of the park. He sat inside, alone, at a wooden table in a small bar. The building was stone and wood, brick and mortar. Niall could sit here with him in relative comfort.

"Dark King." Niall's voice came from behind him.

Irial felt his abyss guardians, shadows that were both part of him and somehow sentient, surge toward him. He felt the twist of guilt, longing, and lust that Niall quickly crushed. And under it all, Irial tasted love. It was buried, but it was still there. With that, Irial's tension lowered just enough to hide his own feelings.

"Did you miss me, love?" Irial said as he glanced back at Niall.

Although it didn't show on Niall's face, Irial could taste it. *Like honied fire.* Niall had always been such fun.

"No guards," Niall asked. His concern had an edge of genuine curiosity now. "I know you summoned me when you heard I was seeking a formal audience."

Irial pushed out a chair. "Sit."

"Not your lackey."

"Please, Niall?"

Whatever he heard in Irial's voice was enough for his curiosity to flare even brighter. He took the chair, although he pulled it back as if Irial couldn't resist touching him.

Irial smiled to himself. Someday, he'd wear down Niall's fears. He no longer looked at the Dark King with only hate in his eyes. The love—and the lust—were always obvious again.

"Do you ever think about the days where no bed was forbidden?" Irial asked. "Where a woman would slide from my arms to yours? Where—"

"Not if I can help it." Niall's expression tightened.

The wave of lust from Niall that washed over Irial was enough to make the Dark King pause. He shook out a cigarette, tapped it on the table. "Do you ever think of children?"

Niall stilled, and for a flicker of a moment, Irial watched

him. He wasn't sure if he could force the question. Did Niall know?

"Have you any?" Irial asked.

Niall took Irial's unlit cigarette and sniffed it. Carefully, he held to his lips and looked at Irial.

Stunned, Irial lit his cigarette. He didn't let himself think of other times when Niall had allowed him other intimacy that ended with cigarettes and silences. "Feeling bold?"

Niall took a long drag and exhaled. "Earlier, my king mentioned that although he does what's needed to fulfill his duties, sometimes, to enable that, he needed to remind himself why."

Irial watched him curiously.

"I am here to tell you that we are in this town, that my king will commence seeking his queen here." Niall smoked and stared at him for several moments. "I am reminded that I risked death to leave you."

"Do you think I wouldn't risk death to tempt you back?" Irial took Niall's cigarette and lit his own with it. After a long moment, Irial asked, "Are you trying to see if I'll seduce you tonight?"

"I'd refuse."

Irial smiled. "Tonight? Probably. You're not meant for the sunlight, though, Niall. We all know that."

"I have no patience with Winter." Niall still held his gaze, as if whatever urge was riding his nerves tonight was going to tempt him toward actions they'd both regret.

"I wouldn't tell you no," Irial whispered. "But the things you're thinking are no good for either of us."

Shame surged in Niall, and Irial drank it down. Such guilt and shame and lust and anger made time with Niall intoxicating.

Despite that, Irial confessed, "I would never refuse the things I see in your expression tonight, *gancanagh*. I miss that."

He clasped his hands together to resist taking Niall's hand or starting a fight that would lead to a way to excuse what Niall was craving. "But what I still want is something else."

Niall scoffed. "I don't recall propositioning you for *anything.*"

"Answer me this: do you have children in this world?" Irial asked, again tasting the feelings that told the truth in a way no words could: Niall was confused. That meant that if those were his relations, Niall knew nothing of them.

Had we both forgotten? Was it Niall's secret and that's why Irial had asked to forget? There was no one else Irial truly loved.

"What game are you playing?" Niall asked, his voice dropping lower in suspicion.

Irial stood, unable to answer and unwilling to lie.

Then Niall grabbed his arm—and Irial let their connection gape open. He shoved his own lust, need, fear, and possessiveness toward Niall. He stood watching Niall shudder as if he was swallowing rich wine.

Niall pulled his hand away.

"Don't grab me unless you want to hold on," Irial whispered. He hated that the only times Niall touched him for centuries were when he was injured and didn't remember their kisses, nights when Keenan summoned him to press shadows into the injured body of the faery he wished he could drag home tonight.

Or anger.

Irial enjoyed both, but neither was enough.

"I will do what I can to protect what you have made, *gancanagh.*" Irial offered his vow, even though Niall wouldn't understand. The vow was binding nonetheless.

Then he slipped into the night, because protecting Niall's child was more important than giving in to the terrible longing in Niall's eyes. Giving in, despite the pleasure it would bring, would make Niall hate him later.

So Irial made his way out of the bar, and as he walked he sent the lust that was boiling over slide along the tendrils of connection with the court. He knew Niall well enough to know he'd return to wherever the Summer Court was staying and find his pleasure with Summer Girls.

"*I am in need of satisfaction.*" Irial sent the invitation to his court. He'd think of his *gancanagh* doing the same elsewhere in this horrible city, and then soon, he'd approach the halflings that his beloved had surely fathered and find a way to protect them from the Summer King.

There was no way that Niall's granddaughter was the mortal who would be Summer Queen. Irial would help her flee Huntsdale, and then in a few years perhaps he could come to terms with the idea that the missing Summer Queen could be a young woman several generations removed from his beloved.

I may have to ask Sorcha to re-curse me.

IRIAL

Playing mortal used to be easier, but knowing this was Niall's family made his plans fall apart. The girl, Moira, was the granddaughter of a *gancanagh*, of his *gancanagh*, and that made everything seem wrong.

She wasn't mortal.

She wasn't a stranger.

Irial knew better than to speak to the girl's mother. That one, Elena, looked at the fey with the clarity of one with the Sight and anger to go with it. She shimmered in that way that the Sighted always did for him, as if they weren't wholly present. A part of him wondered if the Sighted had fey ancestry —but he noticed these two because of the curse or because they were of his court in some way.

"You're staring," she said, pulling Irial's mind to the moment. The girl was braced against a wrought iron fence, and if he had been most faeries, it would intimidate him. The Dark King was immune to the pain of iron.

"You know what I am," Irial said, not even trying to play at being mortal.

"Maybe." Moira tilted her chin defiantly.

"Good." Irial leaned against the iron fence and shook out a cigarette. "Smoke?"

She hesitated, but it didn't last. The girl had Dark Court blood, Niall's blood, *gancanagh* blood. She leaned toward the forbidden. And with a smirk that made him try to remember another face, Moira said, "Light?"

Irial flinched a little and handed her a lighter. She sounded like she was flirting, and Irial . . . couldn't. Although the Dark King was supposed to embrace taboos, the mere thought of debauching this girl appalled him. Moira was likely Niall's grandchild. That was the only explanation he had that would explain his reactions, and it made Irial slide to the side, putting more distance between them.

"Are you why they all watch me?" she asked after lighting her cigarette and pocketing his lighter.

"Any in particular?"

"Icy ones," she whispered. "And the one who glows brighter. Like you but"—she shrugged—"warm?"

Irial nodded. "There was a curse once, a foolish man cursed a girl, and her daughters and her daughters' daughters."

Moira waited. She shrugged again, paused to fling her thick dark hair over her shoulder, and said, "So?"

"So I want to protect you. I need to keep you safe," Irial said, wondering why the need to do so was so urgent. "They must not see you. One, in particular . . ."

"Him."

The Dark King nodded. "When you're ready, I'll help you run."

"I can't leave my mother." Moira folded her arms over her chest. "You don't under—"

"I'll protect her. My court," he swore. "No one will hurt your mother."

Moira Foy stared at him, as if trying to figure something out. "Do you know why? Why the Dark Court—"

"You know who I am." Irial smiled at the girl. By all rights he ought to react much differently to a mortal Seeing and learning of the fey, but she wasn't just a mortal, was she? Moira Foy and her mother Elena had Dark Court fey blood along with mortal blood. Elena, the girl's mother, felt older than she looked. Irial was certain that one was more fey than mortal. He wasn't sure about the girl beside him. If Keenan saw her, she'd become fey as part of the curse.

"She can't know," Moira whispered. "That you're watching her."

Irial nodded. This one was clever for her age. *Niall's blood.* He pushed off the fence. He wasn't about to linger and draw eyes to her too soon.

"Once he sees you it's too late," Irial warned.

Moira said nothing as she turned and walked away. She certainly had the spirit to lead the Summer Court. Irial tried to see a trace of Niall in her walk or her hair or something. He couldn't find it, but with everything he'd learned from Sorcha and his only reactions, the girl had to be Dark Court. These were the descendants of someone he valued enough to seek a curse.

That detail concerned him. The only love he actually felt was romantic love for Niall and brotherly love for Gabriel. And Gabriel's children were not secret to him. That left Niall, but Irial saw none of his traits in the girl.

Watch these two for ever after, Irial thought-ordered his court. *They are of ours.* He let them see Moira and her arrogance despite fear and he let them see of his memory of her mother, Elena, staring at him not in fear but that same arrogance he saw in many of his court. She was a force.

Irial was still watching the street near Moira's house when Beira approached him. She stared at him in a way that reminded him of long-gone days where they were friends of sorts. When she was in love with Summer, when the three regents flitted from court with comfort. Friends. In maudlin moments, he missed *that* version of the Winter Queen as much as he missed the late Summer King.

"There was a time we all laughed," he said to her. "Do you ever laugh that way?"

"I was weak." Beira shrugged it off. "And I suffer still for it."

Irial kept silent. He despised her statements that were openings to either argue or lie. Irial couldn't *say* that Beira's suffering was a choice, and he couldn't *lie* to say she was right. Trust Her Icy Temper to have found a way to make the *geas* on honesty a way to torture him.

"Do you recognize her?" Beira asked, and Irial didn't need the Dark Court ability to taste emotion. Her curiosity was writ large in her voice and posture.

"Some mortal that wanted a cigarette," he said, not technically lying.

"That's all?" Beira prompted. "Any urge to *seduce* the girl?"

He shivered involuntarily.

The Winter Queen leaned close and whispered, "Or *protect* her?"

"From *what*?" Irial scoffed.

Laughter shouldn't ever make him shudder like hers did. Her sharp-edged laugh thing filled him with horror. *Did she somehow know that Moira was the missing mortal? Had she always known?*

Beira pressed her red-painted lips against his cheek, leaving her make-up kiss over a frost-burned mark. Painting her blue lips didn't change how dangerously cold she was. "That child is a halfling, Irial. We both know it."

Irial stared at her. Whatever he'd forgotten, she knew in part.

"Perhaps. Those are Sorcha's interest not mine." The Dark

King could misdirect well, but he saw no need to try to do so when the truth was undeniable. "Talking to a halfling is not the same as *protecting* them."

"Despite her parentage?" Beira asked, somehow sounding both disbelieving and amused simultaneously. "Isn't that why you watch her? Knowing about the *father*?"

"I owe you a gift, Winter Queen, if you do not harass these halflings." Irial met and held her gaze. "My word that the debt I owe is equal to the worth of these halflings."

The weight of his vow was violent. The *value* of these halflings was immense, even if Irial didn't have logical reason to think so. The Dark King's shadows, the abyss guardian, slithered all over him as if they recalled. He wanted to know the thing he'd forgotten, but Sorcha's words that death would come with his knowledge held him back.

"Vow accepted," Beira murmured. "My court will not tell the High Queen about these halflings. Nor will we take their eyes."

"Or tell the Summer King?" he prompted.

"I thought I already killed him," Beira said cheerily. When he stared at her, Beira added, "Fine. I won't tell my child either."

"You underestimate the kingling," Irial warned her. All curses end, and if there was any chance of peace between them, Beira needed to start treating Keenan as an adult.

Beira scoffed. The Winter Queen didn't take any critical word lightly. She also apparently didn't know Moira and Elena's greatest secret, but he still needed assurances that Beira wouldn't draw his gaze their way. Keenan had already been drawn to the city where his intended queen lived.

The curse is weakening.

If Moira stayed, the curse would be broken. Irial knew it, and as much as he was ready for balance, that wasn't best for the Dark Court. They fed on the darker emotions of the fey, and as such they were almost as powerful as Winter currently.

And it'd not be best for the girl.

Irial walked back to the girl's house, waiting for her to gaze down at him. When she did, he tapped his wrist and whispered, "Time to go."

"Her name is Moira Foy," he announced, sounding more certain than he ever had before when they'd done this. "It's *her*, Don. I know it."

"Keenan," Donia snapped, a cloud of frigid air slipping out with her voice. "She doesn't like you."

"She will." Then he said the words that'd sealed so many mortal girls' fates. "I've dreamed about her. She's the one."

Keenan glowed more than she'd seen in fifty years. There was a spark in his eyes, a flicker of fire she hadn't seen when he's looked at the other girls. He grabbed her hands regardless of the pain it caused in her skin and her heart. "Things are going to get better."

"Congratulations . . ."

"She was leaving town, but I asked. She'll be back in a few days." Keenan glimmered with the sunsparks. "I've found her, Don. I'm sure this time."

And Donia was equally sure. This felt different, but she said nothing.

"Once she says 'yes,' we'll both be free. You won't hurt, and

I'll be at my full strength." Keenan brushed his lips over hers. "I feel it. This is the start of the end of the curse. We can still--"

"I still have to convince her not to love you," Donia pointed out. "I'm as bound as you are."

He nodded but he didn't believe her, not truly. She could see it in his eyes, and as she looked at the way he was smiling, Donia had no doubt she could convince Moira Foy to reject him.

Keenan was half-in-love with Moira already.

It was the nature of the curse, even though he was Donia's beloved, he wasn't hers to keep. She could admit to herself that he was and would always be her "one," her fairy tale prince, even though he wasn't destined to be hers.

What we just had was nothing more than a winter dream. And as the Summer King stared at the building, that dream evaporated. A mortal girl was slowly becoming fey, and soon she'd either reject him or take the test.

Either way, Keenan was no longer looking at Donia. The curse made this sudden love he felt for mortal after mortal inevitable, but that didn't mean it didn't hurt.

"You'll see," Keenan swore. "She's the one, Don. Everything will change now!"

And Donia blinked away her tears before leaning in and kissing his cheek. "I believe in you, Keenan."

She did, and even though she would try to convince Moira to refuse Keenan, Donia now also wanted him to succeed. They all needed Winter to stop growing in power, and Donia needed to be free of him before the love in her heart turned to hate.

The End

AUTHOR'S NOTE:

THIS STORY of Ash Foy's mother—as addressed in my first novel, *Wicked Lovely*—is the story of a young woman who ran away from the metaphorical "demons" pursuing her. In Moira's story, those are faeries. In the real world, there are other demons many of us have wanted to run away from, or spite, or defeat. Ash's mom in the story chose death over the Summer Court. I want to remind you though, that this was a fictional world. Out here in the real world, we keep fighting to overcome. We ask for help. We find a resource. I've watched loved ones struggle with depression and with crises. I've lost friends to suicide, to addiction, and to deaths hastened by other kinds of deadly choices. I have considered suicide, but after some rough patches I decided to seek help. Look to your local resources, trusted friend or family, or suicidepreventionlifeline.org.

OLD HABITS

Set after *Ink Exchange*

PROLOGUE

"You're going to make an excellent king," Irial said.

And then, before Niall could react, Irial pressed his mouth to the long scar that he'd once allowed Gabriel to carve on Niall's face. Niall felt his knees give out under him, felt a disquieting new energy flood his body, felt the awareness of countless dark fey like threads in a great tapestry weaving his life to theirs.

"Take good care of the Dark Court. They deserve that. They deserve *you.*" Irial bowed his head. "My King."

"No." Niall stumbled back, tottering on the sidewalk, nearly falling into the traffic. "I don't want this. I've told you—"

"The court needs new energy, Gancanagh. I got us through Beira's reign, found ways to strengthen us. I'm tired—more changed by Leslie than I'll admit, even to you. You may have broken our tie, seared me from her skin, but that doesn't undo what is. I am not fit to lead my court." Irial smiled sadly. "My court—*your court now*—needs a new king. You're the right choice. You have always been the next Dark King."

"Take it back." Niall felt the foolishness of his words, but he couldn't think of anything more intelligible to say.

"if you don't want it—"

"I don't."

"Pick someone worthy to pass it on to, then." Irial's eyes were lightening ever so slightly. The eerily tempting energy that had always clung to him like a haze was less overwhelming now. "In the meantime, I offer you what I've never offered another—my fealty, Gancanagh, my king."

He knelt then, head bowed, there on the busy sidewalk. Mortals craned their necks to stare.

And Niall gaped at him, the last Dark King, as the reality settled on him. He'd just grab the first dark fey he saw and . . . *turn over this kind of power to some random faery? A* dark *faery?* He thought of Bananach and the Ly Ergs circling, seeking war and violence. Irial was moderate in comparison to Bananach's violence. Niall couldn't turn the court over to just anyone, not in good conscience, and Irial knew it.

"The head of the Dark Court has always been chosen from the solitary fey. I waited a long time to find another after you said no. But then I realized I was waiting for you to leave Keenan. You didn't choose me over him, but you chose the harder path." Irial stood then and took Niall's face in his hands, gently but firmly, and kissed his forehead. "You'll do well. And when you are ready to talk, I'll still be here."

Then he disappeared into the throng of mortals winding down the sidewalk, leaving Niall speechless and bewildered.

Several weeks later

Niall walked through Huntsdale, trying to ignore the responses his presence elicited. He'd never walked unnoticed. Over the centuries, he'd been a Gancanagh and the companion to the Dark King; later, he'd been advisor to both the late Summer King and the current Summer King. None of those were roles associated with dismissal. He'd always had influence. When he was with Irial, he hadn't realized that his companion was the Dark King, but that hadn't meant that many of those he'd encountered were unaware. They knew the influence he'd wielded far before he did.

Dark Court faeries—*my faeries now*—scurried around him. They were always in reach, always in sight, always willing to do the least thing that he required. They sought his approval, and despite wishing he was impervious, he couldn't withhold his responses. Being their king meant feeling a connection to them that he'd only ever felt twice—to Irial and to Leslie. Perversely, perhaps, being the Dark King meant he felt even more connected to both the mortal girl and the faery. Leslie, although she'd severed her tie to Irial, was still protected by the

Dark Court, and Irial, while no longer king, was the pulse of the court.

Worse, Niall could taste the emotions of every faery he passed. He knew the things they sought to hide with their implacable expressions. He knew their pains and their hungers. It made the world flex with sensory overloads.

Niall walked through the door of the Crow's Nest, the mortal club where his closest friend waited. Seth didn't stand when he saw Niall; he didn't bow or scurry. He merely nodded and said, "Hey."

The weight of the job Niall didn't want seemed to slip away. He sat down at the small table in the back of the dim building. The jukebox was turned on, but the volume was at a bearable level this early in the day. A few mortals threw darts; others watched a soccer match on the oversized television; and a couple silently drank their beers. It was peaceful.

Seth pushed an ashtray toward Niall. "What's up?"

Niall frowned. He'd unconsciously pulled out a cigarette when he sat. *The habit resumed the moment I was connected to him again.* Niall stared at the cigarette and refused to remember the first time he'd smoked. *Memories of Irial are never good to dwell on.*

"You look worse than usual today," Seth said.

Niall shrugged. "Some days . . . some days I hate Irial."

"And the other ones?"

That was the catch, the other days. Niall took a drag off the cigarette, enjoyed the feel of the smoke sliding into his lungs. He exhaled after a moment. "The other days, I know he was right. I *am* the Dark King and whining about it is futile."

"You could always give it away, right?" Seth leaned back, tilting his chair so it was balanced on the back two legs.

"Sure. If I want to be a fool." Niall signaled the waitress and ordered a drink.

Once the waitress walked away, Seth leaned forward. "So what *aren't* you saying?"

Niall exhaled a plume of smoke. "I called Leslie."

"Why?"

"I thought I could suggest that we could be friends. Leslie and me." Niall paused, but Seth said nothing. The mortal simply stared at him, so Niall continued, "I wasn't calling to suggest we … date."

"Bullshit." Seth shook his head. "You don't want to be her friend. Listen to how carefully you had to phrase that lie."

"If it were a lie, I couldn't say it."

"Really?" Seth quirked one brow. "Try to tell me you just want to be her friend. Go ahead. Say it."

"I don't think that—"

"It would be a lie, wouldn't it?" Seth interrupted. "Telling me you want to be just her friend would be a lie. You can't say it."

"Why are we friends?" Niall muttered.

"Because I don't lie to you *or* pander to you." Seth grinned. "You don't like being adored or disobeyed … which makes you messed up enough to lead a bunch of crazy faeries, but makes you need a few friends who *aren't* crazy faeries."

They sat silently while Niall accepted the drink the waitress delivered. He'd never had much trouble attracting mortal attention, but he'd expected it to lessen now that the Gancanagh addictiveness was negated. Instead, he was able to touch mortals safely, but was no less appealing to them. In his life, the only one who seemed to want absolutely nothing from him was the mortal who watched him now. Unfortunately, Seth wasn't immune to the traits that made Niall interesting to most mortals. He was simply aware of them—and thus better able to know them for what they were. *Which is why he keeps his distance.* Seth was utterly nonjudgmental, but he was also utterly devoted to his beloved, Aislinn. *And completely hetero.*

The Summer King's ploy of encouraging Niall to watch over the mortal had had a few not entirely unexpected consequences. When Niall accepted that charge, he was still a Gancanagh—addictive to mortals. They hadn't discussed it, but Seth knew why he responded so strongly to Niall: Keenan had expected Seth to become addicted to Niall.

Not that I objected then.

The Dark King shook his head. It seemed perverse that the orders he'd carried out for another regent filled him with more guilt than the things he'd done as a king himself. He still spent time with Seth, and he considered the mortal a friend, but there was more than a little evidence that Seth had some degree of addiction to him.

I was following orders. A few touches on his arm, nothing more than an arm around his shoulders. It wasn't as if anything happened.

Niall reassured himself with the lies he could whisper in his mind, but the truth was the truth. He'd injured Seth, and the fallout was that he was dangerous to Seth. He always would be, and it was difficult not to take advantage of the thread of addiction and the new allure that Niall wielded as Dark King.

Niall reached into his pocket and pulled out a nondescript stone. He slid it across the bar table. "Here."

"A rock. You shouldn't have." Seth lifted it between his thumb and index finger. A look of peace came over the mortal's face. "Damn."

"If you don't want it . . ." Niall stretched his hand out.

For the first time since Niall had become the Dark King, Seth didn't move out of reach. He also didn't release the stone. Instead, he curled his hand around it, so the stone was wrapped firmly in his palm.

Seth laid his other hand on Niall's forearm briefly. "I'd say no one's ever given me such a useful gift, but that seems too slight. It's . . . difficult being around the Summer Court, the

Summer Girls especially. . . . They're good about trying not to manipulate me." Seth paused and looked up at Niall. *"Usually."*

Niall smiled at the memory of the Summer Girls' lack of restraint. He missed them, some more than others, but he doubted that the Summer King would support the idea of Niall visiting them. "They aren't used to restraint. It speaks well of their regard for you that they even try."

"And you?" Seth prompted.

"I noticed your tendency to keep a table between us," Niall admitted.

"It's not personal, you know?" Seth flashed an amused smile then, one Niall hadn't seen in weeks. "If you were female, your . . . uhhh . . . *appeal* would be cool. Not that Ash would be good with me doing anything then, either, but I'm not into guys. No offense."

Niall laughed. "None taken."

As they talked, Seth had kept the stone clenched in his hand. He took a deep breath, laid it down in front of him, and reached back to unfasten the chain he wore around his throat. While he did so, he kept his gaze on the stone, and Niall realized then how difficult it must've been for the mortal to be surrounded by so many faeries. *And me.* Niall could write it off as merely a result of Seth's relationship with Aislinn, but it wasn't because of the Summer Queen that Seth sat here at the table with Niall. Aislinn would be happier if Seth severed ties with Niall; Keenan would be happier too—for entirely different reasons.

Seth slid the silver chain through a hole in the stone, and then he fastened the chain around his throat. When he was done, he tucked the stone under his shirt. "It's like the world got more in control all of a sudden. I owe you one." Seth poked at the ring in his lower lip. "Not that I have any idea how to repay *that* kind of gift, but I will."

"It wasn't given with a price attached," Niall pointed out. "It's a gift, freely given. No more, no less."

"Yeah, well, you don't look like . . . let's just say, it was a little weird looking at you and having thoughts that I *know* aren't what I think of you, and" —Seth bit his lip ring as he obviously weighed his words— "let's just say, not everyone has been as unaware of how they could affect me."

Niall felt his temper slip a little. "Will you tell me who?"

"Nope." Seth grinned. "I'm not offering you an excuse to start shit with anyone, and now that I have this, I think those head games will be entertaining for *me* for a change. It's all good."

For a moment, Niall debated pressing the matter, but part of being a friend meant trusting that Seth would speak if he needed help. Niall tapped out another cigarette. "You'll let me know if you need intercession." He looked at Seth as he packed his cigarette. "I have a few faeries who might find it entertaining to assist you."

"Yeah, Ash would be thrilled if I sent the Dark Court knocking." Seth quirked a brow again. "If you want to pick a fight with him, you'll do it on your own. I'm not planning to give you an excuse."

Niall lit his cigarette. "Just don't forget."

"Not today, okay?"

Admitting defeat, Niall held up his hands.

"So how are you?" Seth prodded carefully. "Are you getting along any better with your . . . predecessor?"

The fact was that Niall did want to talk to Seth about that topic, but he didn't quite know what to say, not yet, at least. He took a drink; he smoked in silence.

And Seth drank his own drink and waited.

"He's gone missing regularly, and I don't know what he's doing." Niall shook his head. He was over a millennium old, and he was seeking advice from a mortal child. "Never mind."

"And you don't want to ask what he's doing, but you feel like you should."

Niall said nothing. He couldn't deny it, but he didn't want to admit it either. If Irial had handed all of the court's back-room bargains, illicit investments, and nefarious dealings over to him, he wasn't sure he'd be ready to be the Dark King, but he felt like he *should* know.

"Either let it ride or tell him he needs to report in more. There's not a whole lot else to say, is there?" Seth gestured at the now open dartboards. "Come on. Distraction time."

CHAPTER 2

It had been hours that Sorcha sat unmoving as Devlin brought forth the business that required her attention. One of the mortals that lived among them was mourning. It was a messy business.

"Should I send him back to their world or end his breathing?" Devlin asked her.

"He was a good mortal; he should be allowed to live awhile longer." The High Queen moved one of the figures on her game board. "Remind him that if he's leaving us, he can't be allowed to see us. You will need to gouge his eyes."

"They do dislike that," Devlin remarked.

Sorcha tsked. "There are rules. Explain his options; perhaps it will inspire him to learn to temper his emotions so as to stay here."

Devlin made a note. "He's been weeping for days, but I'll explain it."

"What else?"

"Some of the discarded paintings were left in a warehouse for the mortals to 'discover.'" Devlin stepped closer and moved a figurine carved in a kneeling position.

She nodded.

"I've not heard any more of War's intentions." Devlin's expression didn't alter, but she saw the tension he was restraining. "The Dark Court seems unaware. The Summer Court remains clueless. . . ."

"And Winter?"

"The new Winter Queen is not receiving guests. I was refused entrance." Devlin paused as if the idea of being refused was perplexing to him. He had existed from the beginning of time, so it was somewhere between pleasing and befuddling for him when a faery managed to surprise him. "Her rowan said that I could leave a . . . note."

"So we wait." Sorcha nodded. The newer fey were peculiar; their methods seemed crude to her sometimes, but unlike her brother, she was not amused by it. It simply *was*. Emotional reaction to it was unnecessary. She lifted another figurine and dropped it to the marble floor, where it shattered into dust and pebbles. "That play hasn't worked for centuries, Brother."

Devlin lifted another piece and replaced it in the same square. "Will you take dinner or will you be in cloister?"

"I'll be cloistered."

He bowed and left the hall then, leaving Sorcha alone and free to meditate for the evening. She stood and stretched, and then she, too, left the stillness of the hall. Even the minutiae of business must be handled in the same way they always had been—in austere spaces with reasonable answers.

Only the swish of her skirt disturbed the quiet as Sorcha made her way to the small room where she intended to spend the remainder of the day. It was one of the indoor spaces where she meditated. The gardens were preferable, but tonight she'd opted to forego the openness of such places in favor of the intimacy of a tiny room.

Her slippers made no sound as she entered the empty

chamber, nor did she verbalize the moment of discord she felt when she found the room occupied. "I did not summon you."

Irial stretched on one of the plush chairs she'd had brought in from a local shop. "Relax, love."

She leveled an unyielding look at the former Dark King. "Faeries of your court aren't welcome in my presence—"

"It's not my court. Not now. I've walked away." He stood as he said it, tense as if he had to restrain himself from approaching her. "Do you ever wish you could walk away, Sorch?"

Sorcha cringed at his bastardization of her name, at the familiarity in his tone. "I am the High Court. There is no walking away."

"Nothing lasts forever. Even you can change."

"I do not change, Irial."

"I have." He was barely a pace away from her then, not touching, but close enough that she felt his breath on her skin. It was all she could do not to shudder. He might not be the Dark King anymore, but he was still the embodiment of temptation.

And well aware of it.

He took the advantage. "Have you missed me? Do you think about the last time we—"

"No," she interrupted. "I believe I might've forgotten."

"Ah-ah-ah, fey don't lie, darling."

She backed away, out of reach. "Leave it alone. The details of the last mistake aren't even important enough to be clear anymore."

"I remember. A half-moon, autumn, the air was too cold to be so"—he followed, letting his gaze linger on her, as if her heavy skirts weren't in his way—"exposed, but you were. I'm surprised there wasn't oak imprinted on your skin."

"It wasn't an oak." She shoved him away. "It was a . . ."

"Willow," he murmured at the same time. He looked satisfied, sated, as he walked away.

"What difference does it make? Even queens make mistakes sometimes." Even though he wasn't looking at her, she hid her smile. She had always enjoyed watching him draw her emotions to the surface, enough so that she'd pretended not to know that the Dark Court fed on those emotions. "None of this explains why you are here, Irial."

He lit another of his cigarettes and stood at the open window inhaling the noxious stuff. If she did that, it would pollute her body. Irial—the whole Dark Court—was different in this as well. They took in toxins to no ill effect. For a moment she was envious. He made her feel so many untoward feelings—envy, lust, rage. It was not appropriate for the queen of the Court of Reason to be filled with such things. It was one of the reasons why she'd forbade members of the Dark Court from returning to Faerie. Only the Dark King had consent to approach her.

But he's not the king anymore.

She felt a twinge of regret. She couldn't justify giving in to his presence now, not logically.

And logic is the only thing that should matter. Logic. Order.

Irial kept his back to her while her emotions tumbled out of control. "I want to know why Bananach comes here."

"To bring me news." Sorcha began reasserting her self-control.

Enough indulging.

The former Dark King was kind enough to not look at her as she struggled with her emotions. He stared out the window as he asked, "I don't suppose you'll tell me what news?"

"No. I won't." She took her seat again, calm and in control of her emotions.

"Did it have to do with Niall?" Irial looked at her then. This odd honesty they had shared over the centuries was something she'd miss now that he was no longer the Dark King. No one save her brother and Irial saw this side of her.

"Not directly."

"She is not meant for ruling," Irial reminded her. "When she took the throne before . . . I wasn't there, but I heard the stories from Miach."

"She is a force of destruction that I would not unleash. I will never support her, Irial. I've no quarrel with Niall"—she frowned—"aside from the usual objections to the mere existence of the Dark Court."

And Irial smiled at her, as beautiful and deadly as he'd always been. King or not, he was still a force to fear. *Like Bananach. Like the Summer Queen's mortal.* Often it was the solitary ones who were the most trouble; the tendency toward independence was not something that sat well with the High Queen. It was un-orderly.

He was watching her, tasting the edges of her emotions and believing she was unaware of what he was doing. So she gave him the emotion he craved most from her, need. She couldn't say it, couldn't make the first move. She counted on him to do that. It absolved her of responsibility for the mistake she intended to make.

If he were to realize that she knew the Dark Court's secret, their ability to feed on emotions, she'd lose these rare moments of not being reasonable. That was the prize she purchased with her silence. She kept her faeries out of the Dark Court's reach, hid them away in seclusion—all for this.

The Queen of Reason closed her eyes, unable to look at the temptation in front of her, but unwilling to tell him to depart. She felt him remove the cord that bound her hair.

"You need to say something or give me some clear answer. You know that." His breath tickled her face, her throat. "You can still call it a horrible mistake later."

She opened her eyes to stare directly into his abyss-dark gaze and whispered, "Or now?"

"Or now," he agreed.

"Yes." The word was barely from her lips before she wrapped her arms around him and gave up on being reasonable for a few hours.

Afterward, Sorcha sat and replaited her hair while Irial reclined on the floor next to her. He never provoked her or pointed out the truth of their relationship during these quiet moments.

He smoked silently until she picked up her garments from the floor. When she held the pale cloth to her chest and turned her back to him, he extinguished his cigarette, moved her braid over her shoulder, and fastened the tight bindings.

"Bananach always presses for war . . . but things feel different this time," she admitted.

Part of politics for them had always been admissions that weren't public knowledge. During Beira's reign, Irial had come to her for solace; when he lost Niall, he had come to her for comfort; and when Beira murdered Miach, Irial had come to her—with all his unsettling presence—and together they had mourned the last Summer King. That was the first time she'd opted to indulge in the glorious mistakes they'd shared the past few centuries.

Today is the last time.

Sorcha finished dressing as she asked, "And Gabriel? Where does the Hunt stand?"

"With Niall."

"Good. There are factions enough already. With the trouble between Summer and Winter and between Dark and Summer . . ." Sorcha let the words fade away, not wanting to speak them into being.

"Niall strengthens the Dark Court. Had I stayed king . . . Keenan would've attacked in time. He's not going to forgive my binding him. Nine centuries is a long time for rage to fester." Irial's regret was obvious even if he didn't mention it.

They, and few others, knew the reluctance of his bargain with Beira. Binding Miach's son wasn't something the Dark King had wanted to do, but like any good ruler, he made hard choices. That choice had given his court strength. Sorcha, at the time, was grateful that Beira hadn't set her sights on Faerie. Eventually, she would've, but then . . . then, it was Summer's fall, Dark's entrapment, and her staying silent.

"So we wait." Sorcha reclaimed the calm reserve that was her daily mien. She gestured toward the door. "In the interim, I will send Devlin to greet the new king on my behalf."

Irial did not respond to her warning. Instead, he unlocked the door and left.

CHAPTER 3

*A*fter centuries of making the transition, Irial still found the journey from Faerie to the mortal world jarring. The differently colored landscape, the disconnection of time, and the hordes of mortals all thrilled and displeased him simultaneously. Faerie was unchanged for all of eternity, but the mortal world seemed to alter in a moment. He marveled at the ways it had evolved in the centuries that stretched behind him, and he wondered what would follow their already remarkable progress. Some faeries found mortals to be little more than vermin, but Irial was enthralled by them. *More so since I am no longer a king.* Of course, he was more fascinated by the faery he now approached.

The new Dark King stiffened as Irial came to stand beside him. It was a conscious effort, however: as Dark King, Niall knew where Irial was for several moments prior to this.

The king glanced at him. "Why are you here?"

Irial lowered his gaze respectfully. "I am seeking an audience with the Dark King."

"How did I you know I was here?" Niall asked.

"I know you, Niall. I know your habits. This space"—Irial

73

gestured at the small courtyard outside the mortals' library—"soothes you."

Irial smiled as he thought of the year it had been built. He'd been bored, and while he couldn't create, he could fill the architect's mind with visions.

"Columns?" the man repeated.

"Strange, isn't it?" Irial murmured. "Utterly impractical. Who cares what a place looks like?"

"Right."

Irial continued, "And there were statues, towering nearly naked women; can you imagine?"

Niall stood staring at the columns that stood on either side of the ornate wooden door to the library. "It always looks familiar."

"Indeed."

"The building . . . it's like somewhere I've seen before." Niall prodded, but he kept his attention on the building as he spoke. "Why is that?"

"It's hard to say," Irial demurred.

Niall glanced his way. "I can taste your emotions, Irial. It's not a coincidence that I find it familiar, is it?"

"You know, my King, it's much easier to get answers when you *order* people to obey you." Irial smiled at a young mother with a pair of energetic toddlers. There was something enchanting about the unrestrained enthusiasm of children of any species. He had a fleeting regret that he hadn't any young to indulge, but such regrets were followed by memories of half-mortal Dark Court offspring who were as easily contained as feral beasts. *Beautiful chaotic things, children.* He'd loved several of them as if they were his own.

"Irial." Niall's tone was testy now. "Why does the library look familiar?"

Irial stepped up to stand a bit closer than his king would

find comfortable. "Because a very long time ago, you were happy in the courtyard of a building very like this one."

Niall tensed.

Irial continued as if neither of them noticed Niall's discomfort, "And I was feeling . . . a longing for such moments one day last century when a young architect was staring at his plans. I made a few suggestions to his designs."

The Dark King moved to the side. "Is that to impress me?"

Irial gave him a wry grin. "Well, as it took over a hundred years for you to notice, it obviously *didn't*."

Niall sighed. "I repeat, what are you doing here?"

"Looking for you." Irial walked over to a bench that faced the library and sat down.

As expected, Niall followed. "*Why* are you looking for me?"

"I went to Faerie . . . to see her." Irial stretched his legs out and watched a few mortals slide around on wheeled boards. It was a curious hobby, but he found their agility fascinating.

With a nervous bit of hope, Niall joined him on the bench— at as much of a distance as possible, of course. "You went to see Sorcha."

"I thought she should know that there was a change in the court's leadership."

"She *did* know," Niall snapped. "No one goes there without her consent."

"The Dark King can," Irial corrected.

"You are not the Dark King." Niall's temper flared. "You threw it away."

"Don't be absurd," Irial said. "I gave it to the rightful king."

The emotions coursing through Niall were a delicious treat. Irial had to force his eyes to stay open as the flood of worry, fear, anger, shock, outrage, and a tendril of sorrow washed over him. It was best to not mention that he could read all of this. In theory, only the Dark King could read other regents, but for reasons Irial didn't care to ponder, he had retained that particular trait. Most of his gifts of kingship had vanished: he was vulnerable to any faery who struck him, and he was once again fatally addictive to mortals. The connection to the whole of the court was severed, and the ability to write orders on Gabriel's flesh was erased. These and most every other kingly trait were solely Niall's, but the emotional interpretation was unchanged.

Even as his emotions flickered frantically, Niall spoke very calmly. "If she had wanted to, she could've killed you."

"True."

Several more moments of delicious emotional flux passed before Niall said, "You can't tell me you're going to be my advisor, and then get killed. A good advisor advises. He communicates. He doesn't do idiotic things that can result in infuriating the High Queen."

Innocently, Irial asked, "Does he do idiotic things to infuriate the Dark King?"

"You are far more trouble than you're wor—" Niall's words halted as he tried to speak that which neither true *nor* his true opinion. He scowled and said, "Don't be an ass, Iri."

"Some things are impossible to order, my king." Irial grinned. "Would you like me to apologize?"

"No. I'd like you to do what you said you would—advise me. You can't do that if you piss off Sorcha enough to get killed or imprisoned or—"

"I'm here." Irial reached out, but didn't touch Niall. "I went to find out why Bananach visits her. The High Queen and I have had an . . . understanding these past centuries."

Niall opened his mouth, but no words came out.

Irial continued, "I needed to know that she wouldn't support her sister in any attempts on your throne. I know chaos is good for the court, but I will not sacrifice you for the court if it is ever in my power. Not again."

"A king's duty is to his court," Niall reminded him.

"And that, Gancanagh, is why I am not qualified to be a king," Irial said gently. "It is not a matter of being tired of my court, or throwing it away, or punishing you, or trapping you, or any of those very diabolical things you would like to believe of me. The court requires a regent who will put its needs first."

"And you think I would?" Niall asked.

"I know you would." Irial smiled to let Niall know that this was a *good* thing, but the taste of Niall's guilt was still heavy. Neither of them commented on what that meant about Niall's loyalties—or the choices Irial had made in the past. *Choices that put Niall second to the court.* There was nothing to say that would lessen the ugliness of those choices.

"If you are my advisor, I *will* know where you are. I will *not* need to worry that you are trapped in Faerie or dead by Devlin's hand because you angered Sorcha," Niall said with more of a snarl than Irial expected.

"Yes, my King." Irial knelt. "Do I take this to mean that my *understanding* with Sorcha is discontinued as well?"

Niall dragged his hand over his face. "Nothing's ever simple with you."

"I can ask her permission to visit her in the future . . . or simply remain here. I'm sure I can find other—"

"Until such time as I say otherwise, you will not enter Faerie," Niall interrupted. "What else did you learn?"

Irial remained kneeling, but he lifted his gaze. "Devlin will visit."

"For what purpose?" Niall made an impatient gesture. "And get up. You're far too amused by this posture, and it's not the least bit about re—" The words froze again.

Irial laughed, but he stood. "It is a *little* about showing respect, my king."

"Irial," Niall started.

"Devlin often seeks respite in the mortal world that he cannot find in Faerie. I have long offered him the court's hospitality; however"—Irial stared at his king then—"Sorcha knows of his visits. I am anxious over this first visit with there being a new king. Sorcha would not be remiss in making a statement. As your advisor, I'm strongly suggesting you keep the Hounds in house. You should also have Bananach's staunchest supporters in your presence. Devlin tends to get bloody in his visits, and this could be a particularly . . . energetic visit. We can make use of that to rid ourselves of the disloyal. It serves several purposes—for us and for Sorcha."

"What aren't you telling me?"

"About this? Nothing." Irial shook his head. "I will stand at your side, as will Gabriel, and we will make quite clear that the Dark Court is not weak."

"We *are* weakened. If we weren't, you wouldn't have done the ink exchanges."

Irial stared at Niall. "The violence Devlin will bring will nourish them. It is part of why I make him welcome. This time, it will nourish *your* court, and therefore you."

"I require more than violence."

"Call some of the Summer Girls, summon the Vilas, a Hound"—Irial paused as he weighed the words—"*anyone* you desire is yours. Human or faery or halfling. Gabriel's daughter is strong enough to relax with you."

"No."

Irial repressed a sigh. "You weren't celibate in the Summer Court."

"I'm not ready to—"

"Leslie is gone, Niall." Irial crouched down and looked at his king. "She left. She needs a life in the mortal world, for now at least. You, my *Gancanagh*, require the pleasures you're denying. If I thought you'd forgive me, I'd arrange them delivered to you as they once were. You weren't so reticent then *or* when you were in the Summer Court. You are the king of the Dark Court. They are all yours to command."

"Now that I'm their king, they might not feel free to say no." The fear in Niall's expression was only a tiny portion of the overwhelming fear Irial could taste. Niall lowered his voice, "I don't want them to feel trapped."

"Don't be foolish." Irial caught Niall's gaze. "I would offer you anything you need. They would too. It's not a trap to offer happiness to one's regent." Irial's affection for Niall was not the least bit hidden. "If you worry, I will collect solitaries for you, or perhaps you ought to go see Sorcha yourself. . . . There are those who are not your subjects. Is that what you seek? Tell me, my King, and I will make it so."

"No. I simply don't want . . . emotionless sex." Niall looked away. "After Leslie—"

Irial growled. "She left."

"I *know*." Niall glared. "It's only been a moment, though, and . . . I can't."

"As your advisor, I am strongly suggesting that you listen to my advice. Don't weaken your court by being mawkish. You've never once been monogamous in your life, and if you think you could've been so with her, you're a fool. You were a Gancanagh. Now, you're the King of Temptation. You are what you are."

"You're a bastard. You know that?"

"I do." Irial stood. "By tomorrow Devlin will be here, and if you expect to be your best, I'd strongly recommend that you go get—"

"I hate that you made me their king," Niall said, and then he walked away.

After he was gone, Irial smiled.

That went surprisingly well.

CHAPTER 4

Niall stood at one of the gates to Faerie. Once he'd marveled that mortals didn't cross it more often, but unlike faeries and halflings, most mortals didn't see the gate. The mortals and halflings who ended up in Faerie were taken or stumbled there unawares. *Which isn't much different from Dark Court faeries.* The High Queen wasn't particularly tolerant of uninvited guests, especially those of his court. The Dark Court's exodus from Faerie had happened long enough ago that the whole of Faerie was her domain, while the mortal world was shared among the rest of the faeries.

Not that I'd want to return the court there.

If Irial could hear him, if Keenan could hear him, if most anyone he'd known these past several centuries could hear how easily he was slipping into the role of Dark King, he liked to think they would be shocked. The truth, of course, was that more than a few of them had accepted his new role as easily as he had. *Because it was inevitable.* He understood that now. When Irial had first offered him the throne, Niall had thought it horrific, but time had a way of removing illusions.

The complications of Devlin visiting the Dark Court were

unclear to Niall. There was obviously some element of the situation that Niall didn't know. Irial was a lot of things, but he wasn't prone to exaggeration. If he thought Devlin's visit was significant, it was.

Niall splayed his fingers over the veil that separated the worlds. The insubstantial fabric encased his hand as if it were a living thing. *I could go to her.* Once, Sorcha had been a friend of sorts. Once, Niall had imagined himself half in love with her. He hadn't been, but she was everything Irial wasn't. At the time, that was reason enough to try to call his friendship love.

"Help."

Fingers grabbed his hand and tugged. Someone on the other side clutched him, grabbed hold of his wrist, and clung to him. The voice that seemed to accompany the desperate gesture was thin.

"Please, I can't see."

A second hand grabbed Niall's arm as if to pull him through, and in the instant, any thought of entering Faerie fled. Niall tugged.

An old man came tumbling through the veil. He still held tightly to Niall's arm. "Please."

Niall steadied him and in doing so glanced down and saw the man's face: both of his eyes were missing. The eyelids drooped over empty sockets. "Who are you?"

"No one." The man wept. "I'm no one, and I saw nothing. . . . I promise."

"You're in Huntsdale," Niall said gently. "Do you know where that is?"

The relief on the man's wrinkled face was heartbreaking. He whispered, "I do. Home. This is where I should be. I was wrong before. I thought … I followed someone, but"—he shook his head—"she was an illusion. It was all an illusion."

There was no need to ask which faery he'd followed. It didn't matter. Mortals had been stolen away, misled, trapped, and tricked for as long as the two races coexisted. Niall had been guilty of doing it.

"Let me help you." Niall had no obligation to the man, but he wasn't at ease with walking away. The Dark Court wasn't evil. It would've been easier if they were. A clear division between good and evil, right and wrong, would simplify everything, but life was rarely simple. His court was formed of passions, of shadows, of impulses. The Dark Court—and its king—were that which balanced the High Court. In this instant, balancing the High Court meant offering kindness.

"You're one of them." The man yanked his hand away from Niall. "I'm not going back. She had them take my eyes, said I'd be free . . . . You can't—"

"I have no intention of harming you. Unlike Sorcha, I am not cru—" Niall's words halted: he was capable of cruelty, but the difference was in the motivations. He'd never understood the High Court opposition to mortals knowing of the fey. He certainly never grasped the logic of breaking them for knowing. "You know we don't lie."

The man nodded.

"I offer you my protection. I cannot undo what she did to you, but I can offer you a haven." Niall waited for a moment, trying not to rush the man, but increasingly aware that someone would probably notice that a mortal had exited Faerie without permission. Keeping his voice calm, he added, "You are free to leave anytime you choose. There are no punishments for deciding to leave."

"She said this"—the man touched his face—"wasn't a punishment."

"I will not cause or allow injury done to you." Gently, Niall touched the man's wrist. "If you prefer, I will deliver you to a mortal physician. Either way, we should leave this place."

The man sighed. "I don't think mortals would be much use

against your sort. I'll accept your offer—for the moment at least."

"I'm going to carry you," Niall warned, and then he lifted the old man, cradling him like a child. It was akin to lifting an empty sack, and Niall wondered how long the frail thing had been in Faerie. Once, Sorcha had explained that the blinding was for the mortals' good as well. *Seeing the changed world after so long is troubling to them," she'd said. "This is kinder." He'd disagreed, but Sorcha had merely smiled and added, "The fanciful ones, the artists, are fragile. Seeing us after they've left is far crueler."*

The walk through Huntsdale wasn't long, but it was long enough that solitaries and those of other courts saw him. None spoke to him, but more than a few faeries stared in blatant curiosity. The sensation wasn't displeasing: he was opposing the High Court and doing something that soothed his sense of guilt over past follies.

As he approached his new home, a thistle-fey scurried forward and opened the front door.

"Gabriel," Niall called.

The Hound—who had once been a friend, more recently an enemy, and was currently Niall's most trusted resource— entered the foyer with a silent grace that should've been impossible for such a bulky creature. "My King."

"King?" the man murmured.

"Her opposition," Niall soothed as he lowered the man's feet to the floor. "You are safe here."

Gabriel shook his head. "You trying to start trouble?"

"Perhaps," Niall admitted, "but I don't suppose that's a problem, is it?"

The grin on Gabriel's face was matched by his mellow tone as he said, "Nope, just making sure I understand."

"The High Queen blinded this man. I have offered him safety here." Niall made a beckoning gesture to one of the Vilas who always lingered wherever Gabriel walked. "You can go with this woman. She'll find you a chamber to rest in while you decide what you want."

The man reached out awkwardly, clearly not yet used to his lack of sight.

Niall took the man's hand and started to lead him to the Vila. "This is Natanya and—"

"What's *your* name, king?"

The belligerence in the man's voice made both Niall and Gabriel grin. This wasn't a mortal who would curl into himself and give up. His bravery made him even more worthy of protection.

"Niall."

"Am I safe from her here, Niall?" The man tilted his head. "They might be pretty, but they're monstrous. You know that, don't you?"

"We do," Niall said.

"Are you all pretty too?" the mortal asked.

It was an obvious curiosity, but it stilled everyone all the same. Natanya stared at Niall; Gabriel shrugged. Niall wasn't sure what answer was truth. *Pretty?* Gabriel was akin to a sort of menacing mortal who lingered in disreputable bars: slow to rile, but quick to strike if angered. He was lean, scarred, and silent. The gray-eyed, gray-skinned Vilas were all beautiful; even in violence, their movements were elegant; but they were as likely as not to dab blood on their lips for color. And Niall . . . being fey meant possessing an innate attractiveness to mortals, being a Gancanagh meant he'd been born to seduce. *Pretty?* He'd thought so once, many centuries ago, but that was not a word he'd found fitting for a very long time. He'd been proud of it, though: he kept his hair shorn to emphasize the scar that he was certain made him anything but pretty. The trouble was that Niall didn't see the Dark Court denizens as ugly, either. Even while he hated things that happened in the court, even when he'd found a vast number of its faeries terrifying, he'd never thought them either pretty or ugly. They simply *were*.

"The High Court thinks we are monsters." Niall let his own emotions into the words. "I suspect that if you saw us, you'd think many of us are too. What we aren't, though, is calmly cruel. What we *aren't* is like them."

The man nodded.

Natanya and Gabriel were both smiling, and there was little doubt in Niall's mind that his own acceptance of his court was likely to be repeated throughout their number.

"Natanya?" Gabriel motioned toward the mortal. "Look after him for your king and for me."

"As if he were your own child, Gabriel." The Vila beamed at Gabriel. The silver chains that held her bone-hewn shoes to her feet clattered as she moved across the room to take the mortal's hand in hers. She led the man away, and for a moment Gabriel was silent.

He shot an assessing glance at Niall. "Salt in a wound when they learn that you brought one of Sorcha's discarded mortals here."

"That is true."

"There are only two faeries she could strike that would truly weaken your court—or make you look weaker," Gabriel pointed out. "Those are the logical choices. I'm not going over *there* and if I'm not able to face Devlin, I need replaced as the Gabriel, so I'm not needing protection. The other one . . ."

"He was already over there. That's how I know Devlin's coming here."

"Huh." Gabriel snorted. "Didn't waste any time trying to protect you, did he? Threaten her, seduce her, or both?"

Niall didn't answer that, but he suspected that Gabriel knew the answer well enough. Irial might not have spoken to the Hound yet, but they'd been a team for as long as Niall had known Irial. Before the day was over, Irial would seek Gabriel out, tell him the things he thought necessary, try again to assure that Niall was safe.

And not once think about the way he endangers himself now.

A regent could prevent any of his or her subjects from seeing the gate, and a strong solitary could impose restrictions on weaker fey. A part of Niall thought stealing others' will was wrong, but he understood now that there were times that choices were a matter of opting for the lesser of several wrongs.

"It is my decree that none of the *subjects* of the Dark Court may enter Faerie without my consent." Niall looked at Gabriel's forearms as the command appeared there. "Until such time as I speak otherwise, the gates are unseen to my subjects."

The Hounds didn't offer fealty, so they could go to Faerie. Of course, they wouldn't do so unless Gabriel directed them. Irial, however, could no longer see the gates or enter Faerie.

CHAPTER 5

Sorcha didn't respond when Devlin walked into her gardens. She'd long since stopped acknowledging him when he did so. *As if it will make the future less difficult.* She hated that he was an anomalous creature—almost as much as she treasured it. He would be her undoing if she let him. Perhaps he would be even if she tried to stop him. In some matters the threads of possibility were seemingly determined.

"My queen?"

She didn't turn. Facing him as they lied in their omissions made the whole business even less palatable. "Brother."

"I have blinded the mortal as you commanded." His voice was as empty as it often was, but that too was a lie of sorts. Her brother might pretend to be High Court, but she was under no illusion that he was solely her creature. He was *hers*, though.

"I have business there that needs tending," she said.

He'd expected as much, but he'd hoped otherwise. She could see the resignation in the moment in which he frowned. The expression was gone too fast for most anyone to see, of course, but she saw much that no one else would. The pause before replying was infinitesimal, but it was still there.

"Whatever you command," he said.

She turned. "Indeed?"

Before she could catch his gaze, he dropped to his knees. "Have I failed you?"

Sorcha didn't speak. *Have you?* She knew he would, but had he? Her vision of the past was unclear. The present and future took her focus so fully, and eternity stretched longer than she could grasp. *Have you?* She waited, looking down at the first faery she'd made. Before he existed, there were only two, Discord and Order, twins who had once created one thing together. *You.* She reached down and ran her fingers through his multihued hair. It was unlike that which graced any other faery, and it was resistant to her will. He couldn't be altered by her touch, not now that he was real. Other faeries couldn't either, but they weren't her creations.

They'd stayed this way for hours before. Devlin had the patience and willpower to kneel for as long as she required it. He didn't falter, didn't sleep, didn't wince. He simply waited. She wondered idly if he could outwait her.

"Could we spend decades thus, Brother?" she murmured.

He lifted his gaze. "Sister?"

"If I demanded it, how long would you kneel thusly?" She traced up his cheekbones and down the outside of his jaw with her fingertips. "Would you falter from exhaustion first?"

"You are my queen."

"I am," she agreed. She cupped his face in her hands and held him still. "That's not an answer."

He didn't even try to resist. "Do you require me to falter or to succeed in waiting as long as you wait?"

She smiled then. "Such a wise answer. You will do whatever I require then? You will strive to not fail me? You will serve me forever?"

"As your servant, your Bloodied Hands, your brother, your advisor, I will do all that you demand." He bowed his head, and she loosened her grip to allow it. Then he added, "The last of those questions is unanswerable."

"It is." She turned her back, but she did not release him. She fashioned a chair of flowering vines and sat down. In her hands, a book appeared. She hadn't created it. She had no such skill with art. She had, however, willed it to appear in her hands. Ignoring her brother, she began to read.

He stayed there kneeling for the next three hours as she read.

Sometime into the fourth hour, she lifted her gaze to look at him. "I need you to go to the new Dark King. Give him word of the High Court's acknowledgment of his new station. Stress to him that, while we are not at conflict, I will not hesitate to act as required to keep order."

Devlin stayed silent, awaiting the rest.

"It would be prudent to make clear your willingness to strike at the Dark Court should it be required," she continued. "Perhaps a fight with the former Dark King? The Gabriel? His mate? The action should be something that emphasizes your assets as the High Court's weapon."

"As you will," Devlin murmured.

The brief look of hurt on his face was reason enough for Sorcha to know that her actions were necessary. It would not do for Devlin to be coddled. Reminding him that he was a weapon to be utilized helped keep his tendency toward emotion in check.

It is for the best.

"Do you require death?" he inquired. "That will limit the choice of combatants."

Sorcha paused and sorted through the threads that had come into focus as Devlin spoke. The consequences of some deaths would be disastrous. *Unexpectedly so.* Later, she would mull the import of one such thread, but for now, she said only, "Not of that list. Injure one of them, or injure many. A lesser death is allowable, but not the new king's advisor or thugs. A regent does tend to react poorly to such losses."

The moment was there, and she knew he would ask. In this, as in so many other things, her brother was predictable. He looked directly at her with those unnatural dark eyes and asked, "Would your *thug's* death elicit such a reaction?"

"My assassin is my advisor and my creation"—she pursed her lips in an expression that should convey the dislike she knew was an appropriate emotion—"so I would be sorely inconvenienced by your death. I dislike being inconvenienced."

He bowed his head again. "Of course."

"If I were emotional regarding any faery in my court, it would be you, Brother." She stood and walked over to him. "You have value to me."

The relief evinced in his slight relaxing of posture was noteworthy for him. This was what he required: reminders of his value, of his use, of his proper role. He never spoke of the fact that his choice of her court was a struggle, but she knew. *As does Bananach.* It was in his nature to crave both Discord and Order. In her court, at her hand, by her word, she could give him that. *And keep him from Bananach by doing so.*

"I expect there to be violence enough that the Dark Court will be suitably reminded of my strength," she added.

"As you require."

She expected that this was a moment in which she should offer him comfort. He evoked that in her, an urge to nurture, but it would hasten the seemingly inevitable future. *When he becomes my enemy.* Instead she said, "You will not allow yourself injured, Brother. The High Court is represented by your success in this. Do not fail me."

"I will not." He was still on his knees, still unflinching. "May I depart?"

She set a storm over his head and walked away. "When the next hour ends, you may rise."

As she left, she directed a small bolt of lightning to strike him. There was no cry of pain. A tangle of wild roses grew around him as she opened the gate to exit the garden. The thorns didn't pull him off balance, but they would make his position increasingly unpleasant over the next hour. That pain would be predictable; the flowers' rate of growth would be precise. However, in deference to Devlin's discordant streak, she set the lightning strikes to a random order.

After tending to a few business matters that required negotiations that the Dark King didn't need to know about just yet, Irial finally approached what appeared to be a derelict warehouse to follow up on the last task of the day. The creatures that filled the building evoked fear and discomfort by their mere presence. When they ran, they were a beautiful nightmare—so much so that even the former King of Nightmares felt a flush of terror roll over him. It was a warning that even regents should heed: inside the stable, the Hunt ruled. No kingship, no law in either world, nothing other than Gabriel's word mattered once one entered their domain.

Consequently, it was one of the few places in this world or in Faerie that Irial would approach with caution.

Irial stopped at one of the doors and waited for a moment.

One of the younger Hounds stepped forward and flashed a sulfurous green gaze at Irial.

The sight of the green eyes in the dark was more comforting than menacing, but sharing that detail would elicit an undesired reaction from the Hound. Fighting was rarely one of Irial's preferred hobbies, so he kept his thoughts to himself.

"I would speak with the Gabriel." Irial didn't lower his gaze, but he didn't stare directly at the Hound.

A second Hound, who leaned against the building, crossed his arms. "Don't think Gabriel is expecting you."

"Do you deny me entrance?" Irial held his hand out, palm up, as one would for any number of feral beasts.

The first Hound sniffed Irial's hand. Then, he stepped closer and sniffed the air near Irial's face. "Smells like the other place."

"Faerie," Irial murmured.

The second Hound growled. "Can't run there. *She* says no visits. Wants us asking permissions first."

"I bring word of violence."

At that, both Hounds' attitudes shifted. One pushed off the building and pulled the door open. "Go ahead in. Gabriel's in the ring."

As always, the Hounds' steeds were in various forms. Cars, motorcycles, and beasts waited in wooden stalls. A few of the steeds sat in rafters in various guises. Here, they could adopt whatever form they preferred. Irial felt a twinge of longing for Faerie then. Once, forever ago now, these steeds could wear whatever form they wanted all of the time. At first, they continued to do so in the mortal world, but now, they were more cautious—for obvious reasons: the sight of the vibrant green dragon that slept in the center aisle would alarm most mortals.

The dragon stirred enough that a clear lens flickered over one its massive eyes. It yawned, giving Irial a glimpse of teeth as big as his own arms. Then, scenting him, its nostrils flared. It had awakened.

Both of the creature's eyes were now focused on Irial.

"I'm here to speak with the Gabriel," Irial said. "I bring word of blood for the Hunt. A guest from Faerie will be coming here."

The dragon flicked a thin purple tongue out, not far enough

to touch Irial, but close enough that for a moment, Irial thought he'd misremembered how close one could stand and still be at a safe distance. But then the tongue retracted, and the beast closed its eyes.

Irial resumed walking toward the ring at the far back of the building.

The scent of blood and the cacophony of snarls and rumbling voices were unaltered, but Irial had no doubt that they all knew he approached. The steeds shared nonverbal communication with their riders—and with the Hound who led them all. Everyone in the stable knew what Irial had said to the Hound at the door and to the steed that rested in the form of a dragon. That did not, however, mean that any of them saw reason to interrupt whatever fight was in progress. The Hunt had different priorities than the less feral faeries often understood.

Irial closed the distance, prepared to wait for the match to end. As he reached the edge of the crowd, the Hounds parted to let him walk to the front. At the side of the roped-off ring, Irial stopped and gaped.

There were few things that would be as unexpected as the sight before him: Niall stood in the center of the ring. Blood trickled from a set of teeth marks on his forearm and soaked the denim around a jagged tear on his leg. His opponent, an average-sized Hound, growled as Niall landed a punch that rocked the Hound's head backward. Before the Hound could respond, Niall followed through with a second punch to the throat, which had the Hound toppling to the straw-covered floor.

As Irial stared, Gabriel came up beside him. "Always was a ruthless bastard in a fight."

"Does he do this often?" Irial watched his king put one boot-clad foot on the fallen Hound's chest.

"Most every night since you made him king." Gabriel's emotions tangled between amused and content. "Seems to be taking to the job if you ask me."

"Perhaps I *should've* asked you," Irial murmured. He felt a curious wave of sadness that Gabriel had kept this from him. It wasn't wrong of Gabriel, but it was yet another loss.

Niall looked over his shoulder then to stare at Irial. While the Hounds couldn't taste emotions, the rest of the Dark Court could. Of course, that didn't mean they always *understood* the reason for the emotion—which was abundantly clear in the surge of fury that Niall felt.

The Dark King grabbed the Hound at his feet and hauled him upright. He shoved the injured Hound toward the rope and snarled, "Next."

If they had been any other two faeries, Irial would've pulled his king aside and explained that the sorrow was not over seeing Niall battering the fallen Hound, but over Gabriel's secrecy. They weren't any other faeries though, so Irial did the next best thing: he stepped forward.

"Don't be absurd," Niall ground out.

Without taking his gaze from his king, Irial ducked under the rope. "If you would, Gabe?"

"Hear we're expecting blood. Who's visiting?" Gabriel asked.

"Devlin. Sorcha undoubtedly would like him to make a statement. It *is* traditional." Irial waited for a moment, listening to the receding footsteps and motors already coming to life. The Hunt was vacating the stable, undoubtedly at Gabriel's silent command.

Softly, Irial added, "The pups should stay close to home for a few days."

Gabriel's teeth snapped and a low snarl emanated from him. "My pups are—"

"Safe enough," Irial interrupted, "*if* they stay out of sight. Sorcha has issued orders to take halflings, so just tell them to stay low for a few days."

Niall took a step toward Irial and said in a low voice, "This is why I need you here. You have centuries of dealing with the nuances. The court needs that wisdom." He did not add that he needed Irial too, but the emotion was there for Irial to taste—as was the resentment. "I require your presence and your safety. The gates to Faerie are unseen to you now, Irial."

"Well, this evening is just full of surprises, isn't it?" Irial raised a fist. "You'd leash me then? I went there for—"

Gabriel cleared his throat loudly. "We'll stir up a little nourishment for the court tonight." He paused briefly and then said, "Niall?"

Niall glanced away from Irial.

"Your strength is the court's strength. Don't much matter whether you feed on fury or lust, or who you do that with, but you need to be strong." Gabriel put word to what they all knew. "I'll gather some of the solitaries or the Summer Girls if you'd rather—"

"The Summer Girls are *not* to be given to the court." Niall bared his teeth. "No one is permitted to be touched without their consent."

"We know that," Gabriel said. "The *old* king made that rule. The Hunt brings them, but they choose to stay or go."

Niall gave Irial a curious look, but Irial said nothing. If he'd told Niall, it wouldn't have changed a thing, but it would've started a conversation that neither of them had been ready for in the years that had passed. Knowing Irial regretted being unable to protect Niall didn't undo the past.

Finally, Niall looked away. "Do what you must to bring nourishment for the court."

"And you," Irial added. "A few fights aren't enough and you

know it . . . although I'm glad you *are* fighting at least. Now if you were fu—"

"Stop." Niall's emotions were all over the spectrum. His gaze snapped back to Irial. "Don't think I'm going to be easy to beat just because there were a few Hounds trying to pummel me."

At this, Irial's flash of irritation vanished. He lowered his fist and laughed. "You've never been easy about anything, love."

The fist that slammed into Irial's face was faster than he remembered Niall's punches being, but it had been a very long time since Niall had hit him. Striking a king wasn't tolerated unless it was in an agreed-upon match, and for the past eleven centuries, Niall had known that Irial was a king.

And that I withheld that little detail when we met.

A second punch didn't come.

Niall stared at him. "We're in a ring, Irial. You can strike a king here."

Irial grinned as he heard Gabriel call, "We ride."

As the Hunt started to leave, the stable was a storm of emotions that both he and Niall consumed. While those emotions were still flooding them, Irial said, "Should I have extended that offer to you a second time when you learned that I was a king?"

"Maybe." Niall smiled briefly. "I thought about this often enough."

"Hitting me?"

"No," Niall corrected as he swung at Irial. "Beating you half to death."

Then, they were too busy to argue. Irial wasn't as quick with his fists, but he let every emotion he felt free. Reading Irial's emotions and Niall's own rage-guilt-pleasure over the knowledge put Niall off-center enough that Irial was able to withstand the next hour better than either of them had anticipated.

Eventually, however, Irial was prone on the ground. He couldn't open his left eye, and he was fairly certain that at least one rib was cracked. "I'm done."

Instead of walking away as Irial expected, Niall plopped down on the floor. He was covered in blood and sweat, and he was content.

"It's easier than I thought," Niall said.

"I'm not *that* easy to beat." Irial smiled and then winced as the movement made his lip bleed more freely.

"It's easier being their king than I thought it would be," Niall corrected.

"I knew what you meant." Irial forced himself to sit upright, and immediately reassessed the number of broken ribs to at least three. "You were always their next king. You knew that. I knew it. Hell, Sorcha knew it."

Niall's eyes widened slightly. "She told you that?"

Irial had forgotten how much more open Niall had always been after a fight. "Not directly, but her emotions did."

Hesitantly, Niall asked, "What emotions? The High Queen doesn't . . . *does* she?"

"She does in the presence of the Dark King." Irial held Niall's gaze as best he could with one eye swollen mostly shut. "I asked if you were ever going to be the next king, and she felt both excited and sorrowful. I didn't know for sure then, but I hoped—and now, I think that she knew, that she looked forward to you being this."

They sat silently, but not without communicating. Over the centuries, Irial had read Niall's emotions without his knowledge. Tonight, for the first time, Niall consciously revealed his emotions for the purpose of sharing the things he couldn't verbalize. The years had changed them both, but those changes had only made Niall more suited to being the Dark King. Niall was both relieved and disappointed that this was so. He was also happier than he'd been since he'd left Irial's side more than nine centuries ago.

As am I.

Eventually, Niall stood. "Things will never be like they were before."

"I didn't think they would." Irial stared up at him.

Unexpectedly, Niall extended a hand—and then grinned as he tasted Irial's shock. "You fight better than I remember."

"You broke several ribs." Irial accepted Niall's hand and was pulled to his feet. "I can't see from one eye, and I think something in my knee ripped."

"Exactly." Niall released Irial's hand and grinned.

"Maybe next time I'll do better." Irial regretted the words as soon as they were out, but he wasn't going to admit that. He concealed his emotions and stilled his expression as best he could.

For a moment, Niall said nothing; his emotions were likewise locked down tightly enough that they were out of Irial's reach. Then Niall shrugged. "Maybe."

Irial lifted the rope for Niall to duck under.

They walked out together in silence. Niall did not tell Irial to depart as they walked to the house that had once been Irial's, nor did he invite Irial to stay. At the step, they paused, and for a foolish hopeful moment, Irial waited. Then, Niall reached out to the gargoyle that adorned the door, and Irial left for his current residence. It was a peaceful parting.

Things might be all right after all.

Irial knew they both were keeping secrets that could change the trust they were building, but it was progress. For now, that was enough.

Once we get past the visit from the High Queen's emissary.

What Irial had learned in his conversations with his spies had directed a course of action he'd intended to discuss with

Gabriel tonight, but Irial had long since discovered the importance of improvising. A chance to mend his relationship with Niall outweighed the benefits of informing Gabriel of Irial's plans. He could handle matters quietly, and then apologize to Niall if he was found out.

CHAPTER 7

*D*espite the things left unsaid, Niall knew that the house he lived in had not been intended to go to the new Dark King. If the last king had died, Niall would be entitled to all his predecessor's belongings. The last king, however, was far from dead. *He is very much here. Thankfully.* Niall smiled —and then paused. *Do I forgive everything?* He had set aside centuries of dislike for Irial in a few short weeks. *No.* Niall walked across the foyer, knowing that servants waited in hopes of his needing something, anything. There were those in the Dark Court that seemed to thrive on being given orders. It was perplexing to him. *Forgiving* everything *will never happen.* That didn't mean that Niall could cling to the illusions that he'd held to these past centuries: he couldn't forget the good things any more than the bad.

Ignoring the faeries that waited in every alcove and around every corner, Niall made his way to his chambers. He opened the door and stopped.

"He said you needed me." She stared at him, not moving, not crossing the thick carpet to stand nearer him. Once, she would've. Now, she watched him and said, "The Hound. He brought me here because you needed me."

"No," he corrected. "I needed a *body* to be here. Not you. It's what I am now. I have need of a body."

She shrugged. "I am a body."

"No." He wasn't exactly *happy* to find one of the Summer Girls waiting there. He tried to think of her that way: one of the Summer Girls. He tried not to think of her as someone he'd once protected. It didn't work.

"You could be anyone." He slammed the door closed. "You—"

"You don't need to try to make me upset, Niall." She gave him a sorrowful smile. "Tell me."

"Tell . . ."

"What you need," she supplied. Even in this place, far different from her court, she swayed a little as if she heard music still. The long brown hair that she usually pinned into curls hung straight today. "The last Dark King invited us here often enough. Tonight, though . . . I hoped it was you I was here for when I saw the Hound. I would've come without that hope, but I'm glad to be brought to you."

Niall hadn't thought about it overly much. It made sense, though: the Summer Girls were without Keenan's hatred of the Dark Court. They were creatures of pleasure, the embodiment of only the joys of Summer. Later, he'd ask Gabriel how often the Summer Girls had visited the court—and how often they could visit safely. Even in his fury with Keenan, Niall still believed that the Summer King would not sit idly by if the Summer Girls were harmed. His former liege manipulated as freely as every other powerful faery did—*including me*—but often that was out of the protectiveness he felt for his faeries. The Summer Girls, former mortals who'd been cursed to be faeries dependent on Keenan for their very sustenance, were particularly important to the Summer King.

"He always asked about you. The last king"—she unfastened her sundress—"I thought of telling you sometimes. More than once, he asked me to come to him right after I'd lain in your arms."

Niall stilled. *Did you? Why? How often?* There was nothing he could think to say that didn't sound bizarre—not that she would be fazed by a bizarre statement. The Summer Girls were unflappable. He stared at her as she dropped the dress.

"We knew that one day"—she stepped from the dress that now puddled around her feet—"you'd return to this court."

If she had been any of the other Summer Girls, her words would've surprised him, but Siobhan had always told Niall things he hadn't thought anyone noticed. *She is my friend.* He remembered the years after she'd first joined the Summer Court, when she realized that Keenan's love was as fleeting as his attention had been.

As she watched him, she pulled her hair over her bare shoulder. "I remember when you taught me about this world, Niall. You spoke of them, of *his* court, with a difference in your voice. Your eyes grew dark when you spoke of him. Did you know that?"

The way she watched him was exciting. When he'd been in the Summer Court, he had always favored her, but the Summer Girls never seemed to care whose arms they were in. *Do they, and I just didn't know?* He turned away from her, dismissing her with effort, and walked to the low chest at the foot of his over-sized bed. He propped one foot up and began unlacing his boots.

Without looking back at her, he said, "You could go. There are others—"

She laughed. "I *miss* you. I'm here by choice. My king wouldn't like it, but we are not disloyal to him. We did not speak of our court here . . . except to Irial, and he only asked after you."

"Keenan would not approve," Niall pointed out rather foolishly. What the Summer King approved of wasn't Niall's concern. Even now, the Dark Court was strong enough to withstand any threat the Summer Court offered them. *Unlike the High Court or the Winter Court.* He unlaced his other boot and dropped both boots on the floor. The black of the leather almost blended in with the deep burgundy carpet. *I will not look at her.* He sat on the chest.

"Niall?"

He lifted his gaze.

In an instant, Siobhan had crossed the room and stood in front of him. Carefully, she reached out to touch his face. Gone was the impulsivity he'd known with her as one of the Summer Girls. Instead, she approached him much the way one would approach a wild animal. "You've been fighting."

Until that moment, the fact that he was blood-covered had slipped his mind. He flinched and pulled away from her touch. "You should g—" The untrue words halted. He tried again: "You *could* g—"

"No." Her hand was outstretched, but she did not touch him this time. Her sorrow and her longing and her love flooded him. "I want to be right here."

Love?

He stared at her in wonder.

She stilled. "What?"

Silently, he shook his head. The ability of his court to taste emotions was secret. As carefully as she had, he reached out, and despite the number of times that he'd been with Siobhan, it felt new. He slid his fingers through her hair, brushing it back, letting it slip from his grasp to slide over her skin. "I do want you to stay."

As he touched her, she closed her eyes, and he tried not to notice that the vines that were on her skin wilted as he slid his hand down her bare arm. She was a part of the Summer Court;

he was not. Like everyone else outside of the Summer Court, his touch was not nourishing for her now.

"Niall?"

He traced the wilting vines that trailed across her bare stomach. "You know you can walk away from here."

"I'm here by choice," she repeated softly. "I want to be here."

Her emotions were as clear in her voice as they were in the air around him. Her fear of rejection tangled with need. Even though he was bruised and bloodied, even though he was offering her nothing, she wanted him—and was terrified that he would send her away. He drank down both her terror and her lust as he pulled her onto his lap.

And in doing so, all of her hesitation vanished. She drew his lips to hers and wrapped her legs around him. *This* was the Siobhan he'd taken into his arms so often over the past century. She didn't apologize as she shredded what remained of his bloodied shirt or when she caused him pain by being too impatient with his bruised body.

Unlike every other relationship he'd known, Siobhan was uncomplicated. She didn't think about the future; she didn't ask about the past. *Or cause me to think of those things.* She was here, in this moment, in this place. She was a Summer Girl, demanding the pleasure that she considered her right. She took what she needed, and she shared herself because she wanted to do so. She was who she was, and she didn't try to hide that truth.

And in this, Niall admitted to himself, perhaps the Summer Court and the Dark Court were not so far apart.

CHAPTER 8

The following day, far earlier than the court would gather, Irial was waiting in the alley outside the warehouse Niall had been favoring of late. Much like the changes Niall had made in what used to be Irial's home, this change was both comforting and disconcerting. The court owned plenty of clubs, both mortal and faery focused, but for reasons Niall didn't specify, he'd chosen to have meetings here in a vast warehouse. They'd hired mortals to refit it, removing the excessive steel so that it was bearable and adding wood and stone fixtures. The presence of steel weakened the faeries, but it also meant that only the strongest among them could act out. That, Irial had to admit, was clever. His own solution when he'd ascended the throne had been bloodier, but Niall was a different sort of ruler.

Irial had waited there since the sun rose, but it was not until afternoon that he saw the faery he'd been expecting.

"Irial." Devlin moved with the same ease that shadows did, but rather than take advantage of that, he tried to announce his presence when he arrived—unless he was sent to assassinate someone Sorcha had declared troubling.

"I have made you welcome among us for centuries, but I understand that Her Unchanging Difficultness has sent you to make trouble," Irial murmured.

"My queen is wise in all things." Devlin stiffened. "She seeks to keep order, not promote conflict."

"By striking those in my—*the* Dark Court?" Irial grinned. "The High Court is a twisted place."

"You are no longer king. Nothing should prevent me from striking you." Devlin's voice had no inflection. In most cases, evoking obvious emotion in Sorcha's brother was a challenge.

"If necessary, I would offer myself up for you to take your pound of flesh." Irial gestured to the street. "We can deal with this out here before or after you say what you will to my king."

The expression on Devlin's face seemed to grow even more unreadable, and his already hidden emotions became absent enough that he was as a vacant body. "Regrettably, I think I will decline that offer."

The sound of Hounds approaching didn't evoke so much as a flicker from Devlin. Their steeds' engines growled and snarled; the exhalations—which mortals would see as vehicle exhaust—were tinted the same green as their eyes. While the Hunt did not ride in pursuit of anyone, they made their entrance with the same ferocity as they'd pursue an enemy with. Gabriel's steed was, uncharacteristically, a massive motorcycle with dual exhaust and a growl loud enough that the street shuddered. Gabriel himself snarled as fiercely as the steed, the act of which made his words almost unintelligible. "Irial . . . What. Are. You. Doing."

Irial widened his eyes in faux innocence. "Greeting a guest to the Dark Court. We were both in the street, and—" Irial's words were lost under another growl.

Utterly implacable as always, Devlin merely looked at the assembled Hunt as if they were nothing more than a group of mortal schoolchildren. "On behalf of the Queen of Faerie, I seek audience with the Dark King."

"Irial?" Gabriel said in a slightly clearer voice. "Go inside. Now."

Something in him rankled at being ordered so, but Gabriel had always been prone to treating Irial as an equal instead of as a king. *And now I am not a king.* Irial shrugged, glanced at Devlin, and said, "My offer stands."

The resounding snarls that greeted his words brought a look of true amusement—and matching burst of emotion—to Devlin. "I believe there is some opposition to your suggestion."

Gabriel extended his left arm; on it, the Dark King's commands spiraled out and made quite clear that Irial was to be kept safe. "Inside."

Devlin smiled broadly now. He glanced from the ink on Gabriel's arm to Irial's face. "Your king seems to disapprove of your propensity for protecting him."

At that, Irial shook his head. "Understand this: if you so much as lift a hand to my king, I will bring such destruction into Faerie as would make War in all her fury seem like an infant in a snit. There are more than a few who owe me debts I will not hesitate to call due." Irial lowered his voice, not to hide his words from those standing near him, but in hopes of keeping it from any hidden watchers. "I've spoken to those who carry word of the High Queen's orders. Whether it is now or for the rest of eternity, any who strike at him will answer to me."

"You unman him with such a threat," Devlin remarked.

"No," Irial corrected. "I *protect* him. It is no different than what you would do for your queen."

Devlin paused a heartbeat too long before murmuring, "Perhaps."

"Inside on your own, or they'll move you." Gabriel clamped

a hand on Irial's shoulder. "I will not disobey my king—nor will you."

Several of the Hounds shifted restlessly. They would obey their Gabriel, but after centuries of protecting Irial, they were uneasy at the idea of manhandling him.

"Your words are noted and will be relayed to my queen." Devlin bowed his head, either to hide his expression or out of respect. Irial wasn't sure which.

NIALL WAS FUMING when Irial entered the building. A barricade of solid shadow snapped into place around the two of them, sealing out everyone but them. "What were you thinking? Did you ignore *everything* I said yesterday?"

"No." Irial was unabashed. He put his hand against the shadow-formed wall. "You are able to do things that I struggled with as easily as if you'd been king for several years."

"At least one of us is adjusting well."

At that, Irial paused. "What do you mean?"

"Instead of hiding the fact that you were informed that Devlin was to strike you or Gabriel, you should have told me," Niall said as calmly as he could. "You offered me the court, your fealty, your advice, yet you hide things that, *as your king*, I should be told."

For a moment, Irial stood in silence. "If Gabriel were to be injured, the Hounds could replace him, and we cannot be certain that another Hound would support you as Gabriel will."

"I know."

"So of the two, I am more expendable." Irial shrugged.

"You are not expendable to me . . . . And I couldn't speak it if it were untrue"—Niall held up his hand before Irial could interrupt—"neither could you, so we both believe we speak truths. You told me of this visit, advised me how to proceed, and then undermined me. You should have told me what you learned."

"I'm not very good at serving."

Niall put one hand on Irial's shoulder and pushed him to his knees. "I noticed."

The truth was that even as he was apologizing, Irial was not subservient. Kings weren't meant to become subjects, and after centuries of being a king, Irial wasn't likely to change overnight. *Or at all.* The consequence of that truth, however, was that the one faery in the Dark Court best able to advise Niall was also the one least suited to being anyone's subject.

"We need a solution or you need to go," Niall started.

Irial lifted his gaze. "You would exile me?"

"If you work against me, yes, I will." Niall frowned. "Tell me what you know. Maybe we need to do so every day. A meeting . . . or a memo . . . or I don't know."

Irial started to rise to his feet.

"No," Niall whispered. "You will kneel until I say otherwise."

A slow smile came over Irial's face. "As you will."

"I'm not joking, Irial. Either I'm your king or you are gone. If I am to rule this court, I need you"—Niall paused to let the weight of that sentence settle on both of them—"more than I think I've needed anyone since you failed me. So tell me right now, do you want the court back, do you want to leave, or do you intend to be my advisor in truth?"

"I want to keep you *and* the court safe." Irial looked only at Niall despite the growing number of faeries outside the shadowed barrier. "That means, I cannot be their king."

"Then stop trying to make all of the decisions." Niall ignored the fighting outside the wall as well. A fair number of Ly Ergs stood in front of Devlin, who was steadily throwing them across the room as if they were weightless. "You learned that the High Queen wanted a show strike that would be a noticeable display of her assassin's strength."

"Yes."

"Gabe has arranged that—up to allowing you to act the fool," Niall said.

Irial startled. "I see."

"I sent Gabe to find out which of your spies you'd visited." Niall let his pleasure in the situation be obvious in his voice. "I manipulated you, Irial."

Irial turned away to watch another faery go sailing by the barrier. "May I rise?"

"No." Niall hid a grin. "You will give me your vow."

"On what?"

"I will have your vow that you will tell me when there are threats that you consider protecting me from, threats to me or to the court or to you that you consider withholding, and you will tell me what they are as soon as you are reasonably able to do so." Niall had weighed the words in his mind as he'd sat stewing over Irial's deceit. "You will vow to trust me with ruling this court or you will become solitary, exiled from the court and from my presence until I decide otherwise."

The flash of fear that Irial felt almost made Niall waver. Instead, he continued, "You will spend as much time as I require in my presence, teaching me the secrets that you are even now thinking I can't handle yet."

"There are centuries of secrets," Irial hedged.

"Either you kneel there and give me your vow to all that I just said"—Niall reached out, gripped the underside of Irial's jaw in his hand, and forced his once-friend, once-more, once-enemy to look at him—"or you may stand and walk out the door."

"If I tell you everything, neither of us will sleep or do anything else for months."

Niall squeezed Irial's throat, not hard enough to bruise —much—and asked, "If I directed you to tell me what you hide, would you be able to give me a full answer?"

"In time? Yes. Today? No. Centuries, Niall, I've been dealing in secrets for centuries." Irial stayed motionless in Niall's grasp. "I told you about my understanding with Sorcha. I had Gabe bring you one of—"

"Yes," Niall interrupted, squeezing harder now. "Did they spy for you?"

"Only on you."

With a snarl, Niall shoved him away. "Your vow or go."

Even as he struggled to remain kneeling, Irial didn't hesitate in his words, "My vow . . . and full truth within the decade."

"Within the year."

Irial shook his head. "That is impossible."

"Two years."

"No more than three years," Irial offered. "You have eternity to rule them, three years is but a blink."

For a moment, Niall considered forcing the matter, but if it had taken him centuries to change, it was far from unreasonable for Irial to ask for less than a decade. Niall nodded. "Done."

"May I rise now?" Irial asked.

"Actually, no. You can stay like that. In fact, maybe you should always stay like that when you bring me news." Niall dropped the barrier and launched himself into the fracas.

This, at least, I understand.

CHAPTER 9

*I*rial felt unconscionably proud of his king as Niall
waded into the fight that was now more than a
conflict between Devlin and the Ly Ergs. Niall had always
fought with unrestrained passion. The Dark King was in the
thick of the fight, swinging at Hounds and Ly Ergs and Vilas.

Glass shattered over Irial and rained down on him. With it
came the remains of a bottle of merlot. The dark wine dripped
on Irial, but he stayed exactly where his king had told him to
stay: kneeling in the midst of the chaos of a beautiful bloody
battle.

For several minutes, Irial remained kneeling in the midst of
the fight, which now included a full three score of faeries.
More than a few faeries took advantage of the melee to pelt
things at him or at the walls and ceiling. Debris rained on him.
At least three blows struck him. He didn't ignore them, but
fighting while kneeling was a new challenge.

Finally Niall came over and grabbed him by the upper arm.
"Get up."

Irial obeyed—which was the point of the exercise. He

brushed bits of glass from his arms and shook splinters of wood from his hair.

"Stay next to me or next to Gabe," Niall demanded as he swung at an exuberant thistle fey. "Clear?"

"Yes." Irial grabbed a length of what appeared to be a chair and sent it like a spear toward Devlin.

The High Court assassin knocked it from the air with a nod. He wasn't injured in any visible way, but he was blood-covered and smiling. Devlin might choose to ignore the fact that he was brother to both Order and Chaos, but here in the midst of the Dark Court's violence, it was abundantly clear that he was not truly a creature of the High Court.

Another faery went sailing through the air, knocking into Devlin as if a running leap would make a difference. It didn't. The High Court's Bloodied Hands swatted the faery from the air and moved on to the next opponent.

"They lack structure," a Hound grumbled as she stomped on a fallen Vila's hand. "No plan in the attack."

"Was there supposed to be a plan?" Irial asked.

The Hound looked past him to Niall, who nodded. Then she answered, "No. Gabe thought a bit of sport would be good for everyone. The king agreed." She lowered her voice a touch and added, *"He* fights well enough that I'd follow him."

"He is remarkable." Irial glanced at Niall. The Dark King was enjoying himself as the fight began to evolve into a contest of sorts. In one corner, Devlin stood atop a pile of tables and wood; in another, Gabriel stood with his back to the wall; and beside Irial, Niall stood on a small raised platform. All around the room the Dark Court faeries scrabbled toward one of the three victors. Without speaking, the fight began to resemble nothing so much as a bloodier version of King of the Hill. Everyone wanted to topple one of the three strongest fighters, if even for a moment, and all of them were still having fun.

Devlin had more than held his own against the Dark

Court's fighters, reminding them that he was not to be ignored. All of the faeries in the room had more nourishment than could have been hoped for as a result of the flare of violence and blood sport.

And Niall had made his point.

The new Dark King had played them all like pawns.

Irial started to back away, and the Hound next to him clamped a hand on his arm. Irial glanced from her to Niall, who grinned, dodged a punch from a glaistig, and said, "I don't think you were dismissed."

The Hound and the glaistig both laughed.

I love my court.

"As you wish." Irial stepped around the Hound to lean against a wall out of the fight. He had more than his fill of fighting. If he could fight Niall, it'd be different, but fighting for random sport wasn't his preferred entertainment.

Almost an hour later, Devlin bowed to Gabriel and then to Niall.

The faeries dispersed, limping, bleeding, stumbling—and chortling with glee.

"The High Queen sends her greetings," Devlin said as he approached Niall. "She reminds the new Dark King that he is no different than any other faery and that she expects him to abide by the same restraints the last"—Devlin looked at Irial then—"Dark King observed."

None of them spoke the unspoken truths about the numerous visits that Irial had paid to the High Queen in Faerie, but they all knew of those visits. *Such is the way of it.* Irial kept his gaze on his king rather than reply to Devlin. It was the *king* who needed to answer the invitation implicit in those words.

Niall didn't disappoint.

"Please let Sorcha know that her greeting was received, that her assassin has made her willingness to strike at me and mine abundantly clear, and"—Niall jumped down so he was standing face-to-face with Devlin—"if she ever touches those under my protection without just cause, I will be at her step."

Devlin nodded. "Will you be requesting an audience with her?"

"No," Niall said. "There is nothing and no one in Faerie right now that interests me enough to visit."

For a breath, Irial thought Devlin was going to strike Niall, but the moment passed.

Then, Niall smiled. He gestured behind him, and a Vila escorted a sightless mortal man into the room.

"This"—Niall didn't turn to look at the mortal—"is unacceptable. My court has offered this man protection. He will not be taken to Faerie or otherwise accosted." He kept his gaze on Devlin.

The ghost of a smile flickered on Devlin's face, but all he said was, "I shall relay the message to my queen."

"And any discussion she has on Dark Court matters"—Niall stepped forward—"will be handled between regents or via official emissaries."

Devlin did smile this time. "My queen has only one emissary. Do you have a chosen proxy?"

"As of this moment, no, but"—Niall glanced at Irial—"perhaps that will change *in time*." The Dark King turned his back on all of them then and said only, "Gabriel."

The Hound inclined his head, and Devlin preceded Gabriel toward the door. The two faeries walked out of the building, and then only Irial and Niall were left in the destruction.

Irial waited for the words that went with the frustrated anger that he could taste. He counted a dozen heartbeats before his king turned to face him.

"Don't push me again, Iri," Niall whispered. "I rule this damnable court now, and I'll do it with you on my side—*as you promised*—or with you under my boot."

Irial opened his mouth, but Niall growled.

"You tell me you care about them, and about me, so you better prove it." Niall blinked against a trickle of blood that ran into his eye. "I don't expect you to change today, but you need to trust me more than you have."

"I trust you with my life." Irial ripped the edge of his shirt off and held it out.

"I know that," Niall muttered. "Now, try trusting me with *my* life."

And to that, Irial had no reply. He kept his mouth closed as Niall stomped through the destruction and left. The Dark King was here, truly and fully, and Irial would do what he could to serve his king.

As truthfully as I can.

There was no way to tell Niall everything, but he had three years before he had to be fully honest. An otherwise unoccupied faery could get a lot accomplished in three years, and the sort of king Niall was could get their court in order in far less time than that. All told, the Dark Court was better off than it had been in quite some time.

And so is Niall.

"It is inevitable, Brother," Sorcha said by way of greeting when he finished his report.

"What is?"

"Her ascending to strength." Sorcha could not see her twin's future, but she knew well the results of Chaos' growing stronger. The world was not as it should be. Deaths that Sorcha would mourn, in her way, were coming.

As Sorcha reached into the seemingly empty space in front of her, she plucked at threads of possibilities. She let them slip through her fingers, each one as unsatisfactory as the next: her former lover dead, her brother dead, a pierced mortal dead, her once-friend dead, Faerie blackened. They were only possibilities, but none were pleasing.

"She is not going to be stilled easily," Sorcha whispered.

"You are stronger, Sister." Devlin smelled of blood. It wasn't visible on him, but the lingering scent of violence clung to him.

A weapon to be used to keep Chaos at bay.

"Will you help me?"

"I serve the High Court, my Queen. I cannot fathom any

reason that I would do otherwise." He stared at her as he spoke. "Do you know of a reason I would do otherwise?"

There was no pleasing answer to that question. She knew many reasons that he would do otherwise: he was Bananach's creature too; he wanted things not found in Faerie in centuries; he resented her; he enjoyed violence. None of those were new facts. Logically, none were worth speaking.

"There is a mortal I see."

"An artist? A Sighted one? A halfling?"

Curiously, as Sorcha tried to look at him, the mortal with the metal decorating his face, she saw only blackness. There was nothing. It was akin to attempting to see Devlin's or Bananach's future. *Or my own future.* In the moment between seeing the mortal and speaking of him, he had become part of one of the three of their lives. *He matters.*

"I don't know," she admitted. "Watch for him. He is young but not a child. He will matter to one of us."

Devlin bowed.

Sorcha closed her eyes trying to recall other details, but her glimpse of him had been too brief. "He wears an assortment of metal in his skin."

"Steel?"

"I do not know. I cannot See him now." She opened her eyes. "He was a glimpse, and in that glimpse, he was still and bleeding, lying on the soil here in Faerie."

"Did that please you?"

She shook her head, but did not admit the curious sense she'd had that this mortal's pain *hurt* her. The Queen of Order did not mourn. It was illogical. "I do not believe it did."

Devlin approached her. Silently, he reached out and swiped a tear from her cheek. He lifted it and held it up.

They both looked at it, a silver droplet on the tip of his outstretched finger.

"The body does odd things at times," she whispered.

"It's a tear."

Sorcha lifted her gaze from the oddity to stare at her brother's face. "I do not weep."

"Yes, my Queen." He pulled his hand behind him, and she knew without looking that the tear was still held there.

She nodded and brushed past him. At the doorway, she paused for a servant to appear. She did not speak to him; in order to be worthy of being allowed in her private rooms, those most trusted sacrificed their hearing. At set locations, they waited with eyes downcast so as not to lip-read the words she spoke. The servant saw the hem of her dress on the floor before him, and so stepped forward to pull the tapestry away from the doorway.

"I will find him," Devlin said from behind her. "The mortal."

Her heart felt oddly constricted. "Not all threads are truths, Brother. What is truth is that Chaos grows. Every possibility I See shows me the results of her strength. I need you to be mine."

"My word that I will not fail you if ever it is in my power." Devlin's words were small comfort. He did not say he was hers, that he would stand with her against Bananach—*because he cannot.*

"When you visit their world, watch for a mortal of significance." Then she stepped through the doorway, trying not to ponder the odd reaction she'd had to the thought of one unknown mortal lying motionless in her presence.

STOPPING TIME

Unlike some faeries, *he* didn't bother with a glamour. He sat on a bench across from the tables outside the coffee shop. Their silent late-afternoon meetings had become a routine of sorts the last few months, and each week, the temptation to speak to him grew greater—which was why she'd invited a study group to meet with her this week. Their presence was to be incentive to keep her from talking to him.

It didn't help. These together-but-not times were the closest thing she'd had to a date in months. She looked forward to seeing him, thought about it throughout the week, wondering what he'd be wearing, what he'd be reading, if this week he'd approach her.

He wouldn't. He'd promised her choices, and he wouldn't take them from her. If she spoke to him, it would be because she approached him. If she went to him, it would be of her own volition. If she wanted to stop seeing him, she could stop arriving here every week. That, too, was her choice. So far, she resisted approaching him and speaking to him. She did not, however, stop coming to the precise spot each week at the same time. They had a routine: he read whatever his book of the week was, and she studied.

And tried not to stare . . . or go to him . . . or speak to him.

She couldn't see the cover of his current book at first. His taste was eclectic in genre, but consistent in quality. She glanced at the book several times, trying for subtle, but he noticed.

He still notices everything.

With a grin, he lifted the book—one called *American Gods* this time—higher, hiding his face as a result. The extra benefit of that move was that she could look at him unabashedly while they both pretended he didn't realize she was admiring him. He appeared happier of late, far more so than when she'd left Huntsdale. Ruling the Dark Court had suited him, but advising the new Dark King seemed to suit him better. He hadn't lost his taste for indulgent clothes, though. A silk tee and tailored linen trousers flattered him without being ostentatious. The silver razor blade he'd worn before was accompanied by a small black glass vial. Without asking, she knew it was the same ink that she had in her tattoo.

Maudlin or romantic? She wasn't sure. *Both maybe.*

He lowered the book, taking away her unobserved access, and stared at her for several heartbeats. Often, he stayed invisible when he came to sit near her. This week he was very visible, though. She saw him either way, but when he was visible to others, it was extra difficult to keep her gaze off him. His visibility was an invitation of sorts, an extra temptation to approach him.

It means I could walk over and start talking to him.

"He's got it bad," one of her study partners commented.

Beside her, Michael was silent.

Leslie tore her gaze from Irial and looked at her companions. "He's an old friend."

The curiosity on their faces was obvious. She shouldn't have met them here.

"A friend you don't talk to?" Jill's voice held the doubt that the others were too polite to voice. "What kind of friend is that?"

"One who'd move the earth for me, but"—Leslie glanced back at Irial—"not one who brings out my better side."

His mouth quirked in a just-restrained laugh.

Got to love faery hearing. Leslie watched the girls check him out—as he preened for them. It wasn't overt, but she knew him. His tendency to arrange himself to his best advantage was reflex more than choice.

"Well if you don't want him . . . maybe I should go say hello." Jill flashed her teeth in what passed for a smile.

Leslie shrugged.

Of course, I want *him. Everyone who looks at him* wants *him.*

Anger rose up inside of her as Jill stood and started across the grassy lawn that separated the coffee shop and the bench where Irial waited. Worse still, it embarrassed her to admit that she felt a familiar possessive pang. Irial was *hers*. That hadn't changed, wouldn't change.

Except that it did.

When she left his world—*their world*—she'd made it change. He still watched her, not in a predatory way, or even in an intrusive way, but she'd see him around campus. While Irial watched, Niall respected her requests not to visit; instead, he sent Hounds to guard her. Occasionally Aislinn's rowan-people or the Winter Queen's lupine fey looked in on her too. Leslie was safer than she'd ever been, guarded by the denizens of three faery courts, and pretending not to notice any of them.

That was an implicit understanding: she mostly pretended they weren't there, and they pretended she wasn't ignoring their presence. Sometimes ignoring the fey made her feel a kinship with Aislinn. When Aislinn was mortal, she'd had to pretend not to see them. They hadn't known she had the Sight. Leslie, however, didn't need to pretend.

Except for myself . . . and for him.

She smiled at Irial, letting the illusion slip for a moment—and immediately regretted it. He lowered his book and leaned forward. The question in his expression made her heart ache. She didn't belong in his world, not even now that he was no longer the Dark King. Talking to him was dangerous. Being alone with him was dangerous. It was a line she couldn't cross —not and still retain her distance. If she were to be honest with herself, it was the other reason she'd invited her study group this week. She could speak to them, say things she wanted him to know without admitting she was speaking to him.

Faery logic.

He stood.

She shook her head and turned away. There were moments when she failed, when she talked to the fey, but not to Irial.

Never to him.

Jill was beside him now, and he spoke to her. No doubt he said something charming but dismissive.

Leslie stared at the page, her notes blurring as she tried to look anywhere but at Irial. Resolutely, she read over the words in her notebook. School was the one thing that helped her focus; it was how she had kept it together when she lived in Huntsdale, and it was how she had continued to hold on the past few months. She'd rather hurt and keep trying than hide from her feelings. Irial had helped her see that.

Seeing anyone else near him hurt. Seeing him hurt. *Not seeing him hurts more.* That was the challenge, the dilemma she couldn't resolve: his nearness made her feel safe, made her feel loved and valued, but it reminded her of what she couldn't have. Two faeries, arguably the two most tempting faeries in the world, loved her, and she couldn't be with either of them— not without sacrificing too much. She couldn't be a good person and be in their world. Maybe if they were part of any other faery court or if she were a different sort of person, she could build a life with them, but the future she'd have in the Dark Court wasn't a future that she could accept. Monsters don't become house pets, and she didn't want to become a monster.

"Well"—Jill plopped down in her seat again—"that was interesting."

"What?" Leslie's heart sped. She might have the Sight, but that didn't give her faery hearing or reflexes.

"He said—and I quote—'Tell Leslie that I send my love or anything else she might need.'" Jill folded her arms over her chest, leaned back, and studied Leslie's expression. "Gorgeous guy, apparently loves you, and you—"

"Drop it." Leslie's calm faltered then. Her hand started shaking as she gathered up her notes. "Seriously. He's . . . a part of my past. He's why I moved here. To be away from him."

Michael put a hand on Leslie's arm. "Is he threatening—"

"No. He isn't here to hurt me. He . . . he'd protect me at his own risk. Our situation is just"—she looked in Irial's direction and caught his gaze—"complicated. I needed space."

She didn't look back at her study group. No one spoke, and she couldn't think of anything else to say. The awkwardness of the situation was more than she wanted to deal with. *How do I say that I love and am loved by . . . Dark Kings? Faeries? Monsters?* There weren't words to explain—and the only one there who deserved her explanation already knew it.

She stood. "I'll catch you in class."

She slung her bag over her shoulder and walked away. She paused after she passed him and whispered, "Good night, Irial."

"Be safe, love. I'll be here if you need me," he promised her. There was no censure in his words; he gave her the reassurances he knew she needed: that he loved her, that he protected her, and that he did so from a distance.

Faeries don't lie, he'd once told her, *so listen carefully to what we* actually *say.*

By every mortal standard, the worst faeries in the world were those in the Dark Court. They fed on the baser emotions; they engaged in activities that the other—also amoral—faery courts repudiated. They were also the only ones she truly trusted or understood.

. ◆ .

IRIAL WATCHED her walk away until he was sure that she was within sight of her guards. She grew stronger every week. If any mortal could've survived the Dark Court, it was his Leslie. Her strength awed him, even as it manifested in choosing to continue loving two faeries but to be with neither of them. Few mortals had the mettle that she did.

But being strong didn't mean that she should hurt. If he had his way, she'd spend the rest of her life cosseted. *And that life would be as long as Niall's.* Irial had learned centuries ago that the world didn't always bend to his will. *Unfortunately.*

After he was sure Leslie was far enough away that she wouldn't think he was stalking her, he walked away from the coffee shop. There were always guards near enough to hear her if she cried out for help. He'd prefer that there were guards walking alongside her, but she would suffer more for that. Their visible presence saddened her, so the guards had been ordered not to crowd her. *At least not all of the time.* It was a delicate dance, watching her but not being too present. In this, as in so many other things, Leslie was an anomaly. She accepted their guardianship, but not their omnipresence. She accepted their love, but not their companionship.

Everything on her terms or not at all. Just like Niall.

He walked only a block before he saw Gabriel leaning against his steed, which was currently in the form of a deep-green classic Mustang. If Irial asked, Gabriel could spout off the year, engine, and modifications his steed was currently adopting, and for a moment, Irial considered doing just that. It would be more entertaining than a lecture.

Gabriel pushed away from the car. "What are you doing?"

Irial shrugged. "Checking on her."

"And if Niall finds out . . . your *king* who told you to stay away from her? What do you think he'll say?" Gabriel joined him, walking in the direction Irial had already been going. The car didn't follow.

"I suppose he'd be angry." Irial smiled to himself. Angry Niall was far more fun than sulking Niall. If it wasn't so counterproductive, Irial'd spend more time actively trying to provoke his new king. *My only king.* Sometimes the fact that he had a king amused Irial to perverse degrees. After centuries of leading the Dark Court, he was monarch no more. He'd returned to what he was before, a Gancanagh, fatally addictive to mortals, solitary by nature—except that Irial had never really been one to follow anyone's conventions but his own. Rather than resume solitary status, as was typical of former Dark Kings or Queens, he swore fealty and stayed in his court as advisor to his new king.

Gabriel scowled at him. "Seriously, Iri, you can't see her if you want to stay in the court . . . and you know he needs you. You don't expect him to put up with this, do you?"

"I wasn't planning to tell him. Are *you* planning on spilling my secrets?" Irial stopped and stepped in front of his friend and former advisor. "Tell him the things I do when I'm not dutifully awaiting his attention?"

"Don't be an ass." Gabriel punched Irial. The force of it knocked Irial backward. Blood trickled from Irial's lip. The Hound had always hit with enough force to draw blood.

Several garish rings on his hand assured that every punch would wound—or leave behind distinct bruises.

"Now that you've made your point"—Irial licked the blood from his lips—"tell me: have you found her father? Or the wretch?"

Gabriel shook his head. "Niall didn't want you knowing about that."

"Niall doesn't always get what he wants though, does he?" Irial watched a pair of coeds sizing Gabriel up. He spared them a smile that had them changing their path to approach—until Gabriel snarled at them.

The moment evoked a longing for simpler days, when he'd first met Niall and the three of them had traveled together. Various Hounds and Dark Court fey joined them here or there, but Gabriel was always with them to keep Irial safe. Niall was an innocent of sorts: he'd had no idea that he traveled with the Dark King, no idea that he himself was a Gancanagh. He was young and foolish, trusting and forgiving.

Until he met me.

Gabriel shrugged. His loyalty was to his Hounds first and then to the Dark King. A former Dark King, friend or not, fell somewhere after that. "I'm not disobeying my king, Iri, not even for you. If he wants to tell you, he will. Come on. Let's go back to Huntsdale before he—"

"No." Irial wasn't in the mood to argue, at least not with Gabriel. The Hound was obstinate on his best days. "I'm not with Leslie, so you don't need to intercede for the king. Unless he sent you after me?"

Gabriel held out his bare arms where Irial's commands had once been written out, where Niall's would now appear. "There are no orders here."

"So go."

Gabriel shook his head. "I thought *he* was an ass when he was with the Summer Court and trying to stay away from you, but you're both a pain these days. Either work your shit out or walk away from the court, Iri, because this isn't how you obey your king *or* work anything out with the one you claim to love."

Irial didn't answer. There wasn't anything to say. His feelings for Niall and his feelings for Leslie were tangled together. He wanted Leslie to live surrounded by the protection of the Dark Court, indulged and cosseted while she lived out her mortal life. He wanted Niall to woo her and bring her home. He couldn't truly have a relationship with either of them, but he'd done what he could to make them safe to have one with each other. If they were together, he'd have both of his beloveds in one house. It was the closest to a relationship with them that he thought possible. It was also what would make them happiest. They were just too damn difficult to take the obvious path.

Which is part of why I love them.

Leslie let herself into the building, wishing for a moment that Irial had walked her home or followed her. She knew she was safe, knew that her building was secure, knew the logical things that should make her feel okay. She still had panic attacks, though. Her therapist assured her that she was making great progress, but the hypervigilance was worse at night. *And in close spaces. And in strange spaces. And in the dark when I am alone.* Sometimes, she thought about inviting her faery guardians in so 'she wasn't alone: *My very own monsters to chase away the fears.*

Now that she felt her own emotions, she wished she could give him the ones that left her shaking in cold sweats from nightmares she barely remembered. She wished she could give him the edge of the bad emotions—to nourish him and to let her get sleep.

It didn't work like that, though. Since she'd severed her connection to Irial, she was left with mere mortal solutions. She went into her apartment, turned the door lock, but not the bolt. *Not yet.* She flicked on a light and then another. Then she checked each window. She opened the closets, peered under the bed, and pushed the shower curtain aside. It was obvious that no one would fit under the bed: there was no room. It was impossible to hide behind the shower curtain: it was gathered. Still, if she didn't check, she'd be unable to rest. Once she was confident that she was alone, she turned the bolt.

Her pepper spray stayed in reach though. *Always.* Her phone was in reach too. The therapist, the girls in group, they talked about the difference between being cautious and being unwell. They claimed that she was being rational, that caution wasn't bad, but she didn't feel very rational.

"I'm afraid," she whispered. "But it's okay to be afraid. It's normal. I'm normal."

Silently she fixed a salad and took it into the living room. She slipped a DVD into the machine, so the silence wasn't as weighty. The opening of *Buffy the Vampire Slayer,* a show that she'd found on DVD and loved, made her smile. It was a strange security blanket, but it never failed to remind her that she could be strong. *That I am strong.*

The phone rang. She picked it up. No one was there. She laid it down. It rang again.

"Hello?"

Again, no one was there.

Twice more it rang. *Unknown Caller* her readout showed. Every time, the caller didn't speak. It wasn't the first time she'd had weird calls. It had happened a few times the past month.

Logic said it was nothing, but caution meant she was feeling twitchy.

Resolutely, she ignored the next few calls. Her door buzzer went off twice. She paced as the calls continued for almost thirty more minutes.

So when the phone rang again after ten minutes of silence, she was frazzled. "What? Who do you think you are?"

"Leslie? Are you okay?" Niall was on the other end of the line. "I don't . . . are you all right?"

"I'm sorry." She put her hand over her mouth, trying not to let her hysterical burst of laughter out, and walked to the door again. It was secure. She was safe in her apartment.

"What's going on?"

For a moment, she didn't want to tell him. Whoever was harassing her wasn't a faery. Very few of them even used phones, and none of them would have her number. *Or reason to call.* This was a human problem.

Not a faery issue. Not Niall's issue.

"Talk to me?" he asked. "Please?"

So she did.

When she was done, Niall was silent for so long that she wondered if they'd been disconnected. Her heart beat too loudly as she clutched her phone. "Niall?"

"Let me come stay there or send someone. Just until we—"

"I can't. We've talked about this." Leslie sank down onto her sofa. "If there were a faery threat, it would be different."

"*Any* threat is unacceptable, Leslie," he interrupted, with a new darkness in his voice. It was the unflinching power of the Dark King, and she liked it. "You don't need to deal with this. Let me—"

"No." She closed her eyes. "I'll change the number. It's probably just some drunk misdialing."

"And if it's not?"

"I'll go to the police." She pulled a blanket over her as if it would stop the shivering that had started. "It's not a Dark Court concern."

"*You* are a Dark Court concern, and that's not going to change," Niall reminded her gently. "Your safety and your happiness will always be our concern. Irial and I both—"

"If doing so negates my happiness, will you still interfere, Niall?"

Niall was silent for several moments. Only his measured breathing made clear that he was still listening. Finally he said, "You are a difficult person to reason with sometimes."

"I know." Her grip on the phone loosened a little. For all of the passions that drove him, Niall would do his best to let her have her distance. On that, he and Irial seemed to agree. Of course, if she so much as hinted that she wanted them to intervene, people could die at a word. The reality of that power wasn't something she liked to ponder overmuch. Instead, she asked, "Talk to me about something else?"

Niall, however, wasn't eager to let the topic drop, not entirely. "You know I want to respect your need to be away from us, but Gabe is in the area. He had to see someone. If you needed anyone . . ."

"What I need is a friend who talks to me so I can think about something good." Leslie stretched out on the sofa, pepper spray in reach on the coffee table, Buffy staking monsters on the television, and Niall's voice in her ear. "Be my friend? Please? Talk to me?"

He sighed. "There was a new exhibit at the gallery I was telling you about last month."

Niall wouldn't ignore the issue, but he would cooperate to a degree. And knowing he was out there protecting her made Leslie feel a little safer too. *They both are.* She felt guilty sometimes for the way they both continued to try to take care of her, but she also knew that having the protection of the Dark Kings was all that kept her safe from being drawn back into faery politics or becoming a victim of the strong solitary faeries. There were those who would happily destroy her if they learned that she was beloved of both the current Dark King and the last Dark King.

For a breath she hoped that whoever called, if they were trying to upset her, was a faery. If it was a faery, Irial or Niall would find out. They would fix it.

The reality of how easily she could sanction violence made her pause. *That,* she thought, *is exactly why I can't come back to either of you.* She forced the thought aside. Friendship was all she could have with them, and even that was tenuous. She kept barriers in place: no speaking to Irial, no seeing Niall, and no touching either one of them. At first, she'd thought she could put them in her past and that they would forget about her, and maybe someday they would reach that point.

"Did you buy anything this time?" she asked.

"What? You think I can't go to a gallery without buying something?" His voice was teasing, sweet, calming.

"I do."

"Three prints," he said.

She laughed, letting herself enjoy the comfort he offered. "*Someone* has a problem."

"Oh, but you should see them," he began, and then he told her about each print in loving detail, and then about others he saw but didn't buy, and by the time he was done, she was smiling and yawning and able to sleep.

IRIAL SAW THE BOY, Michael, lurking outside the building. He stayed to the shadows, making it obvious that he was trying to be stealthy. He stood in a spot where the streetlights didn't eliminate the cover of darkness, yet still had a clear line of sight to the entrance to the building. The mortal had a large cup of coffee, a jacket, and dark clothes. The combination made Irial aware that the boy intended to stay there for some time.

Why? He'd seemed tense earlier, and Irial hadn't missed the glares aimed at him. The glares were not unwarranted; jealousy was a mortal trait. Setting up watch outside Leslie's building seemed overreactive. *Usually.* Irial spared himself a wry smile. *Watching over her is overreactive unless it's me doing it or ordering it.* The difference was that Irial knew the horrors that existed in the world around them—had, in fact, ordered horrors committed—so his cautious streak where Leslie was concerned was logical.

"Why are you here?" he asked.

Michael startled.

He wasn't fey, nor did he have the Sight, so Irial made himself visible. At this hour, Leslie wouldn't be coming outside. *And if she did . . .* Irial smiled. She wouldn't expect him to act any differently. Leslie saw him for who he was, for what he was, and loved him still. Despite being what nightmares are made of, Irial wasn't frightening to her.

It wasn't Leslie who saw him, though. Between one step and the next, he made himself seen to another mortal. If Michael had been a threat, Irial wouldn't do so.

The boy swallowed nervously, took a step backward, and blinked several times. To his credit, he didn't run or scream or do anything awkward. It spoke well of Leslie's character judgment that she'd selected the mortal as a friend.

"What are you doing here?" Irial asked as gently as he could. "Why are you at this place? At this hour? Hiding in the dark?"

"Checking on her." The mortal straightened his shoulders, stood still enough to almost hide his trembling. "What *are* you? You just *appeared.* Right? You did."

"I did." Irial repressed a smile at the boy's bravery. Many

mortals did not handle the shock of seeing the impossible become manifest. Leslie had chosen well when she'd made friends with this one.

"It doesn't matter. I won't let you hurt her," Michael said.

Irial waited. Silence often proved to be more incentive than questions.

"I saw you earlier. Everyone did. You're the one stalking her," Michael accused.

Irial let the shadows around him shift visibly, let his wings become seen. "No, I'm *visiting* her, watching out for her. She knows where I am. She expects me to be here. Does she know you're here?"

"No." The boy's gaze flickered nervously to the ground, back to Irial, and then to the building. "I worry, though. She's so . . . fragile."

"No one will hurt her. *Ever.*" Irial shook his head. "Once, I was the King of Nightmares. Now, I'm something else. No matter what I am, I'll be here keeping her safe as long as we both live."

Michael narrowed his gaze. "You're not human."

"She is," Irial said. "And she needs human friends . . . like you."

"Michael." The boy held out his hand. "I'm Michael."

"Irial." Irial shook the mortal's hand. "I know. I watch when you can't see me too. You care for her."

Michael didn't reply, but he didn't need to. Irial had watched the mortal talk to her, escort her to her building, say things that made her smile. He was a good human. Unfortunately for him, he was also half in love with Leslie, ready to protect her from threats. Irial had seen that clearly several weeks ago when he'd watched them walking at night. If Irial cared overmuch for humans, he'd feel sympathy for the boy; as it was, Irial was practical: Michael's emotions made him useful.

"Tell me why you are here," Irial encouraged.

"Someone's been calling her at weird hours," Michael blurted. "After the way you were watching her, I thought maybe it was you. She says not to worry, but she . . . I just . . ."

"I understand." Irial smiled and dropped an arm around the boy's shoulders. "These are the sorts of things I'd like you to tell me, Michael. Come sit with me."

Michael glanced at her building. "Shouldn't we . . . you at least . . . stay *here?*"

"I have a flat across the street for when I'm in town." Irial led the boy to a nondescript building. "That way I'm close if she needs me. If not me, there are others near enough to hear her should she call for us."

"Oh." Michael looked at him for a moment. His gaze was assessing, albeit far too trusting.

In another era, in another life, walking off blindly with a Gancanagh was foolish. *Perhaps it still is.* Irial meant the boy no harm. He was merely a tool, a useful resource. Leslie was what mattered. But for one other in all the world, everyone else was fair game for whatever he needed in order to assure her happiness and safety.

· ◆ ·

WHEN LESLIE WOKE the next morning, she was still holding the phone. She didn't hear a dial tone, so she asked, "Hello?"

"Good morning," Niall said.

"You stayed on the phone while I *slept?*" She sat up.

Niall laughed. "You don't talk in your sleep."

"I snore."

"A little," he admitted. "But I liked being there to hear it."

"Weirdo." She felt safe, though. Having him there—even

only on the phone—made her feel protected. "I'm glad you were . . . here."

"I wish I was really *there.*"

"I . . . I know." She never knew the right words to reply to such things. They all fell short, partly because they weren't the whole truth. She wanted to be with him—*and Irial*—but doing so would mean being in the Dark Court.

They stayed silent. She heard him breathing, heard him waiting for something she couldn't give him.

"We should stop talking." She clutched the phone. "I can't . . . I'm not . . . I need time to live, and your court . . ."

I know." His voice was gentle. "You're too good to live here with us."

"I didn't say that!" She felt the tears threaten. She missed them, missed Niall, Irial, Gabriel, Ani, Tish, Rabbit . . . her court, her *family.*

"I said it," Niall murmured. "I love you."

"You too," she whispered.

"Be safe. If you need anything—"

"I know." She disconnected then. What she needed was to let go; what she wanted was to hold on tighter. Irial was addictive to touch, and Niall had to stay with his court. Being with Irial would kill her. Being with Niall would mean living in the Dark Court. She couldn't have a normal mortal life in the middle of the Dark Court; she couldn't let herself become the person she would be if she lived there. She wasn't ever going to be anything other than human, and humans didn't thrive in their world. They died.

Self-pity doesn't fix a thing, she lectured.

So she got up and got ready for class, and she knew that somewhere out there in the streets faeries watched to guard her, that Irial waited somewhere to protect her, that farther away Niall waited to listen and help her believe in herself. She was not alone, but she was still lonely.

· ◆ ·

IRIAL FOLLOWED Leslie without her knowing. It felt wrong to hide himself from her, but he was quick enough to slip out of sight when she turned to glance over her shoulder.

"I'm sorry, love," he whispered each time. It felt too near to a lie, but if she saw him following her so closely she would be alarmed. They'd never spoken any agreement, but he kept himself out of sight except for their once-a-week silent meetings. If she saw him so near, she'd know that he'd learned of her disquieting calls or she'd suspect that something else was amiss. He'd rather not upset her if he could avoid doing so.

When she went into the red brick building, he waited and watched the courtyard. Mortals fascinated him far more now that he was a Gancanagh again. Their flirty laughs and knowing smiles, their defiant gazes and inviting postures—it was not an easy thing to resist so much potential. He didn't remember being so easily intrigued by them, but it had been a lifetime since he was a Gancanagh. Being Dark King had nullified that for him, just as it now did for Niall.

Niall . . . who would beat me half to death if I indulged.

Irial grinned at the thought. It had been too long since Niall had been willing to fight with him. Perhaps when this matter was resolved, he'd tell the Dark King that he'd been pondering enjoying some sport with mortals.

Business before fun.

So Irial waited until Leslie was safely in the building and then he went to find Gabriel. Her class lasted for not quite an hour, but he'd be back well before that. It wouldn't take long to find someone who could locate Gabriel. Then, they'd need to decide if Niall should be involved in locating whoever was upsetting Leslie or if the matter could be handled with more discretion.

· ◆ ·

CLASS HAD ONLY JUST BEGUN when Leslie felt the vibrations from her phone. The professor had a strict "no phones in class" policy, so she tried to ignore the phone, but after the fourth time, she began to worry. It rang silently in her pocket. Text messages came in, making it vibrate again.

Carefully, she slid it out of her pocket and glanced at the message.

"Time's up," the first message read.

She didn't know the number it came from.

The second one read, "If you want Them exposed ignore me. If not come down NOW."

Them? There weren't a lot of threats that would make her panic, but danger to Irial or Niall was near the top of the list. The threats were vague. There was no reason to assume that the *Them* meant Irial and Niall. She shivered.

The third text added, "I know WHAT they are."

Her hand tightened on the phone for a moment, and then she shoved it into her pocket, got up, and walked out of class. There was no way she was going to keep her regular routine if someone was out there threatening her. Her hands were shaking as she accessed her voice mail. *Faeries don't leave creepy messages. Faeries don't text threats.*

She knew it wasn't a faery.

She stepped into the sunlight outside the building and saw him—her mystery harasser.

Cherub-pretty and too familiar, her brother sat on one of the tables in the small courtyard outside Davis Hall. His feet were on the bench, and he had one arm across his middle. His unzipped jacket covered his hand; the other hand rested on his knee. He didn't stand when he saw her approaching, but there was little likelihood that she'd be offering him a sisterly embrace. Despite the irritation of seeing him, it was almost a relief. She might not like him, might not have anything but loathing left for him, but he was her brother.

"What the hell, Ren?" She folded her arms over her chest to hide the shaking. "You think you're funny calling and—"

"No." Ren grinned. "I think I'm smart. You get spooked, and your little friends will show up. Do you know how much I can get paid once I prove that there are *monsters* living around us?"

He stood, his arm still against his chest.

Leslie forced a laugh. "Monsters? Really?" She gestured around her. "The only monster I see is *you.*"

For an odd moment, she realized that it was true: No Dark Court faeries were in sight. *Because I'm supposed to be in class.* She thought about screaming. One of them was surely in hearing range. *He's my brother.* If they came, if they saw him near her, they'd hurt him. Despite everything, that wasn't her first choice.

"Your boyfriend wasn't human, Les." Ren stepped forward, grabbed her arm, and pulled her closer. When they were near enough that it looked like they should embrace, he let go and pulled his jacket open. Inside, he held a gun, hidden from view by both the jacket and her proximity. "Scream or fight, and I'll shoot you, Sis."

Leslie stared at the gun for a long moment. She knew nothing about guns, nothing about make or model, nothing about their effect on faeries. When she pulled her gaze away, she looked at her brother's face. "Why?"

"Nothing personal." Ren smiled, and it wasn't a reassuring look. "You think I *like* working with low-end dealers? I can make a pretty sum if I collect a freak. Business is business."

"I don't know what you think they are—"

"Don't care. Smile, now." Ren dropped his arm over her shoulders and started walking. She felt the gun muzzle pressing against her side.

"This is a mistake." Leslie didn't look around. *He's my brother. He won't actually shoot me.* Ren was a lot of things, had done horrific things, but he'd never had the stomach to dirty his hands directly. Like everything in his life, he half-assed this too.

"Let's go home, Les." Ren kissed her cheek and reminded her, "Smile. I'm not intending to shoot you if I don't have to. You're just bait."

She smiled, trying her best to look convincing. "Why?"

"Met a guy. He had a business offer." Ren lifted one shoulder in a shrug. "I saw the pictures. You were living like a freaking celebrity. Looked like you were having a killer time. . . ." He paused and laughed at his own weak joke. "The man who pays more gets the prize. Your old man wants to ante up, I don't shoot him or take him in. He doesn't want to pay, I go with the original plan."

Blackmail Irial?

The thought of it was ludicrous: Irial would kill Ren. Maybe Niall would find a solution, but Niall wasn't nearby. For all she knew, Irial wasn't either. She saw him once a week. *Last night.* Today, he was who knew where. *This isn't their fault, not their problem.* If they got hurt because of her, she wouldn't be able to recover from that.

Leslie stumbled.

Ren pulled her tighter to him and shoved the gun tighter into her side. "Don't be stupid. You're not strong enough to escape *or* fast enough to outrun a bullet."

"I'm . . . not. I *tripped*, Ren." She tried to keep the waver from her voice.

What do I do?

Letting him into her home seemed stupid. Calling out for help seemed dangerous. Her brother had been behind the horrors she couldn't forget. *If I call for them, they'll kill him.* Once, she had wanted to believe he was sick, that he could get well if he got help. *Addiction is a disease*, that's what she'd reminded herself. It didn't mean the things he'd done, the thing he was currently doing, were okay, though. *Not every addict wants to get well.*

"We'll go to your place, and you can call them," Ren said. "He can pay me more, or I can take him to them. His choice."

Leslie felt numb as she walked with her brother. If she called Niall, help would come. Irial would know too. Gabriel would know.

And my brother will die.

If she didn't call, she wasn't sure what would happen. Niall would call her sooner, or later; Irial would notice when she wasn't at the coffee shop; and the guards would notice. Neither Dark King would invade her privacy—unless she was in danger. She knew that. *What would happen if Ren shot them? If he knows what they are, what sort of bullets does he have?* She thought about seeing Niall when he was sick from steel exposure. If the bullets were iron or steel, if that entered a faery's body—any other than a regent—it would be horrific. Leslie wasn't ready to make the decisions she felt like she had to make, nor was she able to ignore them. Ren was here.

THE TANGLES of panic and fear and guilt hit Irial like an unwelcome banquet. If they were anyone else's fears, it would be a welcomed treat, but the emotions that assailed him were hers.

They'd come flooding toward him over his mostly severed connection with Leslie.

No. He hadn't figured her pursuer would enter her classroom. Most mortals didn't escalate from a few calls to a dangerous public scene that quickly.

"Leslie needs help. Get Niall," Irial snarled. "Now."

Mortals paused and shuddered, but they didn't hear.

Only faeries heard his order—and he knew that Dark Court faeries would obey as quickly as they had when he was still a king.

He ran to Leslie's classroom; she wasn't there.

Leslie, he called, hoping that the thread that bound them was still alive enough to let her hear him. Once in a while a fleeting moment of connection flared in it. He'd felt her panic. Now he needed to feel *her,* to know where she was. He called louder, *LESLIE.*

The thread that once bound them lay silent.

Irial felt a surge of terror. In the centuries he'd led the Dark Court, Irial had only felt true terror one other time. Then, it had been Niall in danger; then, he had been useless. Now, he felt much the same: she was in danger, and he hadn't been there to stop it.

Abject terror filled him as he ran through the streets seeking her, listening for her voice.

Then he heard her: "Ren, this is a mistake."

Irial moved through the streets toward her voice, and just outside her door, he stopped. Leslie's brother stood with a gun barrel shoved into her side. Irial could smell it, the bitter tang of cold steel. Steel wouldn't kill him, nor would the copper and lead of the bullets inside the weapon. They would *hurt,* but faeries—especially strong ones—healed from such things. Mortals didn't. Leslie wouldn't.

If she were fey, he could safely pull her out of reach. If she were fey, she'd likely heal from a gunshot. She wasn't.

Should've killed the boy then. He had watched over her, had guards at the ready, yet Ren had escorted her away. *If I'd have killed him then . . .* Irial winced at the thought of Niall's pain—at *our* pain—if Leslie was hurt by his prior decision to let Ren live.

"I'll remedy that mistake," Irial murmured.

. ◆ .

LESLIE'S HAND shook so much that she dropped the key.

Ren smacked her with one hand while keeping the gun steadily pressed into her side. "Pick it up. Don't try anything, Les. Really."

"I don't know how you think this is going to work." She snatched up her keys. "You think my ex is going to just show up?"

Ren gave her an unreadable look. "No. I think you're going to find a way to reach him or one of them—I don't care which of them—and until one of them comes through your door, we'll sit in your dive of an apartment and wait."

She shoved the key in the lock and glared at him. "Then prepare to wait because *unlike you* I don't sacrifice other people to protect myself."

A look of what seemed like regret crossed his face, but it passed in a breath. "We all do what we have to."

Leslie opened the door, and for a brief moment as she stepped inside the building, the gun wasn't against her. It didn't last long enough to be of use.

She jumped as Ren closed the building door.

He gestured with the gun. "Up."

"If I had said the word, he would've killed you," Leslie said.

Ren followed her up the stairs. "Why didn't you?"

"I'm not sure, Ren." She paused on the last stair and glanced back at him. "Because real family protects each other?"

Could I push him down the stairs? Am I fast enough to get away while he falls? Letting him inside her apartment seemed like a sure way to be trapped. *He'll sleep, though.* She thought about it, escaping while he slept, but then just as quickly thought about him jacked up and paranoid. He was terrible when he was strung out.

She shoved as hard as she could with both hands and then she ran.

"Bitch!" Ren cursed and stumbled.

"Pleasepleaseplease." She jammed the key into her apartment door and slammed it behind her. She threw the bolt with a shaking hand, and then retreated farther into the apartment.

She couldn't leave. She couldn't be sure whether he'd shoot through the door. She couldn't think beyond the fear wrapped around her.

Irial. She started to speak as they once had, but their metaphysical bond was gone—burned away by her own choice.

This isn't a faery matter.

But it was. If Ren was looking for Irial, if he was looking for Niall, for Gabriel, for her Dark Court family, it did concern them. She pulled out her phone and pressed the button she'd programmed but never dialed, closed her eyes, and waited.

"Leslie." Relief laced Irial's voice. "Are you . . . safe?"

"Did you see him?" she started, and then quickly added, "Don't come here!"

"Where are you?"

"My apartment," she said.

"Alone?"

"I am the only one inside my apartment." She shivered His voice made her want to cry, even now. *Especially now.* He was every monstrous thing she shouldn't miss, every nightmare she shouldn't crave.

"Are you hurt?"

She shook her head, as if he could see. Memories of the way he'd held her when she wept came flooding back. "No," she whispered.

"Stay, inside. I'll fix this."

Tears slipped down her cheeks. Hearing his kindness and his darkness made her miss him as intensely as she had those first days after their bond was severed. "Don't come. He wants to hurt you. Someone told him about you, about faeries. He's here to . . . he says he'd let you pay more for his silence, but you can't trust him. You *can't* . . . and I can't . . . if you were hurt, if Niall . . ."

Irial sighed. "My beautiful Shadow Girl . . . no mortal will hurt me *or* our Niall. I promise."

A sob escaped her lips. "Ren's in my building. He has a gun. I should call the police. I couldn't . . . if you were hurt . . . I just . . . I don't want him to ever hurt you, either of you. Neither of you can come in here. Someone else . . . I can't ask anyone else to either. I just—"

"Hush, now," Irial soothed. "I'll stay exactly where I am. This will be fixed, and neither I nor Niall will be injured."

"Promise?"

"We will not be injured by Ren, and I won't move a step. I promise." Irial's voice was the same comforting croon that had kept her steady when she felt the horrible emotions that he had once funneled through her body.

She whispered, "I wish I was with you instead of here."

Irial didn't hesitate, didn't make her regret her admission. He said, "Talk to me, love. Just talk to me while we wait."

IRIAL WANTED to rip the door from its frame, but to do so would mean that the building would be vulnerable. He stepped away from the doorway to her apartment building as Gabriel and Niall approached.

"Push the button to open the door, Leslie," he said.

She gasped.

"Open the door," he repeated.

"You said you wouldn't move." She pushed the button even as she said it.

"I didn't. I said I wouldn't take a step, and I didn't." Irial put one hand to the window in front of him, wishing he could move, wishing he could be the one to enter her building. He'd promised. He'd assured her that he wouldn't move. He didn't intend to twist his words with either Leslie or Niall if he could help it. If Niall were going in there alone, Irial wouldn't be waiting so calmly, but Niall had Gabriel at his side, and the Hound would keep their king safe.

A weak laugh from Leslie made him smile. "You said 'a step,' didn't you? A lot of steps doesn't break the vow."

"Indeed," he murmured. "My clever girl."

"I couldn't stand playing word games all the time," she said, "but I'll try again. Promise me Ren won't hurt you. Promise me you are safe right now."

Irial watched the Dark King in all of his furious majesty drag Ren into the street. Mortal and faery were invisible as long as Niall had his hands on Ren—and he did. One of Niall's hands was on Ren's throat.

"I am safe, love," Irial promised. "So are you now."

"You always keep me safe, don't you?" Leslie whispered. "Even when I'm not aware of it, you're here. I want to tell you that you don't have to, but—"

"Shush. I needed a hobby now that I have all this free time." He felt a burst of love in the tattered remains of their connection. "I'm lousy at knitting."

She sighed. "You need to let go."

"Never. I'm yours as long as I live. You knew that when you left me."

In the street between the buildings, Gabriel waited. Oghams appeared on his forearms as the Dark King's orders became manifest.

For a moment, Leslie was silent. Then, she whispered so low that it was more breath than words, "I'm glad you were here today."

Gabriel spoke softly enough that Leslie wouldn't hear him through the phone line: "Is she uninjured?"

"I'll be here." Irial walked into the doorway of the building where he had his no-longer-secret apartment and stared up at her window. "But you didn't need me, did you? You'd already got yourself to safety."

"If I call the police now . . ."

Gently, Irial told her, "There's no one for them to collect, love."

"Sometimes, I sleep better knowing you . . . and Niall . . ." She faltered.

"Love you from a safe distance," he finished.

"Yes."

"And we always will. Whatever distance—however far or near you want us—that's where we will both be as long as we live." Irial paused, knowing the time was wrong, but not knowing if she'd ever call him again. "Niall will be here tonight. Let him comfort you. Let yourself comfort him."

Gabriel stood scowling.

Irial held up a hand for silence. "I need to go deal with things. Think about seeing Niall?"

He glanced up at the window where Leslie now stood watching him. When her emotions were this raw, she drew upon their residual connection like a starving thing. He shivered at the feelings roiling inside of her. He couldn't drink them, not now that she'd cut apart their bond, but he could still feel them.

"I . . ." Leslie started, but she couldn't say the words. She put her hand on the window as if to touch him through the glass and distance.

"I know." Irial disconnected and then silently added, *I love you too, Shadow Girl.*

Then he slid the phone into his pocket and stepped up to Gabriel. "Well?"

Extending his arm so Irial could only see part of the orders, Gabriel gestured to the street in front of them. "Walk."

• ◆ •

ONCE THEY REACHED the sidewalk café, Irial waited until Gabriel left before taking a seat across the table from his king. When it was just the two of them, he asked, "Shall we try to enjoy lunch? Or do you want to try to reprimand me for the error of my ways?"

The look Niall gave him was assessing. "I'm not sure which of those would please you more."

Irial shrugged. "Both are tempting."

"I asked you to stay away from her." Niall's possessiveness beat against Irial's skin like moth wings.

"I have trouble with authority," Irial said. "She's safe, though, isn't she?"

Niall smiled, reluctantly. "She is. From *him* . . ."

"Good."

The waitress had already delivered a drink. Niall's allure to mortals did result in superb service.

Irial glanced up and a waitress appeared. "Another of these."

He pointed at Niall's glass. "Fresh bread. Cheese tray. No menus just now."

Once she was gone, he sat back and waited.

Niall stared at him for several breaths before getting to the inevitable issue. "You gave me your vow of *fealty*."

"True." Irial reached out and took Niall's glass.

When Niall didn't react, Irial drank from it.

The Dark King still didn't respond. So, Irial leaned forward, flipped open the front of Niall's jacket, and retrieved the cigarette case from the inside pocket. To his credit, Niall didn't flinch when Irial's fingers grazed Niall's chest.

Silently, Irial extracted a cigarette, packed it, and held it to his lips.

Niall scowled, but he extended a lighter nonetheless.

Irial took a long drag from the now lit cigarette before speaking. "I'm better at this game, Niall. You can be the intimidating, bad-tempered king to everyone but me. We *both* know that I wouldn't raise a hand to stop you if you wanted to take all of your tempers out on me. There's only one person I'd protect at your expense . . . and her life span is but a blink of ours."

"You're addictive to mortals now."

"I know," Irial agreed. "That's why I won't touch her. Not ever again."

"You still love her."

Irial took another drag on his cigarette. "Yet I did the one thing that would assure that I can't be with her. I am quite capable of continuing to love someone"—he caught Niall's gaze—"without touching them. You, of everyone in this world, know that."

As always, Niall was the first to look away. *That* subject was forbidden. Niall might understand now why Irial had not stepped in when Niall offered himself over to the court's abuse centuries ago, but he didn't forgive—not completely.

Maybe in another twelve centuries.

"She is sad," Irial said, drawing Niall's gaze back, "as you are."

"She doesn't want . . ." The words died before Niall could complete the lie. "She *says* she doesn't want a relationship with either of us."

Irial flicked his ash onto the sidewalk. "Sometimes you need to accept what a person—or faery—can offer. Do you think I'd come see her if she didn't want me to?"

Niall stilled.

"Every week she is at the same place at the same time." Irial offered back Niall's half-empty glass.

Once Niall took it and drank, Irial continued, "If she wanted to not see me, she'd have only to change one detail. I didn't come one week, and a faery—one whose name I will not share—came in my stead to watch her response. She looked for me. She couldn't focus—and the next week? She was relieved when she saw me. I tasted it."

Niall startled. "I thought that you were . . . the ink exchange was severed."

"It was severed enough that we are unbound," Irial assured him. "I don't weaken her." He didn't add that Leslie weakened him, that he came to watch her each week so she could do just that. It wasn't conscious on her part, but she drew strength from him. Irial also suspected that his own longevity decreased as hers increased. That wasn't something Niall needed to know.

"You are hiding things." Niall took the cigarette from Irial's hand and crushed it in the ashtray. He slid forward one of the full glasses that a waitress had wordlessly delivered.

"Nothing that harms Leslie." Irial accepted the glass. "That's the only answer you'll get."

"Because you don't want to know how I'll feel about what you've done." Niall lifted not the untouched glass but the one from which Irial had drunk. "If your actions harm *you,* I would be upset. I hate that it's true, but it is."

"I'm glad." Irial reached out so his hand hovered over Niall's. He avoided touching the Dark King during such conversations if possible. *Because I am a coward.* "Go see her. I cannot give you what you'd like in this life, but I can promise that I mean her—and you—only happiness."

"Life was easier before."

"For you, perhaps. I could taste all of your emotions then," Irial reminded him. It wasn't a lie; he *had* been able to taste them. He just didn't mention that he still could. "You never hated me."

"It was easier when I thought you didn't know that." Niall watched mortals walking along the street. "I still don't like that you see her."

"You are my king. You could command me to stop seeing her."

Niall turned his gaze to Irial. "What would you do?"

"Blind myself, if you were foolish enough to use *those* words." Irial stood, pulled out a few bills, and tucked them under the ashtray. "If not? Break my oath to you."

"What good is fealty if I can't command you?"

"I would follow any order you gave me, Niall, as long as it didn't endanger Leslie . . . or you." Irial emptied the glass. "Ask me to carve out my heart. Tell me to betray our court, the court I've lived to serve and protect for longer than you've existed, and I would obey you. You are my king."

The intensity of Niall's earlier anger was equaled now by hope and fear in even measures.

"You both need me, and"—Irial set the glass down, pushed in his chair, and let the moment stretch out just a bit longer as Niall's hope overwhelmed his fear—"I will not fail either of you ever again."

The Dark King didn't speak, but he didn't have to: Irial

could taste the relief, the confusion, and the growing sliver of contentment.

"Go see her. Be her friend if nothing else. *You* are safe for her to touch now. I made sure of it." Irial paused. "And Niall? Let her believe it was me who solved her problem."

Niall's expression was unwavering; he admitted nothing in look or word.

Irial crouched down in front of him and caught his gaze.

"She won't think less of me for it. It's you she still sees as tamer than we are. Let her keep that."

"Why?"

"Because you both need the illusion"—Irial put a hand on Niall's knee as he stood, testing the ever-changing boundaries —"and because you need each other."

Niall looked away. "And you."

Irial lifted one shoulder in a dismissive shrug. "Love works like that."

For a moment, they simply stared at each other. Then Niall stood, intentionally invading Irial's space. "It does."

Irial froze. *An admission?* He stayed as motionless as he could, waiting. "Niall?"

Niall shook his head. "I can't forget. I wish I could. . . ."

"Me too," Irial whispered. "I'd give you anything I have to undo the past. I couldn't protect you. Not from yourself, not from my—"

"*Our,*" Niall interjected.

"*Our* court." Irial leaned his forehead against Niall's. "I would, though. Not for a touch. Not for a forgetting. I just want to take away the scars."

Niall froze, then.

Irial smiled. He reached up to touch the scar on Niall's face. "Not that you are any *less* for them, but because they mean you were hurt."

"Regrets are foolish." Niall smiled, tentatively. "We had other . . . things I remember too."

"We did." Irial hadn't ever felt as careful, as hopeful, as he'd been these past few months.

"You taste so afraid right now," Niall. whispered. "You gave me all the power. The court, your fealty . . ."

"You could sentence me to death on a whim."

"Why?" Niall sounded, in that moment, as young as he'd been when they first met.

"If that's what would make you finally forgive me—"

"Not *that* . . . You stood by. You let me offer myself to the court. *You* didn't hurt me." Niall shuddered.

"I didn't stop it either."

"I forgive you." Niall's words were shaky. "I know you don't understand why I made that bargain. I didn't understand why you didn't step in—"

"They'd have killed you," Irial interrupted. "If I tried to unmake your offer, they'd have killed you, the mortals you were trying to save. . . . The court wasn't as orderly then as they are now. They're not an easy people to rule. If I could've talked to you without them knowing, if I could've stopped you, if I had told you what you were, if I wasn't *me* . . . There are a lot of ifs, love, but the fact is that it was twelve centuries ago. I've been doing penance as best I could."

"And then a few grand gestures since I wasn't noticing?" Niall laughed. "Give me a court. Give me away to be with Leslie. . . ."

Irial shrugged. "Some people like grand gestures."

"I noticed the smaller ones too," Niall admitted.

Without letting himself think on it too much, Irial leaned in and brushed his lips over Niall's. It was no more than a feather touch, but he felt both of their hearts race. He stepped away. "Go see her."

Niall reached out as if he'd touch Irial, but he didn't close the distance. "Move back into the house?"

Irial stilled. "Into . . .?"

"Your old room. Not mine." Niall did reach out then. He put his hand on Irial's arm. "I can't offer more, but . . ."

The hope and fear inside the Dark King were dizzying. It was enough that Irial wasn't sure which answer Niall really wanted.

Neither is he.

"Come home?" Niall added.

Irial pressed another kiss, no longer than the last, to Niall's lips. Then, he pushed him gently away. "Go to her. She needs to be reminded that she is loved."

Niall didn't move, so Irial started walking back toward Leslie's building. He made it several yards before Niall joined him. They walked in silence until they were almost at the door.

"You could take the court back," Niall said. "I'd give it to you."

"Then neither of you would be able to have what you need." Irial frowned. "And it's not best for the court."

"If you weren't addictive—"

"I'd still be unhealthy for her." Irial shoved him gently toward the building.

Niall didn't press the button. He lifted his hand, stopped, and lowered it. "Will you be at the house?"

"Yes." Then Irial walked away.

· ◆ ·

LESLIE PACED IN HER APARTMENT. Some tendril of the vine that connected her to Irial still lived. It wasn't the thing that stole her emotions; it was almost an extra sense that allowed her to taste others' emotions—and to get glimpses of Irial's feelings sometimes.

She knew that he was with Niall: his feelings for Niall were always amplified.

Like mine.

She looked out her front window again. If Irial was with Niall, that meant Niall was near. If he was near . . . She pushed the thought away. Him, she could speak to. *Not that I should.* With Irial, she had difficulty not simply throwing herself into his arms and letting go. She let herself be near him, but they didn't speak. Talking to Irial would be the first step in not-talking, and mortals who lay down with Gancanaghs became addicted. Unfortunately, knowing that didn't remove the temptation. Knowing didn't help her forget how much pleasure she'd felt when he held her. Her relationship with Niall, on the other hand, had never reached that place, so . . .

Who am I kidding?

She snorted at the rationalization she was indulging in: she shouldn't be alone with either of them. It was why she didn't talk to Irial. It was why she didn't accept five out of six of Niall's calls.

The buzzer for the downstairs door rang. She pushed the speaker on, knowing full well who was there.

"Leslie?"

For a moment, she couldn't speak, but then she asked, "Are you alone?"

"Right now, I am . . . . Can I come up?"

"You shouldn't."

"Can you come down?"

"I shouldn't either." She'd already had her shoes on, though, and she grabbed her keys from the hook by the door.

She saw him watching her through the front door of the building as she came down the stairs. It wasn't like seeing Irial, not now, not ever. With Irial, she was sure; they knew each other intimately. With Niall, she was still nervous; they'd never moved beyond kisses and what-ifs.

She opened the door—and paused. The awkwardness, the urge to touch and not-touch, the where-does-one-go-now wasn't something they'd figured out. They both froze, and the moment of greeting passed. Then, it was too late to touch without being *more* awkward.

He stepped to the side, but reflexively offered her his elbow. It was basic civility for him, but he caught himself as soon as he did it. She could see his doubts, his fear that he'd crossed a line already.

Leslie slid her hand into the crook of his arm. "Should I pretend to be surprised?"

He smiled, and all of the tension fled. "Harbingers of my visit or just the fact that I was in town?"

"Did Gabe send for you?" She didn't look around them. "Someone . . . else?"

"Why didn't you tell me he visits?" Niall's tone was more curious than hurt as he asked.

"Because I want you two to get along," she admitted. "I want . . . I don't know . . . I just like the idea that you are at peace with one another. That you can be there for each other."

Niall gave her a curious look.

"What?"

He shook his head. "I'd move the court here if it made you come back to . . . *either* of us."

"I know." She leaned her head on his shoulder. "And if he thought it would work, he'd be trying to manipulate you to do so. Sometimes I think he wants me in your life more than in his."

Niall paused. "You'd be in both of our lives if—"

"I can't." Leslie's voice wavered embarrassingly.

"So . . ."

She leaned in and kissed him. "So we take tonight for what

it is, and then you return to our court, to him. You need him in your life. I can't live my life in the Dark Court. That's not where I belong."

"Maybe there will be someone else who can be king." He stroked her hair.

"How long was Iri the Dark King?" Leslie kissed his throat. "You know better."

"I want to tell you to be with him," Niall whispered. "He could keep you safe and you'd be away from the court . . . and maybe someday . . ."

"You need him with you, and I don't want to be addicted to *anyone*." Leslie wrapped her arms around him, leaned closer into his embrace. "Sometimes things simply aren't meant to be. I'm not able to live in the Dark Court right now. I'd lose myself if I lived there. You might not see that, but I know myself."

He pulled back and stared into her eyes. "What if—"

"If I thought I could live there, I would," she interrupted. "Being there with both of you . . . it's tempting. More so than I want to admit. I want to ignore the things that happen in the court, not be changed by what I remember. People die. Mortals were killed for sport. Violence is play. Excess is normalcy. I can't live in that without changing in ways I don't want to."

Leslie felt relief at having this conversation finally. She'd expected that she'd be embarrassed by the admission that it wasn't simple horror that stopped her. *That* she knew Niall would accept, expect even, but her real reason was less honorable. She could accept the cruelty and excess of the Dark Court, and that terrified her.

Niall frowned. "I wish I could lie to you. I want to tell you that none of the horrible things happen anymore."

"They do. If you aren't doing the worst of them, he is. Don't think that he's changed. He'd do anything to protect you . . . including protecting you from yourself." Leslie kept her voice gentle. She knew that there was one time when Irial hadn't been able to protect Niall, but it wasn't something any of them discussed. "He will do whatever it takes to keep you happy, so if you aren't able to do . . ." Her words faded as Niall looked away.

"I know that there are parts of being the Dark King that he still handles." Niall's expression clouded. "I hate being this . . . almost as much as I enjoy it. Some of the ugly things, though, deals and cruelties . . . I can't."

"So he does."

Niall nodded. "There are things I don't see. If we could make it so you didn't see . . ."

She ignored that suggestion. "You know what happened with Ren?"

Niall didn't answer for a moment. Then he nodded. "I do."

"I want to be sorry. I want to be the sweet girl you think I am. I want to say I'm sorry that Irial—" she paused, trying to find delicate words for what she knew had to have happened "—got rid of Ren."

For a moment, Niall stared at her. He didn't speak.

"I'm not that girl," Leslie admitted. "Any more than you're Summer Court. You belong in the Dark Court. With Irial."

"And you."

"No." She sighed the word. "The person I would become in the court isn't who I want to be right now. I could be. I could be crueler than you are right now. There are reasons that Irial chose me, that I chose his tattoo, and even if you don't see them. *I do.* If I stay away from the court, I can be something else too."

"I'll love you either way," Niall promised. "He would too."

"I wouldn't." She laced her fingers through his, and they stood there quietly for several moments.

He didn't look away. Cars passed on the street. People walked by. The world kept moving, but they alone were still.

Finally, he asked, "So should I go?"

"Not tonight. Can we pretend tonight? That you're not the

Dark King? That I'm not afraid of the things I learned about myself in your court? For tonight, can we just be two people who don't know that tomorrow isn't ours?" She felt tears on her cheeks. She wasn't well yet, but she was sure that she couldn't go back to the world of faeries without destroying all the progress she was making. Maybe if the two faeries she loved were of any other court, she could.

They aren't. They never will be. And we would've never been together if they were.

"What are you saying?" Niall asked.

"I can't return to the court, but I can't pretend that you aren't in my life. I *see* you. All of you." Leslie didn't move any closer to him, but she didn't back away either. "I need my life to be out here—away from the courts—but I look forward to your calls, to his visits. I want to talk to him, and I want to . . ."

"What?" Niall prompted.

At the end of the block, Irial stood watching. She'd known he was there, known that he'd be closer if he could, and known that he had made this night possible. She was safe from Ren because of Irial. She was in Niall's arms because of Irial.

She concentrated on the tendril of connection she had to him, trying to let it open enough to feel him—and for him to feel her emotions. She wasn't sure if it worked, but he blew her a kiss.

"Leslie?" Niall looked as tentative as he had when they'd first met. "What do you want?"

"I want you to come upstairs with me. Tonight."

Irial smiled.

Niall stepped back, but he took her hand in his. "Are you sure?"

"Yes. Give us tonight. Tomorrow"—she looked past him to let her gaze rest on Irial—"tomorrow, you go back to your court, and I continue my life. Tonight, though . . ."

"I can love without touching." Niall looked behind him, as if he'd known where Irial was all along, and added, "I learned that lesson centuries ago."

"Tomorrow you can love me from a safe-distance." Leslie opened the door; then, she looked back at the faery standing in the shadows watching the two of them. "But it's okay to stop time every so often to be with someone you love."

Niall paused. "You make it sound so easy."

"No." She led him inside. "It's not easy. Letting you go in the morning will hurt, but I don't mind hurting a little if it's for something beautiful."

A shadow passed through Niall's eyes.

"He wouldn't ask you to change who you are, anything between you, if you stopped time *there* either." Leslie started up the stairs, holding on to Niall's hand as she did so. "But not tonight."

"No, not tonight." Niall kissed her until she was breathless.

And then they let time—and worries and fears and the rest of the things that meant they couldn't have forever—stop for the night.

LOVE HURTS

Irial looked at the letters that had been delivered to the current house in Huntsdale. He stood in the doorway, exposed in his bare feet and bare chest. Spring, fortunately, was a true and reliable event the past few years. If anything, the former Dark King was wondering if the season had come a touch early this year. Trees were erupting in new growth, and the ground seemed speckled with flowers. If not for the curious, hand-delivered package, he'd be debating popping over to Winter's abode and asking for a last frost, just a brief freezing before the Summer Queen had her way with nature.

Not that he minded an early summer, of course, simply that he *was* the embodiment of Discord. Stirring a minor tiff over the greenery seemed the right path. It had, in fact, been his plan. Now, though, he couldn't focus. In his hand was what appeared to be the key to his unraveling. Yellowed pages were covered in protective sheaths. It was the word on the top that left him, the man who had led the Court of Nightmares and Monsters, terrified.

Da

Dadaih.

Athair.

Father.

Irial was the embodiment of chaos, of discord. He'd fought, slain, and even died. He'd loved and lost—more than once. His first love, Niall, abandoned him for many centuries. His next love, Thelma, left and died without their even reuniting. The third love, Leslie, had risked death to leave him.

Dadaih.

The script went from childish to mature. The sophistication of the words changed, and the tone grew cold.

Father.

With a jolt, Irial realized that the door was still open. Still, he stood at the threshold of his home, a house he shared with the current Dark King, and read. Flowers bloomed outside, and the sky was clear. Somehow, Irial felt as if a storm was about to erupt. Sadly, his was not a court of nature, as the Winter Court and Summer Court were. He could not send storms free to vent his feelings. All he could do was draw shadows to his skin.

Da.

Irial read that one word in all its forms repeatedly. He didn't need to read the pages that were stacked in the other envelope to know that sender's name. Thelma was the only of the three people he'd loved who had died. She was gone.

And between leaving me and dying, she had my child.

NIALL STOOD in the grand lobby of the Benedum Center, appreciating the now-familiar chandeliers of theater. In the latter part of the 1900s, it had been a concert hall of a different sort. He'd seen both Prince and Bob Marley there in the '80s. These days, it housed both opera and ballet, and as much as *some* faeries mocked his fondness for both, the current Dark King knew that anyone who doubted the appeal of opera simply hadn't been paying attention. It was often terribly tragic stuff, rife with manipulation, murder, and mayhem. Any faery worth his salt would like theatre.

Luckily, even the fey like the Hounds, who might not understand his love of *this* type of art, appreciated arts and music in general. Even better, Leslie shared his interest. Typically, Irial did, too.

Tonight, they had planned to see *Faust,* a French opera of the medieval scholar who makes an ill-fated deal with a devil. Niall had, not so secretly, always wondered if Méphistophélès was inspired by Irial. An unwise bargain with a "devil" who is clever . . . the idea seemed rather more fitting than a mortal dealing with the fey, and although Irial never owned up to it, Niall recalled the years the courts all gathered in Germany. Goethe met fey creatures.

Of that, Niall was certain.

But the devil in question, Irial, had made excuses to miss the opera tonight. Worse yet, he'd done so badly. Now, Niall was left trying to convince Leslie that all was well—an illusion neither she nor he believed.

A glass of wine. A smile. A stroll under beautiful chandeliers that sparkled in the high-ceilinged lobby that was filled with mortals and more than a few fey things. It should've been lovely.

"You look beautiful," he told his date again.

"And you look handsome," Leslie replied.

This is when Irial would've made an inappropriate remark, fished for praise, or simply kissed one of them. His absence rankled. The lights all seemed to dim at once as shadows swarmed to Niall like a ripple of midnight seeping into the evening.

Leslie's hand tightened on his arm, and Niall sent his emotions like a nourishing elixir toward the rest of his court. Some of his faeries perched in nooks in the high ceiling, and others languished in the room, dressed in human guises, pretending to be nothing more than ruffians amongst the gentry in their fine dresses. It was far from the theatre of the past, where everyone was bedecked in gems and formal attire, but it was still very much a crowd where those who *have* wanted to be clear that they were superior.

Or maybe they were as smitten by the grand spectacle of the opera as he was. His box seat was not a statement of status. It was simply a space where he could have privacy. No one not *with* him was in the box. The idea of reserving only a few seats in the box seemed odd. Privacy mattered.

He and Leslie made their way to the Dark Court's seasonal box and took their seats.

She was silent, uncharacteristically so, but he was attempting to respect that. They were never awkward, with or without Irial at their sides, but tonight things were tense in a palpable way. Irial had asked Niall to excuse him, had put Niall in the position of misleading Leslie. There was no good answer, so Niall had chosen evasiveness as his solution to the mess.

Leslie vibrated with tension at his side. The lights dimmed, and he thought that the moment of risk was over. Then she leaned closer.

"He's not ill?"

And as much as Niall wished he could lie, he could not do so. "No."

"Injured?"

As much as he did not want the former Dark King to be ill,

he could not help the flicker that came over him in that moment. "Not yet."

Leslie smiled wanly.

"I don't understand either," Niall admitted. "He's avoiding me."

The show began, and with every tear that trickled down Leslie's cheek, Niall thought about strangling Irial. Avoiding *him* Niall could forgive. Avoiding her? There was no excuse that Niall could imagine accepting.

After the show, Niall and Leslie walked to the street, and there a steed waited. It was a living creature, one that had the heart of a wild steed but chose to serve as Leslie's personal guard. Not quite a horse, not exactly a car, it was a member of the Hunt, but was riderless and technically remained so. Leslie was not a Hound, so she couldn't be its rider—and the steed tolerated no other unless Leslie was there, too. Tonight, it wore the illusion of being a fire-red convertible.

Leslie caressed the side of the car, much the way one greets a beloved pet. The fact that this particular "pet" was a monstrous beast with fire glimmering where eyes ought to be was immaterial. She was beloved by the whole of the Dark Court.

"He'll explain, or we'll *make* him," Niall swore to her as he walked around to the passenger seat.

The engine roared when Leslie's hands touched the steering wheel. She didn't steer, not really. The steed carried her home or wherever else she wanted, as if it were a car. And Niall chose not to linger long on the thought that this once-mortal woman had tamed a steed so thoroughly that it functioned as her car— and seemed quite content to do so.

When they reached the apartment where she lived—in a building he'd recently and stealthily bought when the landlord was causing her anxiety—Leslie stayed in the car, as it purred loudly enough to mimic a fine engine. She stroked the dashboard and steering wheel. After a moment she announced, "I'll handle Irial."

And Niall wasn't fool enough to argue. If anything, he was certain that when he returned from his trip the issue would be resolved. Leslie wasn't meek, and she'd become downright formidable these last few years.

"Should I warn him?" Niall asked lightly.

"Not unless you want to get caught in the crossfire." Leslie stepped out of the car. "I won't have him ruin our night, though. Join me?"

If Méphistophélès were a woman, she'd be no more tempting than Leslie as she held out a hand. Niall would give her his soul, his vow, whatever she wanted. He was certain Irial would, too.

"Forever," Niall told Leslie as he took her hand.

And she smiled with a sweet darkness that made him wonder how he could have earned such love.

The weekend would come, and they would confront the secretive faery they both loved. Whatever Irial was hiding was something they could figure out together. First, Niall would attend to business, and Leslie to her classes.

IRIAL WAS NO CLOSER to knowing what to do about the news of his child than the day he'd learned the news. Niall was away, and Leslie should be in class. Irial had counted on that time to figure it all out.

The doors to the study opened with a thunderous noise.

"You're avoiding me." Leslie stood in the doorway to the library after flinging open the doors in a burst of temper. Her once-blonde hair had become increasingly shadow-dark over the last three years, finally reaching the black of the ink that Rabbit had once tattooed in her skin.

College would end soon, and their lives would change. Irial wasn't sure how—and he was afraid to ask.

What if she wants to move away?

He did not stand. "What do you mean?"

"The opera?"

"Ah." Irial nodded. "You weren't alone, though."

She sighed. "Is it because you are feeling guilty?

Irial shrugged. Guilt? Perhaps. He'd unknowingly abandoned a child—and he was hiding it from both Niall and Leslie. He paused. "Aren't you to be in classes today?"

Leslie scowled. "I couldn't concentrate." She stared at him. "You promised not to meddle. I know there aren't threats like there used to be. Bananach is dead. Ren is . . . "

"Apparently missing," Irial filled in helpfully.

She'd never asked, and he'd never volunteered an answer on that particular situation. Ren had threatened Leslie, *their* Leslie, in order to draw out the faeries who loved her. They'd been drawn out, and when they had, Niall had removed the threat to their shadow girl.

"I don't want you to meddle, but if you do . . . don't avoid me afterward," she ordered.

One of the abyss guardians—sentient shadows that were typically only tied to the Dark King or his consort—slithered over to encase Leslie.

"Hello, sweetie," she whispered to the shadow-wrought creature as she came into the room and pulled the door behind her.

The soft snick of the door catching was loud in the still of the room, and Irial felt strangely like prey for a moment.

"I don't only need you when there's trouble," she announced. "Don't you understand that?"

Mutely, Irial nodded. The shadows glided back to the walls as if they'd only ever been the ordinary shadows any lamp or shelf would cast.

After a moment, Leslie crossed her arms and held his gaze. "What are you hiding?"

"Hiding?" Irial echoed. The sight of her, the sheer force of her mortal self striding through the house of monsters, left him longing.

"I know you, Irial," Leslie said.

"That you do, shadow girl." Truth be told, he'd slaughter near every being in the world at her whim. Leslie's very existence was a balsam on a soul that felt increasingly shredded these last few decades. Denying her was physically painful.

Of course, seeing her today ripped at his heart more than he expected. Thinking about her inevitable death seemed impossible now that he was thinking of Thelma, and tangled into that was the thought of a child. His child.

Half-fey children lived much longer than mortals, but not as long as faeries. Would he want that? Would Leslie? Would Niall?

A child would be complicated, but the thought of watching his own daughter or son grow up made Irial struggle to breath. He had never had that, and according to the letters he'd received, he should have. The closest he'd come was the half-fey children that Gabriel had sired. He was an "uncle" of sorts to many halflings, but the thought of his own child suddenly filled him with longing.

As she walked toward Irial, her footsteps were muffled by the overly thick burgundy and gold rug. Shadows puddled where she stepped as if to soak up some sort of magic in her very touch.

"I do not ask you to be my tiger on a leash," Leslie explained softly.

"Mmmm."

She paused, despite the catch in her breathing and the widening of her eyes. The control she had made him certain that she could rule a nation of pirates . . . or monsters. Leslie was not immune to his allure, but if he didn't know better, he might think she was.

The sound of her breathing, of her trying not to run to him, was enough to make him have to resist leaning forward. For all of his centuries of living, only one other mortal had made him feel so oddly *human*. That was over a century before Leslie had been born, and he still wondered if he ought to mention it to her.

Niall knew. Gabriel had known. The only others who remembered his brief relationship were fey of his court, those who would not share his secret—even with Leslie.

"You're staring," she teased, voice breathless as he felt.

"As are you."

"It's been three weeks since I saw you. Staring is sort of inevitable."

"Ah, and here I worried you were immune by now," he kept his voice teasing, but they both knew that he could not lie.

It *was* a fear—one of many these days. The gazes of others, fey and mortal, still raked over him. From thistle-skinned creatures of the Dark Court to the Scrimshaw Sisters of the Winter Court to the vine-bedecked Summer Girls, faeries watched him as if he was every dream they had. Although he knew Leslie wanted him, she could—and did—leave for weeks.

Niall did the same. It made Irial prone to waves of melancholy. If those who loved him didn't long for every moment with him, was he . . . lacking?

"Immune? To you?" Leslie laughed softly. "We both know that's impossible. Staring would be just as unavoidable if I'd seen you last week. I always want to see you, Iri. That's part of love."

"I *do* love you," he assured her.

There was a question in her words, though, one he was trying to avoid answering. Telling her she had his heart didn't seem to be enough this time. Niall had delivered Irial's excuses to Leslie, but neither of them believed him. The difference, of course, was that Niall was more tolerant of Irial's tendency toward secrecy. They lived together more peacefully than he'd hoped possible because they both kept more than a few boxes of secrets hidden away.

Leslie had no such patience.

She stood in front of Irial now, her knees not quite touching his, and he had to resist the dual urges to reach out and to run away. "But you could've come with Niall last week. Perhaps *I* am not irresistible these days . . . ?"

"He told you that I wasn't able to come," Irial hedged.

"He *told* me a bunch of excuses, and I'm not so innocent as to believe them. Lies are lies, Iri, even when they are delivered by someone who knows how to distract me." Leslie caressed his face. "Why don't *you* tell me you weren't able to come, Irial? Say those words to me."

The half-accusing, half-angry tone in her words made his resolve falter. He couldn't lie outright, and those words were a lie.

"I would say them if I could," he admitted. "I chose not to visit."

Leslie withdrew her hand, leaving him wishing he could lean closer, but too proud to do so. "Because? Tell me, Irial. Is it because of threatening my landlord? He offered to extend my lease suddenly. And there was some error, apparently. I no longer owe back rent. Are you feeling guilty?"

The former king leaned away, more to resist his own temptations than anything else.

"I know you can't help yourself sometimes," Leslie allowed.

"If I have meddled, I'm certain it was justified." He'd far rather discuss his supposed sins than his actual ones. Then, at least, he could be truthful with her. He hadn't avoided her from guilt, so there was no harm in owning whatever she thought him guilty of this time.

His reasons for avoiding her were harder to discuss.

Once, almost four years ago, they were bound together by blood and ink. Her emotions were the food that sustained him, the wine that intoxicated him, but their bond changed him even as it nourished him. She'd severed all but the barest thread of their connection, setting him adrift in the world, feeling like a strange new version of himself. Back then, Irial had been willing to give up everything . . . except her. Now, he was facing the possibility of losing her. It was an intolerable fate.

"You're *hiding* something," she announced.

"Trying."

"Failing." She reached out again, hand not quite touching him but near enough to make him feel like a hapless insect drawn to destruction.

"Don't ask me why I didn't visit," he half-begged, half-ordered. "Tell me how to atone for this meddling you say I did."

He'd ruled the monsters that were only spoken of in whispers, but for the second time in his life, a human girl held power over him.

"You didn't do it, did you?"

Irial shrugged. There was no harm in being held accountable for what Niall had likely done. From all of his years in the Summer Court, Niall carried an impulsiveness that sometimes made him unable to use caution or common sense—and those outside the Dark Court thought Irial guilty of many an ill-thought out act that was Niall's doing.

"So. . . not you."

"I didn't say that, love. I am guilty of all manner of things. I simply asked which has you in this mood." He lit a cigarette, pulling the smoke into his lungs with the comfort of a man who will never weaken or die from the poisonous stuff. It was a pleasant perk of being fey.

"No. I can feel your emotions, Irial. It's not the same as

before, but it's growing stronger the past few months." Leslie spoke carefully as if she were weighing the words, sliding invisible fingers over the tendrils that flowed between their bodies again. "When I . . . cut the ties, it was like a ghost that passed by me sometimes, but now, it's like I can feel you more and more every month."

"Not enough to know whether I'm truly guilty, though."

"True," she murmured.

He caught her hand and pressed it to his cheek. "Does that help?"

Leslie laughed before saying, "Touching you always *helps*, but it doesn't always make you easier to read."

She caressed his face for a moment before settling onto his lap. There was no doubt in her, no insecurity as there had been when he'd first seen her. Back then she was a broken doll hiding her fears behind a false bravado. She'd survived an assault that left her screaming inside and trying desperately to pretend she was untouched by the pain. She'd been everything he needed for a conduit to feed the Dark Court: all but destroyed but still fierce inside.

For the past several years, the Dark Court had been her home. The monsters she'd saved would willingly kill or die for her. Admittedly, they'd also willingly kill for a cookie, but they wouldn't *die* for just anyone. They'd donned glamours and cheered her every victory while she was at university. They'd been planning a party for her upcoming graduation that even Irial thought might be a bit over the top, but he wasn't their king anymore and their current king would agree to any excess if he thought it would please Leslie.

"Niall's away," Irial said, trying to remember that she wasn't only his, not now.

"I know. I saw him last week. *He* isn't avoiding me." She slid her hand from Irial's cheek to his throat. "I'm here to see you, Iri. You can't hide from me if I'm in here with you."

Possessiveness flared at the thought of a few uninterrupted days with her. He ground his unfinished cigarette. No amount of time with Leslie was ever enough, could ever be enough. She was too mortal, too fleeting, and fate had a horrible habit of stealing those he loved.

As Leslie twined her arms around him and pulled him into a kiss, Irial stopped thinking. She was here now, touching him, and that was more than he'd ever expected when they'd first been bonded. Ink exchanges were often fatal, so by the time he realized he loved her, he'd expected her to die. When she severed their bond, it held a likelihood of killing her. When he'd been poisoned, he hadn't even had time to see her before he slipped into a comatose state. So to be kissing her several years later was . . . whatever came *after* miracles.

And like all miracles, he couldn't even quite believe this was real. He'd been the thing that led the worst of Faerie's monsters for over a millennium, the embodiment of Discord for the past few years, and his greatest fear was losing the two people he loved.

He'd done so once. Twice. Three times. Centuries ago, he'd lost the faery he now shared his home with, and then he lost the mortal he'd loved, and then he'd lost Leslie briefly, and then he'd died.

Dying ended up being a temporary state, but he felt the finiteness of life since that unfortunate event.

Losing a loved one always hurt, but with Niall and Leslie, they were still alive even when they weren't *his*. He'd been separated, partly, from them when he died. That, too, was bearable. Death of a loved one, on the other hand, was a far uglier thing. He'd gone through it once, and he'd thought the madness of losing the only other mortal he'd loved would break him. He wouldn't do it again.

"You must *never* die," he whispered to the woman in his arms.

Leslie smiled, kissed him again, but she made no such promises.

Mortals age. They die. And Leslie thought she was mortal still. He hoped she was wrong, but he wasn't sure. The thought that *he* might be wrong made him pull her tighter to him. "Never. Ever. Leave. Me."

~

NOT LONG AFTER, both of them half-drunk of kisses, Leslie watched Irial decided what and how much he could still misdirect her. It was a lie, but he had been king of the Dark Court for literal centuries. He was good at lying by way of omission, misdirection, and other subterfuge.

"I need answers," she nudged.

From the comfort of the sofa, Leslie watched the centuries' old faery pace as he acted only slightly older than the boys at university. Faeries age slower than mortals, and Irial had been a creature of self-indulgence so long that he reacted to restrictions, rules, or confusions with a mix of temper and embarrassment.

"Time to talk," she announced.

"Fine." He sulked—and she tried not to laugh. Learning to live with the Dark Court meant learning that the monsters were often not as scary as people thought, and not nearly as scary as they pretended. At least it seemed that way to her.

Certainly, after the battle between the courts in which Bananach died, Leslie could admit that there was a violence to them that she rarely saw.

"I graduate in a few weeks," she nudged. "Is *that* what has you upset?"

"No." Irial poured himself a drink.

Lightly she said, "Sometimes I swear you have single-malt bottles in every room."

He grinned, drank, and refilled his glass. "I usually do, but *this* is the study. What sort of study lacks liquor? Or books? Or a comfortable sofa?"

As Leslie was stretched out on said sofa, she wasn't likely to argue. "Fair enough."

He shook the glass. "Drink?"

Leslie shook her head. She was legal now, but she didn't often drink. "My liver isn't as eternal as yours."

His face darkened.

"Is *that* what this is all about?" Leslie stared at him. "My lack of eternity?"

"Perhaps." Irial downed his drink. "I dislike how easily and quickly mortals die."

"I'm here right now." She stood, hands on her hips, but regretfully not terribly intimidating. "I'm in my *second* decade of life, Iri. Second."

"And unless something changes, you only have a handful left. Not even a century." His voice grew louder, not quite yelling but far louder than normal speech.

Leslie took a step back. He was far from perfect, but it wasn't like him to yell. He was calm, sardonic, charming, and a million other things. He could be irritating, and on a few occasions, she'd seen him seem cold or cruel when he and Niall were at odds.

Never to her, though.

"Something else is going on." She stepped toward him, approaching as if he were a feral animal that might flee.

"I don't know if I can do this again," he said quietly. He bowed his head.

"Do *what*?" Leslie reached out, and he withdrew further.

"Love someone who is going to die," he admitted.

As pieces started to click together, she stared, mouth agape. *Again.*

He was afraid to love someone again who would die. Foolishly, she'd assumed there had only been Niall. He'd lived for centuries, though. No one was sure how many. He was older than Keenan, the reigning Winter King and former Summer King, and Keenan was over nine hundred years old.

"A human?" she asked.

At first, Irial simply stared at her. Then he gave a nod.

"I had no idea," she said, as gently as she could.

Irial shrugged. "I don't discuss her."

Leslie felt like her heart would break as his wave of sorrow washed over her. The ties that bound them were still fragile things, but even the edge of his grief brought tears to her eyes. Once, before them, Irial had loved deeply. Not Niall. Not her. A stranger. The thought of it made her understand his attempts to withdraw from her. What was confusing was why now? Why did he feel so much fear now when she had always been mortal?

"How old was she?"

Irial smiled sadly. "Young when we met. Older than you, but times were different then." He took Leslie's hand in his. "You are very different people. . . and I've lived longer than I can fathom. Do not feel jealous, love."

Leslie kissed him gently. "I am *well* aware that I am not the first woman in your life, Iri."

He nodded, and they were together quietly for a moment longer.

Then, sheepishly, she admitted, "I just figured that you hadn't *loved* any of them."

He lit a cigarette and paced. His energy, the sheer emotional chaos that rode in his expression, reminded her that while he was gentler with her, he was still something of a caged tiger.

"I almost started a war over her," he said quietly. "When I lost her, I wondered why I ought not start it anyhow."

There was little that she could do. His withdrawal and her

healing connection to him— Leslie had to wonder if it was all connected.

"I am not good at grieving," Irial said lightly, as if she had forgotten how devastating grief could be.

Leslie thought back to Niall when he'd been grieving.

She walked into the room to find Niall holding a fire poker which he'd just tried to shove into Seth's eye. There was a madness there that she'd not ever seen before, but struggled to forget. Inside one of the two faeries she loved was a darkness that was more unstable than Irial's calculated coldness.

"You are not this person," Leslie told Niall.

He dropped the poker to the warehouse floor when he saw her.

Slowly, carefully, Leslie walked farther into the room. Niall's skin sizzled from gripping the poker, and Seth's face was burned. The smell was unsettling, but not as much as the lost look on Niall's face.

She stepped in front of the cage that held Seth, the beloved of the Summer King and friend to Niall until today.

"Niall? You don't really want to hurt yourself . . . or him."

Niall looked lost, as if his very world had vanished. He stared at her. "Seth Sees things. He knew and . . . He knew that Irial . . ."

"I heard what happened." Leslie approached Niall with her hand outstretched, as if she could touch him and heal him with it. She understood as no one in the world did. Irial wasn't the sort of person who could be replaced, who could be lost without a ravine in the middle of her heart. She knew what Niall felt because she felt it too.

"Ash called me. Donia called me. . . . You sent for me. Do you remember that, Niall? You sent Hounds."

"I didn't want to tell you," he whispered.

"I'm here." Leslie looked over her shoulder.

Behind her, a Hound stood in the open doorway. She wasn't sure if he was there for her safety or Niall's. It was all the same though. The court—and it was her court, too—was in pain. They were grieving, and their new king was unraveling.

"I am here with my court," she assured Niall. "I am here with you . . . because you needed me. They need me to be here with you."

She took Niall's uninjured hand in hers, careful not to look at the burned flesh on the other hand, and used the only words she was sure would matter just then: "Irial wouldn't want you to hurt. You know that."

Leslie remembered that sorrow, how it had nearly destroyed the entire Dark Court.

Her own grief was less horrifying in its results, but she would never forget that utter terror that washed over her at the thought of never again touching or laughing with Irial.

She reached out and caressed his cheek. "You're in pain, and I understand."

He stared at her.

"I lost *you* once, Irial. In all the world, there is no one like you, and you were dead. . . and I love Niall as fully as I love you, and *he* was grieving." She felt tears escape her eyes. "Do you think I don't understand your fear?"

SEVERAL HOURS LATER, Leslie lifted her head from his chest and stared at him. "Are you okay?"

At some point in their lovemaking, Irial felt a tear slip from his face to hers, and he hoped she hadn't noticed. He hadn't *wept*, but in the moment of union, he was overwhelmed.

"Mmm." He pulled her down and kissed her, enjoying the sheer novelty of trusting a woman enough to have her on top of him.

She'd gotten far too able to read between his words, so his default with her was typically distraction. It was an excellent plan, if he did say so himself. Kissing Leslie was high on his list of favorite pastimes, alongside touching Leslie and making love with Leslie. Luckily for him, she didn't seem to object.

When she pulled away for real finally, she kissed both of his cheeks and his forehead affectionately before straightening back to a seated position and saying, "I'm never sure if I should be offended that you think I'm that easy to sidetrack. It doesn't work on Niall either, by the way."

Irial shrugged as best he was able with her on top of him and offered her his most innocent look. "You're the one who closed the door and attacked me."

She pressed her lips together and narrowed her gaze. "That's your summary of our day?"

"You made accusations, and we talked. Then you seduced me—after insisting I ought not meddle. So I was merely *not* meddling in your obvious plans to seduce me," Irial continued with the closest approximation of innocence he could muster.

"You might be delusional."

"I've been accused of far worse." Absently, he traced the tattoo of his eyes and the wings that still graced her back. He could feel the inky tendrils that once bound them snaking out to answer his touch.

"It's healing," she said. "The tattoo is almost healed."

"I know."

"That's why I feel you." She leaned back so his hand was tighter against the tattoo. The smoky threads that had stretched out to meet his touch tightened like vines grabbing his hand. The sensation rocked through him, burning along pathways that she'd once yanked out in her—quite justified—anger and fear.

He shivered, the wash of emotions that he felt from Leslie catching him off guard and bringing his own tangled mess of emotions surging to the surface. "Steady, love."

She didn't listen, though. She reached back and held his hand to her skin. He could've jerked away, but . . . he also *couldn't*. She could read his feelings as if he were a book open before her. He wouldn't reject her and risk her turning away from him.

Once Irial and Niall had been gancanaghs, addictive to mortals. When Niall became Dark King and Irial became the embodiment of Discord, they were no longer addictive. Irial had wondered more than a few times over the past few years if fate had a sense of humor. Leslie could stay away from them, but they both craved her nearness the way junkies craved their drugs.

"You're afraid," Leslie murmured, her voice heavy with shock.

Instead of speaking, Irial let her taste his emotions.

"It didn't used to work this way." Her voice was wonder-filled then. "You're worried that I'll leave, that I'm hurt, that I'll die, and . . ." She paused and closed her eyes. She bit her lip, and then opened her eyes and looked directly at him. "You love me more than before. When we were connected, you didn't love me like this."

"I loved you then," he objected weakly.

"Not *this* much." She studied him in silence for a long moment before adding, "You let down a wall, unwillingly, and it scares you."

At that, Irial came to his feet and had the unexpected urge to don his trousers, as if clothing would somehow shield him. After tugging clothes onto his bottom half, he walked away to pour himself a drink. It was bad enough that he had to deal with Niall's ability to read his every emotion; adding Leslie to the mix meant that he would have no walls left to shelter him. Sometimes a faery simply didn't want to have his heart laid bare on the table.

"Come to New Orleans?" he asked Leslie, turning to face her once more.

"New Orleans?"

The former Dark King nodded. "Once, a century or so ago, I lived there."

She smiled, and in a drawl far too like his own, said, "Of course you did."

~

ONE OF THE Hounds pounded on the door. It was not Gabriel, who had been lost to the same forces that had nearly taken Irial, but one of his brothers who rumbled through their home with the same sense of force and thunder.

"The rest of the boxes from the buildings that were flooded are here," he announced as he shoved the door open.

Irial started, "Good, but—"

"Leslie!" Cam grinned at seeing her. He held his arms wide open to hug her.

"Cam," she said, not rising.

Irial pinched the bridge of his nose. "Cameron, close your damn eyes before I pluck them out and feed them to you."

The massive man frowned. "Why?"

"Because I'm naked, Cam," Leslie said, visibly trying not to laugh at either Cam's confusion or Irial's frustration. Her gaze floated between them, and the shadows from the floor zigzagged toward her.

Cam closed his eyes quickly. He nodded, and eyes still tightly closed, he fumbled for the door. In the process, he knocked a painting from the wall and set a floor lamp to rocking precariously.

Abruptly, he paused and turned back, frowning. Without opening his eyes, he asked, "How come you're not naked then, king? I mean, Discord. Err, Irial?"

"Because I have already pulled my trousers on, Cam," Irial said with exaggerated patience. Cam was a fine Hound. He simply lacked the common sense of an average goose.

Leslie giggled.

Cam waved in her general direction—still not opening his eyes—and said, "Good to see you . . ." He paused and amended quickly. "Umm, not that I could *see* you."

Irial sighed again. "Goodbye, Cameron!"

And Leslie's giggles turned into belly laughs as Irial watched. This, this moment, was what she deserved: happiness. He wasn't sure how to make sure she always had it, but he wanted to do so. He didn't want any distance, any secrets between them.

When she stopped, Irial blurted out his great secret: "I think I had a child."

Leslie stared at him.

"I don't know if I meddled in your life, but if I did, I'm sure I had a reason," he added to fill the silence.

After a long minute of staring in silence, Leslie said, "I think I need clothes for this conversation. You do, too."

She tossed his shirt at him, and all Irial could do was think that an event in his past was about to destroy his present happiness. He had no idea that Leslie would react this way. "Before you," he added quickly. "The child was before you were ever even alive, shadow girl."

"Oh, Irial! I'm not angry. I just find all of that"—she gestured at him—"a bit distracting, and I need to focus, especially if I am going to need to buy baby supplies."

The wave of relief that rolled over him was palpable.

Leslie trailed her fingers down his bare chest and pause at his trouser buttons. "Nothing will make me reject you, Iri. Nothing. Don't you realize that yet?"

He exhaled loudly, fears he'd not yet named falling away briefly. He still needed to tell Niall. Hell, he still needed to decide if he'd look up his descendants in person if they existed. One disaster at a time, though. A man doesn't discover children and lost years with them every day.

He pulled his shirt on and watched Leslie dress. It never ceased to amaze him that even the act of dressing was enticing with her. He'd forgotten that charm in the centuries between Niall and Thelma, and the decades between Thelma and Leslie. With most people he'd had in his bed, his interest was only held in the disrobing. Once the present was unwrapped, his interest faded quickly and inevitably.

With Leslie, Irial was as enchanted by her dressing as with the way she covered her mouth as if to keep the giggles from escaping. He could paint her on every canvas he found, and still he wouldn't grow tired of studying her. It was unsettling after so many years of solitude. Now, he had her and Niall in his home, and he felt unmoored.

Once she was dressed, she stood in front of him and said, "Spill."

"Once, many years ago, there was a girl. Human. Unusual." Irial smiled remembering Thelma. "She was bookish when most women were focused on husbands and homes."

Leslie nodded.

"I came near to starting a war. There were people seeking her, and—"

"Irial." Leslie gave him the sort of look that came from knowing him better than most people could imagine. "What people?"

"Influential ones," he hedged.

"Influential as in . . . mafia or as in rich parent or politicians or . . .?"

"Politicians of a sort." He turned away, hand on the glass door knob to open the door and flee. Admitting who Thelma was, who had pursued her, would add complications he'd rather she could avoid. In as casual a voice as he could summon, he said, "Let's not talk about that. What matters is that I protected her, and I did so because I was developing a fondness. Who *they* were is not the point."

Behind him, Leslie put a hand on his back, stilling him, stopping him. "Are you asking me not to ask who pursued her?"

He nodded. Without looking back at her, Irial added, "He didn't deserve her. He wasn't going to love her as I did. Sometimes . . . I am impulsive."

Leslie's arms slid around him, and she kissed his back. "You're an absolute fool when you love." She squeezed. "And I am grateful for it. As is Niall. I suspect your missing love was, too."

Irial hoped so. The day he'd decided to pursue Thelma was as clear as if it had been that morning. The downside of near immortal lives was that he couldn't always keep track of time. That day, though, was one he hadn't forgotten.

Gabriel's steed shifted into a handsome horse-drawn carriage, one fit for nobility or the American equivalent of it.

"Well come on then." Gabriel climbed aboard and took the reins, although they weren't technically necessary with the bond between Hound and steed.

"No horseless carriage then?" Irial teased.

"Bah."

The new mode of transportation irritated Gabriel for reasons that seemed to be primarily a matter of loving his steed in its natural equine-like form. Irial, unlike a lot of faeries, was fascinated by technological advances. He'd even had several images of himself made in the last few decades, including a daguerreotype and a tintype. In time, Irial intended to own several horseless carriages as well. What was the point in immortality if one continued to live as if it were centuries past?

"Without being seen," Irial ordered.

Gabriel gave him another raised brow look, but said nothing.

"I don't want her to feel stalked," Irial explained.

Ignoring Gabriel's snort, Irial continued, "I simply need to move to the house in the city for a short time."

"And the Hunt?"

"It's not as if you cannot fetch me if needs be," Irial stated.

"Or we can come with you, Irial." The rumbling in Gabriel's voice clarified that even as he pretended to be suggesting the answer, he was actually demanding it.

"Fine. You can come, too."

As the steed swept by the girl who was walking toward the city, Irial wished he could pull her to him. It was foolish. A wise man would vacate the city, ignore the mortal, stay as far from the quarrel between Beira and Keenan as he could. This one, though, had looked right at him.

"I ought to leave the state," Irial said aloud.

"Are you going to do so?"

"No."

"I'm not going to lecture you, Iri." Gabriel grinned, all teeth and menace, and added, "You're more use when you're not pouting."

"I don't . . ." Irial made a crude gesture at his closest friend and added, "I am not pouting, Gabe. I am simply enjoying a vibrant city, filled with music and distractions. A favorite city, as you know."

Gabriel laughed.

Prostitution was newly legal in New Orleans now. The Crescent City was the first city to legalize it in this country, and the Dark Court enjoyed the profits of that law. His fey fed on darker emotions, and the so-called Storyville District added to the court's already-deep coffers.

"She might simply be a distraction," Irial claimed, careful to phrase his words in such a way that they were not a statement of absolutes. Lying, after all, was not possible for a faery.

"Or a way to cope with your guilt," Gabriel added.

"Or boredom," Irial admitted.

Or something else. He didn't say that aloud though. Far better to think of guilt or boredom as motivators.

Irial smiled. Thelma—much like Niall before her and Leslie

after her—was far from boring. Irial, if he did say so himself, had excellent taste.

"I treasured her," he said. "And she hid my child."

~

LATER THAT AFTERNOON, Leslie and Irial rode to the airport in the company of assorted Hounds. There was something about feeling so cherished that never grew old for her. The massive fey creatures, looking for all the world like a multicultural biker gang, escorted them to the ticket counters.

Cam carried the small bags that she and Irial had packed. In truth, she was surprised that Irial had agreed to pack things. He had the ridiculous habit of believing that a credit card and a whim would suffice when it came to most clothes. His suits, of course, were tailored, but things like jeans or shirts were a matter of little concern.

"No time for stores?" she asked.

"I need all the time to research," Irial murmured, not even looking up from the latest of the letters he'd retrieved from a locked fireproof box and slipped into his Italian leather satchel.

The pages were yellowed, ink faded, but each letter was in a protective sleeve, as if a careful librarian had stored them. Leslie wanted to read them, to know his every secret, but her life with Irial and Niall worked because she had the ability to be patient—and the ability to be brash. She knew the two men well enough to know which trait she needed, and right now, the living embodiment of Discord needed her support and her patience.

They checked their bags, cleared security, and went to stand at a gate. The Hounds, of course, still stood like fierce guards around them. The difference was that no one saw them now. However, in that way of such fey things, they radiated a kind of terror that meant no one came near Irial.

"You really want us to stay here?" Cam asked.

Irial lifted his eyes, met Cam's gaze, and nodded once. To anyone looking their way, it would appear as if he nodded to himself upon reading something pertinent.

"King's not going to approve," another Hound muttered.

"Does Niall know?" Leslie asked, even though she knew exactly what Irial would say.

Or not say.

Irial lifted a shoulder in a small shrug.

Leslie texted: "With Iri. Airport. NOLA. Love."

Then she looked at Irial, back at the Hounds, and said, "Go."

"Leslie?" Cam asked in apparent confusion.

"We need a little time to ourselves," she said, leaning into Irial even with the metal arm rest jabbing into her side. "Just us."

To a bystander, she seemed to be talking to Irial, but the Hounds knew what she was saying. They—like most of the Dark Court—acted as if she were their queen. No one really pressed the matter, and she was cautious not to issue orders. Today, though, she was taking advantage of their obedience to her.

"Just the two of us," she repeated with emphasis.

Irial lifted his gaze, looked around at the fey creatures that were standing there watching over them. Hounds were stronger than many faeries, but this much steel had to be unpleasant for some of them.

"Begone," Irial ordered.

They rolled through the airport boarding areas, an invisible wave of discomfort that the observant could track simply by noting the ripple of fear and anxiety that the passengers' faces showed. Even seasoned businesspeople seemed suddenly ill-at-ease. The trick for those without the Sight was to notice waves of joy, or fear, or chills that seemed to roll across a crowd or street. That was often the result of passing faeries.

Once they were gone, and Leslie saw no other lurking faeries in the area, she turned to Irial and gently prompted, "Tell me what's happening."

Silently, he slipped the letter back into his case.

"A very long time ago, Thelma asked me not to seek her out. She was mortal, and I was not," he paused and smiled. "*Am* not. Will never be. I knew she lived a long life because I looked her up from time to time."

He leaned forward.

"I gave her a vow. In fact I gave her"—he laughed as if there was a joke she hadn't heard—"quite a number of them. The first before we acknowledged that she knew what I was, but the last vow . . . I never saw her again after it. Never spoke."

All traces of laughter were gone, and Leslie felt waves of loss assail her.

"And so I never knew, and she never sent word. I don't know how she could've, but if she had . . . I'd have known my daughter."

Leslie stared at him. "She intentionally hid your child from you?"

"I don't know," he whispered.

Leslie reached over and took his hand. There weren't a lot of words. Being a woman meant that her child—if she had one —would not be a secret. One notices such things. For men, though, the fear that a child out there might be yours, that you might never know, was a real possibility.

"She lived in New Orleans?"

He nodded. "A long time ago, I was there, and she was there, and we met, and . . . if things had been different . . ." Irial shook his head and simply noted, "I would have liked to know my daughter."

They sat in silence, Leslie feeling his emotions and trying to send calm his way, until the plane boarded. They remained the same on the flight to the city at the mouth of the Mississippi

River. She'd never been there, although it was on her list of places to see, but not like this.

By the time they landed, Leslie no longer worried that Irial's sorrow would drown her. So she asked, "What year?"

He looked her way.

"When did you know her?" Leslie clarified.

"We last spoke at the turn of the century."

"Which one?" Leslie kept her voice pitched low.

"In the 1800s, love," he said. "She's dust and ash now. Gone from me."

Irial stared at her so intently that Leslie worried that he was about to become inappropriately affectionate—not that she ever minded, but ending up naked in the middle of a deplaning crowd would be awkward.

"You must never die," he said, not even trying to be quiet. "I couldn't live without you. Swear it."

A nearby older couple looked at them curiously.

"Love . . ." Leslie started.

Irial pulled her to him and kissed her breath away. They were still both dressed when he released her, but the aisle was filled with people who were waiting for the doors to open.

"Newlyweds?" a woman asked.

Leslie leaned against Irial and said, "Close."

Behind her, he was holding her hips in his hands now, as if to keep her from flying or pull her closer to his affections. His fingers tightened, and she was suddenly more than ready to be off the plane and in the French Quarter hotel he'd booked.

"Niall's madness would be two-fold if you died," Irial whispered. "Mine would rival his, *exceed* it, demolish the world."

"I am right here." She covered his hands with hers and glanced over her shoulder at him. "Healthy. Yours. I *love* you."

He nodded, but he looked far from convinced. "Mortals die in a blink. Like mayflies and falling stars. You expire so soon."

When they'd left the plane and were walking from the gate to baggage, Leslie kept her hand in his.

"Do we even know I'm still mortal?" she asked.

She hated to bring up the ink exchange, but she was—quite literally—the only mortal who had survived it. No one expected her to live. Irial had hoped, but even he had thought she'd perish. "It's grown back, roots in my flesh, tendrils stretching to you."

"I'm not sure. Maybe it will tie your life to mine. That was the initial intent." Irial shrugged. "But you burned it, severed it, so I have no idea what it means."

This time Leslie shrugged. "So, love, you may be stuck with me for centuries."

She didn't mention her fears that she had grown less emotional again because of it. What was different now was that she had still chosen to be involved with both Niall and Irial when she was clear-minded. They were what she wanted, and who could blame her? After being loved by them, how could she go back to dating mortals? Being loved by the former Dark King and the current Dark King had taught her that she needed a partner—or partners—who were a little bit feral.

The way she'd handled the monsters she'd met because of them convinced her that she had a spine that was wrought of whatever was stronger than steel. Leslie was able to find the monster in herself when those she loved were threatened, and because of them, she learned that although love can be scary, it can also be empowering.

They'd encouraged her to go to university, respected her desire to not accept their money, and not because they thought she would change her mind but because they'd have done the same. In a stubborn ass contest between the three of them, she wasn't sure who'd win. The only real difference was that Niall attempted to avoid conflicts whereas Irial thrived on it.

~

MILES AWAY IN NEW JERSEY, Niall was ready for a long, peaceful weekend—one that didn't require a suit or manners. He loosened his tie and looked at his mobile. In the assorted messages from Seth, Chela, and Donia was one that stood out: "With Iri. Airport. NOLA. Love."

The text Leslie had sent a few hours ago had plenty of information, but no actual answers. The Dark King lit a cigarette and pondered. He'd never understood the appeal of drawing burning toxins into his body as much as he did now. The Dark King, the whole of the Dark Court, was made for poison.

Shadows from the coming evening crouched at his sides, drawn to whatever strange thing made him a king. Shadows ought not move on their own, but they did. None so often as the abyss guardians that traveled from one shadow to another anywhere in the world. Right now, the same guardians that had touched Leslie earlier that day were now slithering along his arms. He could sense her skin as they did so; the taste of her sweat and perfume lingered in these shadows.

She was safer than most anywhere if she was with Irial.

On the other hand, the man was now the embodiment of Discord. He'd protect Leslie, but that didn't mean he was making wise choices in general—at least not wise by Niall's standards.

For all that was right in his life, Niall was unable to have a single month without drama. This time—hell, a *lot* of times—it originated in the faery who had bequeathed the court to him. Niall stood in the hotel lobby where he'd finished up sorting out the accounting discrepancies at the two new Atlantic City casinos the Dark Court financed. For all his comfort with the dark, Niall preferred when vices were controlled.

Irial's voice, from when they'd first met, came echoing over the years: *You like them. Mortals, that is. Genuinely* like *them.*

Some things were unchanged. Irial wasn't prone to liking humans. He'd bedded his share, but genuine fondness for them was as rare as a blizzard in the Mojave. It could happen, but now that the last Winter Queen had been replaced, it was unlikely.

He looked again at the text Leslie had sent a few hours ago: "With Iri. Airport. NOLA. Love."

He could reply, but getting answers when Discord was involved was as likely as turning coal to diamonds. It could happen, but not without a degree of pressure that Niall was unwilling to apply via another person.

Niall glanced at the time. By now, they were on the ground. *Why?* That was the real question. Of all the cities in the world, that was one of the few Irial avoided. That hadn't always been the case. Niall remembered seeing him there, thinking that it was a city positively designed for the Dark Court. Back then, Niall had been advisor to the Summer King, and Keenan had toted the court there in pursuit of a potential Summer Queen —one who'd vanished.

He called Irial. Once. Twice. Tried Leslie's number, too.

Then he did what any sane Dark King did when Discord was not easily located: he booked a trip of his own. His, however, was a bit more primal than steel tubes hurtling through the air as if by magic.

"Chela?" He spoke the word into the air, the shadow slithered across the ground, and the word moved at the speed of darkness. He ought to call her by her title, but he'd known her too long for that. Before her, her mate—Gabriel—had led the Hunt, but upon his death, Chela assumed the mantle.

"Gabriela," Niall added, using the title out of respect.

Then he ordered a coffee. There was no way to keep up with Irial in New Orleans of all places and catch a bit of much needed sleep. Coffee was the best solution. Again. Some days, Niall wondered if he'd have flat-out refused the crown if he knew how little rest there would be.

Before an hour had passed, Niall could feel them: The Hunt rode. The earth itself seemed to quake, as if the soil would shake loose the dead. The weight of the fear that rolled out before them made the very air heavier, thicker, as if moving was impossible. Several mortals in the street shivered. The roll of terror that surrounded the Hunt made more than a few passing mortals look to the sky as if a storm rode overhead.

"We come," the voices echoed. No mortal ear would hear. No human eye could see.

Chela and the Hounds never moved at a saunter.

When they arrived, Chela did not get off her steed, Alba, who appeared to be a massive lion currently. Chela's shifted shapes the way some people changed clothes. Alba expressed his feelings with his shape. Since Gabriel's death, Alba was often leonine, feral and ready to hunt anything that threatened Chela—or looked as if it could.

None of the steeds were in car form. Instead, they looked like a deadly menagerie: an oversized lion snarled next to a lizard-like beast; something that resembled a dragon paced next to a chimera; and scattered among them all were skeletal horses and emaciated red dogs. Atop the steeds were equally fierce Hounds.

The leader, Chela, dipped her chin. It was the closest to a bow that most Hounds offered. They weren't strangers to the etiquette of court, but they weren't *subjects* of any court either —and Chela was keen on reminding him of that truth. They stayed because she chose to stay. The fears they roused by their very presence were nourishing to the Dark Court. The terror that rolled off their skins was like the finest wine. And they, not shockingly, liked to be appreciated.

"Home?" The Hound paused and grinned. "Or has the old King done something troubling again?"

Niall walked up to her and said, "I don't know, but I need to go find out."

Chela grinned. "Where to?"

"New Orleans."

Her pause would've escaped his notice if several of the Hounds accompanying her hadn't frozen, too. For one extended moment, they all seemed to stop moving, as if time itself had held its breath. Then, with a falsely casual expression, Chela said, "Sure. We haven't been there in ages. A little bayou excursion sounds good." She motioned him toward her. "We'll drop you at the house and go—"

"The house?"

Several Hounds exchanged glances.

"In the Garden District . . .? I thought Iri would be at the house," Chela said haltingly.

"*What* house?" Niall rubbed his temples and lit another cigarette. At some point, Niall figured he might know all the secrets the last Dark King held, but some days he suspected that was impossible.

"You visited," a Hound said.

"The court *owns* that house?" Niall clarified. He remembered. It was an ostentatious Garden District mansion, but he'd assumed that Irial had merely rented it as most courts did in most cities.

More shuffling and their glances went everywhere but him. Niall couldn't order them to obey him. The Hounds only obeyed Chela.

"Sentimental reasons," Chela offered. "We all do things for reasons other than logic, don't we?" She glanced at the steed that kept pace with her, riderless still.

The steed that had belonged to Gabriel had remained in the form of a giant black horse with a reptilian head. It flashed pit-viper fangs at Niall, not in threat but in a smile of sorts. Aside from Chela, the steed had only allowed him, Irial, and Leslie to ride. Niall suspected the Winter Queen could, but she simply visited the nameless creature from time-to-time.

Chela could order it to shift or choose a new master, but she had done neither.

"Why do I feel like there is more you could tell me?" Niall asked.

"Because you're not as dim as I once believed." Chela watched as Gabriel's steed stomped over to him.

A rush of sheer exhilaration rolled over Niall as the beast nickered through those pit-viper fangs and tossed its head.

"I'm coming," he murmured. With a leap he was astride, and the steed was already tensed for motion.

"New Orleans," Chela said as soon as he was mostly, but not quite, seated.

And the world blurred in a way that was both dizzying and beautiful.

LESLIE SAID nothing as Irial opened a door to a house that seemed more haunted than anywhere she'd been. If a building could be melancholy, it would be this one. The building was in immaculate condition, the marble floors inside the door gleamed as if they'd been polished that morning. The tall wooden balusters lining the upper floor had the patina of hands gliding over them often. The Turkish rugs seemed as bright as if they were new.

But as she followed Irial into the house, she saw that every room was filled with sheet draped furniture. No one lived here. Irial pulled a few sheets away, revealing books that were still open to assorted pages on end tables. An empty tea cup sat next to a pair of hundred-year-old glasses.

And Irial looked into corners as if his memory and will alone could summon a body from the past.

Faeries were magical creatures, capable of any manner of impossible things, but not returning faces from the past or making ghost breathe again. The look of sheer pain on Irial's face made Leslie wrap her arms around him. There were no words, but she could offer him comfort.

At first he said nothing, simply pulled her closer to his side like a child holding a stuffed toy. Then a few moments later, he said, "I loved her. I would've loved my child, too. I *do* even though I've never met her."

Leslie couldn't pretend to understand his pain, but she listened and she held him.

Then, they went to the dining room and uncovered a table that would seat a dozen guests. There, Irial spread out the letters and files he had, and they began to read.

WHEN NIALL ARRIVED, the last thing he expected to see was what looked like a midnight study session. Containers of take-out, a bottle of wine, and the unmistakable scent of chicory coffee assailed him when he opened the door of the Garden District house he hadn't entered since the late 1800s.

"The door was unlocked," he said in lieu of a greeting.

Irial nodded. "I figured you'd be here sooner or later since she texted."

Leslie was more enthusiastic. She crossed the few feet between them and pulled him into her usual welcoming hug and kiss. Exhaustion fled in that moment. He was home— because home was wherever these two baffling creatures were.

Mutely, Irial kicked out a chair and resumed reading.

At Niall's querying look to Leslie, the calmest of the three, she sighed and quietly walked over and plunked her hand over the middle of the letter Irial was reading.

"Talk. To. Him."

Irial stood and paced across the room, where several bottles of whiskey had been hidden under another sheet. "Whisky? Gin?"

Niall nodded. He didn't simply grab Irial and kiss the answers out of him as he might if they were alone. Sometimes there was a wall that they kept around Leslie still—not that they lacked affection in front of her, but faeries who were well over a thousand years old could be more violent in their affection than he thought Leslie would understand.

"You're stalling," Leslie said.

Niall smothered a grin with a sudden need to cough.

"I have—had—a child," Irial announced as he handed Niall a beautiful crystal highball glass that would've hit the floor if not for Irial's reflexes. He handed the still-full glass back to Niall. "Thelma had a babe."

"Thelma? The young . . . the potential Summer Queen you spirited away?" Niall emptied his glass and stalked past Irial to refill it.

"The *what?*" Leslie asked. Her arms folded. "The people who were seeking her were faeries?"

Irial shrugged.

And Niall knew. He knew the secret that Irial hadn't shared back then. "You made the curse."

"True."

"Did you always know?" Niall stared at the faery he'd finally started to figure out the past handful of years.

Again Irial shrugged.

Niall half-fell into the chair Irial had offered when he'd arrived. "So you shagged the woman who would have been the Summer Queen if Keenan had found her, and she had your *child?*"

Again Irial shrugged.

"We suffered over a hundred more years of winter because you felt like *hiding the queen?*" Niall wanted to throttle him, simply squeeze until Irial had sense in him, but as such a thing was neither possible nor wise—and the events were all in the past—he simply stared at Irial.

~

AFTER A FEW MOMENTS, Irial stood and walked away. Niall wasn't wrong, and Irial was sure that from the outside it probably seemed like a heinous thing he'd done. It wasn't that simple, though.

Thelma was special.

He didn't risk the wrath of both Summer and Winter casually. Admittedly, such a thing wasn't out of character for him, but he wasn't foolish.

Except when it comes to love.

He turned the door knob, feeling a sharp edge of the glass knob, a memento from when he'd thrown a few things in anger. Just inside the room, Irial paused. The last time he stood here was the day after Thelma left. The room had still smelled of her perfume. Her sheets had smelled the same.

He'd brought her beignets and coffee, as they had shared the first time they had a meal together, and for the first time in centuries, Irial was truly happy. He had been well aware of her mortality, of the fact that loving her as he'd allowed himself to do could only end badly. He'd been equally aware that the then-weak Summer Court and the over-strong Winter Court would both have him skinned alive if they knew that the missing Summer Queen was nestled in his sheets.

What he hadn't know was that Thelma would leave so soon.

"You weren't trying to thwart Summer, were you?" Niall's voice came from the doorway to the room.

Irial had heard his steps, known that the first wave of anger would pass once Niall tasted Irial's feelings.

"Iri? I was rash," Niall said, not quite an apology, but they'd never been much for such words.

Irial shrugged. When he'd met Niall, Irial could taste every feeling, every glorious bit of desire, of hope, of joy. It was a skill unique to the Dark King. He romanced Niall, Thelma, Leslie, and then Niall again with the unfair ability to taste what they felt. He negotiated with kings and queens with that same gift. It had made him formidable. And still he lost more often than made sense. Sometimes knowledge—or love—was not enough to overcome fears or doubts.

"I hadn't planned to love her," Irial admitted, back still to Niall. "Or you. Or Leslie. I'm terrible at it, you know?"

"No," Niall corrected. "You are terrible at dealing with the fears that come with loving, not at *being* in love."

Irial walked over to the bathtub, a claw-footed indulgence that Thelma had thought the single most remarkable part of the house. . . other than books. She'd read the way most mortals breathed or slept, as if death himself would come if she went too long without words.

"I had a child," Irial repeated. The letters that had been delivered the week prior, the strange missives from the past that had been all addressed to him but never sent, had finally arrived a century late.

Irial turned to face Niall. "My daughter wrote to me, and Thelma saved each letter. She wrote, too."

Memories of the past crowded in as Irial tried to contain the massive well of loss, of anger, of confusion that threatened to swallow him.

They stood, awkwardly in silence, until Leslie joined them. Her hand was shaking when she held up a letter.

"This was delivered to the house," she said. Before he could panic much at the thought of Leslie unprotected, she added, "Chela brought it to me."

Irial opened it and pulled out a single page of spidery handwriting.

Father,

I grew up hearing of you. I wrote letters as soon as I could write—at Mother's order. Mother wrote as well, but she often wept when she did. I don't know how things ended, but I know that she never married. As I grew older, never quite aging as children should, we moved a lot. We stayed clear of fey things, and she often spoke in terrified words of the Summer King . . . and of my father, a beautiful man who saved her.

What she failed to tell me, of course, was that the man who saved her was also the Dark King. I knew your name, but not what role you filled in that world. Had I known, I would not have written.

When the Summer King—the same faery that you saved my mother from—came to my door for my daughter, Moira, I tried to figure out how to find you. I discovered then that my beloved grandfather, a *good faery* in a sea of monsters, was the king of the worst of fey. Still I was prepared to reach you, but Moira died, and she left behind a child. No tale my mother told was enough for me to risk that love had blinded her, that you were as awful as I feared.

I believe you are already acquainted with your great granddaughter, Aislinn.

Ash is powerful enough that I thought about writing to you when she became fey.

At the least I wanted you to have the letters I wrote before I knew what you were. I decided that if you came to the house where I was conceived, I would tell you. Mother said you left the house boarded up because you could not bear to be there without her. Every so often, I would check to see if it stood empty. One of my granddaughter's faeries has been watching it for me—the whims of an old lady--so if you ever read this, I believe you've proven that Mother was right, that you loved her. If so, some day, if you would like, I would welcome the chance to meet you.

I have questions about my longevity that sooner or later I'll need to address with Ash. I was old (despite appearance and strength) when my own daughter was born, and I seem to age no further despite the passing of years. I've learned to appear to age, but often I simply moved. Now, though, I'd rather not leave Ash. Perhaps it is time for meeting.

your daughter,
   Elena Foy

IRIAL HANDED the paper to Niall. "My daughter is alive."

As Niall and Leslie read, Irial knew when they understood the import of what the letter contained.

"Of all the people in the world, why did it have to be *her*?" Niall muttered.

"So the women in Ash's family were always the ones who would be the Summer Queen," Leslie pronounced. "Grams, Ash's mother, Ash."

"And Thelma," Niall added.

"Thelma had the Sight," Irial said. "She *saw* me, and she still chose me."

The three stood in silence as the sheer enormity of the thing settled on them. He was blood family to the Summer Queen. Aislinn Foy, the Summer Queen, was Thelma's great-granddaughter. *His* great-granddaughter. How in the name of all that he held sacred was he going to navigate that relationship? He couldn't fathom her taking that well.

Her partner, at least, tolerated him. He and Seth weren't *friends* precisely, but they had a relatively congenial acquaintance.

Then Irial grinned. "Wait till the whelp realizes you're his stepfather-in-law!"

"Not quite how that works," Niall pointed out.

But Irial was, in his heart of hearts, the embodiment of Discord. He wasn't going to do anything to hurt his daughter or great-granddaughter, of course, but his mind was already spinning on the possibilities of teasing Seth and on strengthening the alliance between Dark and Summer. It might not seem like *discord* or chaos, but it strengthened some court alliances, which necessarily weakened others.

"Shall we go out on the town to celebrate parenthood?" Irial draped an arm around both of his beloveds. The issue of Leslie's mortality still lingered as a fear, but that was a trouble for tomorrow.

"Stepdad. Stepmom. We have so many years to make up for with Elena," Irial said.

"I'm *not* her stepmom. She's Ash's *grandmother*," Leslie objected.

"I think I should start with a house," Irial mused. "This house. And a pony. Kids like ponies." He frowned. "Kelpie or steed?"

Niall and Leslie exchanged a look of horror that Irial pretended not to see.

～

"THINK of it as preparation for our little ones," Niall said.

Irial stopped. Leslie froze, but Niall could taste her hope, her joy at such thoughts.

"Come now," Niall said mildly. "Leslie said she wants children. Once she's finished with school and moves in—"

"She's moving in?" Irial said with raw hope. He stared at Leslie as if he'd just been granted a gift. "There will be *children*."

"Eventually," Leslie murmured.

"Oh, when Ani and Tish were tiny, I bought them this little toy shoppe in Philadelphia."

"No," Leslie said firmly. Her flood of amusement surged toward Niall, and undoubtedly to Irial, too, through their ink connection. Leslie folded her arms and announced, "Our children will not get their own stores."

"So just one store," Irial said. "We could do that."

"Not what—"

"We really ought to think about buying more property," Irial announced. "For Ash. For Elena. For Elena's half sisters and brothers."

In a faux whisper Leslie asked, "He does realize that Ash may not be as excited by this as he is, right?"

"Pish!" Irial gave them both big smacking kisses. "What about water parks? How old do the children need to be before we buy that?"

"I'm not pregnant," Leslie reminded him.

Irial waved his hand, as if to brush the objection away. "When you're ready, love." He motioned toward the stairs. "For now, I shall dote on Elena and Ash. My girls."

They followed him down the steps, all but tumbling when he came to an abrupt halt. "They should have guards. Give me a moment to talk to Chela before--"

"They have guards," Niall reminded him. "Summer Queen. Her grandmother."

"More guards!" Irial went to see Chela.

Niall and Leslie stood in the house. He glanced at her. "Have you told him yet that you're moving in after graduation?"

"Not yet. He hasn't been visiting, and . . ." Her words faded, and she shrugged. "He'll figure it out when I stop leaving."

Not a single month without drama, but Niall loved them both. Petulant. Mercurial. All around maddening. Riddled with complications he couldn't imagine. They were everything he could want in life.

"Perhaps we should ask Seth to use that future-seeing of his about your mortality or semi-fey nature *before* Irial tells them he's Ash's great-grandfather," Niall suggested.

"Agreed," Leslie said with a laugh.

Then they went to join the new father to enjoy a rare, beautiful event in anyone's life: celebrating life and parenthood.

The End

SUMMER BOUND

Set after the Wicked Lovely series

Siobhan flinched as Tavish took another blow to the face from Tracie. Her Summer Court co-advisor, on the other hand, smiled joyously as he rarely did in public. Their makeshift gymnasium was filled with cool air and the soothing sounds of soft jazz. It had not been designed to encourage the fighting they were there to do.

Most of the others had left. Only Siobhan, Tracie, and Tavish were still there. Siobhan wanted to be left alone with him, and he'd demanded Tracie stay.

"Are you afraid of Siobhan?" Tracie taunted as she kicked out at him.

He caught her ankle. Blood already dotted his typically impeccable clothes, and strands of tinsel-like hair fell into his face. The plait that usually bound his silver hair tightly back had become loosened after several hours of training the small group.

"Not bad for a Summer Girl," Tavish said, shoving Tracie

toward the ground before he sneered at Siobhan. "Unlike you, Siobhan. Unable to hit me?"

Siobhan winced. He was intentionally being a prick. Tracie, one of the few of the former Summer Girls who had become a guard, was ruthless, though. Kicks followed punches, and Tavish blocked almost all of them.

Unlike Siobhan, Tracie seemed to be making up for their centuries of semi-dizzy lust with bursts of rage. She had found her place as guard, and Siobhan felt pride in seeing one of her own flourish. They had never been competitors. The Summer Girls were bound by Summer, trapped by the Summer King, and they had a bond that was unbroken still—even as a number of their group left.

Tracie stayed. Eliza did, too. A few became solitary, and a few went to the High Court. Siobhan had stayed with the Summer Court, but not as a guard. She'd become an advisor, not interested in unnecessary violence after the fight between the courts had ended.

Not that Tavish cared.

"And here, I'd heard that the Summer Girls were only good for—"

Tracie's fists flew, and Siobhan watched as the other woman hit Tavish repeatedly and say, "I am not. a. Girl. Asshole."

"And you?" Tavish dodged Tracie's last blow and snaked out his leg to pull Siobhan off balance. She toppled to the ground in their makeshift gymnasium.

"What use are you, Siobhan?" he asked.

Siobhan glared at him as she launched to her feet. "Jerk. I serve Ash by advising her, and I learned enough to stay safe."

"Pay attention. If someone comes here, you're vulnerable," he said, as if forgetting the guards that kept watch over the doors—and the queen herself, who was as fierce as any faery in any court.

Several centuries of playing at foolishness made Siobhan

instinctively pout. It wasn't an act that worked on Tavish anymore, though. His next punch was hard enough to knock her backwards.

"I'm not a guard, Tavish." Siobhan spread her feet to give herself a more stable stance and shot her fist forward with as much force as she could. Her punch wasn't enough to knock him backward, but it did distract him. "I don't like to hit anyone."

He was smiling, now. "Even me?"

Then, Tracie landed a solid blow across his throat. Tracie grinned. "I like hitting you, or anyone else I can."

Tavish coughed hard, hand to his throat, not far from the black sun tattoo there. No one knew exactly how or why it had been put there. With his stern expressions and tightly bound hair, he didn't seem the type for a tattoo on his throat, but one night over a lot of tequila, he'd told Siobhan that it was older than the then-king and had been applied when Miach, father to Keenan, ruled. That made it over nine hundred years old.

"Are you injured?" Siobhan asked

Rather than being upset, Tavish beamed at Tracie and said, "Well done."

"Thanks, boss." Tracie rolled her shoulders and asked, "Are we done?"

"You are," Tavish said.

Then he turned to look at Siobhan. His approving smile vanished. "You can stay. You need to be able to defend yourself. What if you're alone or with our queen and—"

"When am I ever alone?"

Tracie leaned up and kissed Tavish's cheek. It meant nothing. Theirs was a court with little hesitation about affection. For a horrible moment, Siobhan hated Tracie for being the recipient of the approval she coveted. It was foolishness, but the more time she spent with him, the more his rare sweet words charmed her. She knew better. Faeries—especially

Summer Court faeries—were notoriously fickle in their affection.

Far better to dream of a solitary, a Winter fey, a Dark fey. Not Tavish. Siobhan knew better.

She thought about all of the reasons he was precisely not what she should want. Tavish was the Summer Queen's advisor, head of the guard, and—as far as Siobhan knew—the oldest member of the court. And, Siobhan was the second advisor to the queen; she was expected to stand in opposition to Tavish's advice when necessary.

Tracie paused and kissed both of Siobhan's cheeks. Then she whispered, "Kick his ass."

Tavish made a sound of disbelief. Obviously, he'd heard. He didn't respect Siobhan in any way, as far as she could tell. How could he? She'd gone from frivolous member of the Summer King's harem, one of the many women who were wooed by him in his search for the queen, to the advisor to the Summer Queen.

"If you can land three solid blows—"

"No." Siobhan shook her head. "I've proven that I can hit you, Tavish. I'm not here for games. I come to these sessions to show support of you, but in this court, I advise. I do not like to fight."

"You are no longer some helpless mortal, Siobhan." Tavish raised his fists in a boxer's pose. "Or hapless plaything."

"Plaything?" she echoed. "Is that what you thought of me all these years?"

"You didn't even have the ambition to try to be queen." He shrugged. "You chose his harem. Why would I think you more?"

"Because you know me," she said. In fact, Tavish knew her when she was mortal, when she refused the test to be Summer Queen, when she was sent by their king to seduce another king. He'd once been the faery she'd wept on when she was newly cursed.

"I was a spy for the king," she reminded him. "That's a fair bit more than hapless."

"But you were a seductress there, too." He stared at her. "You can't kiss your way out of every crisis. What if--"

"You'll never truly see me as an equal, will you?" she asked, although the question wasn't one he could answer. It was hard to recreate her identity when he knew her so well. He was the reminder of what had been. Of the original trio of power in the Summer Court, only Tavish remained. Niall was the Dark King, and Keenan was the Winter King. But Tavish remained— and they had centuries of history that meant he still saw her as someone who didn't matter.

All of which means that he's not going to form an attachment to me. Or even see me as a worthy advisor.

Siobhan met Tavish's cool gaze. "I am done for the day."

He frowned, but was silent for several moments as she gathered her things. The blood dripping from his cut lip seemed not to bother him, but Siobhan found it irritating— more so because she was not the cause.

"Is it wrong to want you to be safe?" he asked.

Despite logic, Siobhan paused. "I am safe, Tavish." She reached out to wipe the blood drop away.

Tavish caught her wrist. "No."

"You didn't used to mind my touch." Siobhan wasn't sure she'd ever been among his favorites, but they had memories over the years. Blurry ones, admittedly, but they'd enjoyed each other. "If all you think of me is as a seductress, perhaps—"

"You weren't an advisor to my queen then." Tavish squeezed her wrist, holding her in place. They stayed, caught in some silent battle for control until he asked, "Do you still visit the Dark? Do you still spend time in *their* court?"

And that was the trigger to her rage. She wrapped her leg around his knee and punched his shoulder with her free hand, using the push and pull of the combined motions to knock him to the ground.

"Do you doubt my loyalty? Or are you jealous?" she asked.

He tugged her forward, not releasing her wrist even as he fell, and she landed atop him. Chest-to-chest. Hip-to-hip. "My duty is to the Summer Court."

"Not an answer," she said, glaring down at him.

"Do you still warm the Dark King's sheets?" he asked.

She tugged her wrist free, hating that she could only do so because he allowed it. A part of her thought he was jealous, but such a thing wasn't normal for a Summer Court faery. If he was jealous, he was a fool. She had interest in exactly one faery —and unfortunately, he was the one who was currently insulting and rejecting her.

"I answer to the queen, Tavish. Not you."

THE NEXT DAY was no better. Tavish was already in a foul mood when Irial himself arrived at the loft where the advisors and queen of the Summer Court made their home. He stood in the doorway as if posing for cameras, dark eyes sparkling and a smile that could only lead to trouble.

The guards parted at Siobhan's nod.

"Irial," Siobhan greeted. She knew him well enough to know that the king who had become Chaos was not here without reason.

"May I enter?"

The guard at the door looked toward Tavish and Siobhan. It wasn't as if they could refuse him, not truly, but seeing him seemed to evoke unease in those who had been born fey.

"No," Tavish said, just as Siobhan said, "Yes."

Siobhan muttered a curse that had Irial laughing aloud. He strolled into the room.

"Lovely to see you, too." Irial was no longer the Dark King, and in truth, he had a unique status among their kind. As Chaos, he could not properly be refused welcome in any court. "It has been too long, lovely."

Siobhan gave him a look no one else could see, and his smile grew cunning. After his death, he'd managed to finagle resurrection as the embodiment of Chaos, and he had the unique position of also being the unofficial consort of the current Dark King.

"Irial. My regards to your better halves."

He laughed. "Oh, but if they are both my better halves, they've fulfilled all the good I could be. Does that leave me nothing but wickedness?"

"If memory serves, that always was a particular gift of yours." Siobhan stepped closer and allowed his familiar embrace, knowing well that he was harmless to her. No one who knew him would be surprised that he dipped her for a kiss.

While Irial's kiss was fairly chaste, it undoubtedly looked otherwise, and the wink he gave her made clear that he intended as much.

Siobhan bit back a smile as Tavish jerked her away from Irial.

"Why are you here?" Tavish asked. "I have no record of a meeting."

Irial grinned. "Niall kicked me out of the house for being 'absurdly cheerful,' so I thought I'd visit the other courts." He looked around expectantly. "Is the queen around? I'd like to pay my respects."

"On behalf of . . ." Tavish prompted.

"Chaos, it is what I am," Irial answered with a cheeriness that was slightly out of character. "Why else would I possibly be here?"

"Are you drunk?" Siobhan asked softly.

Irial laughed gleefully and said, "Not yet, my dear. A glass of Summer Wine wouldn't go amiss, though. Would you fetch me one?"

"Siobhan is not a cocktail maid. She is an advisor to Her Majesty, Aislinn, Queen of the Summer Court and—"

"I was asking you, Tavish." Irial looked at Siobhan's counterpart with an innocent smile that was about as convincing as kelpie claiming to be vegetarian. The innocence fled after a moment, and there instead was a faery to fear. Taunting. Powerful. Far too proud to back down, despite—or perhaps because of—centuries of encounters.

"Summer Wine is for those of our court." Tavish glared, eyes as black as Irial's now. The two could be brothers, opposing twins: Tavish spun-silver hair and Irial shadow-dark strands.

"I belong to all courts," Irial stated.

"Or none." Tavish held Irial's gaze and added, "Our queen is busy. One makes an appointment, requests a convenient time—"

"Are you refusing me access to the Summer Queen?"

"No."

"To the Summer Wine, then?" Irial taunted. "Are you afraid I'll become drunken and difficult, Tavish? Afraid that I cannot control myself? Surely, you are not worried for my well-being."

"You are not of our court," Tavish said, not backing down at all. "Summer Wine is the drink of the court of light. You are a thing of shadows."

If Siobhan didn't know him so well, she would've missed the rage in his form and voice. Even then, however, she would not miss the accusations in his voice. The history between the courts was tense, and Tavish saw no beauty in the Dark.

But while the Dark Court was never a place of sparkling light and joyous laughter, Siobhan knew well that it wasn't evil. She had many fond memories of nights in black sheets with the shadows touching her skin. There was joy there, too, as in her own court.

She looked between the two faeries. Whatever grudges they had meant that this could turn ugly.

"Perhaps, we could—"

"Why would the Dark King want sunlight?" Tavish bit off, speaking over her.

"I am no longer the Dark King, old boy. Your liquid sunlight is no longer deadly to me." Irial held his arms wide. "Let us drink and be friends. I am no longer a creature that must fear sunlight."

"You are still him," Tavish said. "The past is unchanged. Call yourself something else, but you are still monstrous. I remember the countless nights Niall wept. I remember the laughter when my king was bound and weakened. You are still that monster."

"No forgiveness, then?"

Her co-advisor ignored the question and said only, "My queen is not without obligation. She may be indisposed or--"

"Come now, Tavish. I know Seth is not due back from Faerie for several days." Irial's casual drawl barely disguised his growing temper. "And I am in rather immediate need of seeing Aislinn. You have no grounds to refuse me audience . . . or drink, for that matter. There are laws. Surely, you aren't going to ignore them, old boy."

"As you will," Tavish said.

Siobhan stared at Tavish. There was something off in the way he spoke the queen's name, the sheer weight of it was strange.

Irial caught her eye and looked at her as if daring her to speak.

When she didn't, he said, "Then will one of you please tell the queen that I request an audience, and"—he stared at Tavish then—"that I am here waiting? I will be here until she has the time to speak with me."

"I will wait with Irial," Siobhan offered. "Perhaps you could see if Aislinn is available. . .?"

"As you say." Tavish gave a curt nod and left.

His disdain could not be any more obvious if he screamed the words, and Siobhan wanted to follow him, to explain that she was not being disloyal to their court or queen. The queen herself welcomed Chaos to the table regularly. He might not be welcome at their revels, but Siobhan thought that might be as much the decision of the current Dark King as anything else.

Siobhan motioned for the guards to leave the room. "Wait outside the door. I am at no risk from him."

Once they departed, Irial's demeanor shifted. He wasn't as languid or seductive as he had once been with her, but he visibly relaxed. "You always were a clever one."

Siobhan glanced at him from the corner of her eye, emboldened by his trust, and said, "It may be presumptuous, but I do believe, after all this time, that I am safe in your presence."

"You always were. Well"—he gave her a wicked smile that once promised more—"as safe as you wanted to be. You're not as tame as some faeries."

She motioned to a seat, not taking up that thread, but Irial remained where he was. "Tavish seems increasingly stern. Is he considering a transition to the High Court? Niall has spoken to him of it, but would not reveal his thoughts. Should I press the queen on it? Despite what they think, I do not wish danger to your queen. I never have. If Tavish is not adept--"

"He is fine." Siobhan looked to where the silver haired faery had vanished. "Tavish is not without Summer's passion. He simply hides it well for reasons that are his own."

"So that's how it is." Irial plucked at a tendril of her hair. "Are you pining, love? Or are you helping him kindle that passion?"

She sighed. "I fear he sees me as a fool . . . or worse."

Siobhan pushed aside a drape of flowering vines, behind which was an inset bar. She gestured to the cut glass decanters and assorted bottles of wines, whiskies, and liqueurs. "We have drinks that are more to your usual interest."

"No. I want sunlight. I want to understand it." Irial walked over to stand next to her at the hidden sideboard and poured himself a generous drink of the liquid sunshine that was the drink of the Summer Court. His hand trembled slightly.

If Siobhan hadn't seen it herself, she'd never have believed it. Whatever his business with the queen, Irial was not nearly as calm as he pretended—or perhaps it was the fear of burning up if he was not, in fact, safe from the sunlight.

"Irial? Are you . . . well?"

"Shush, Siobhan. A little fear makes us alive," Irial whispered.

"The Dark King might think so, but you . . . are no longer that." Siobhan reached out and squeezed his arm. "If it does not endanger my queen, I am still your friend."

He nodded, and then a moment later, his grin returned. "Mustn't let your beau realize I'm not nearly as awful as he thinks . . . or perhaps we should."

"I care for him, Irial," she warned.

"I see, but"--he tilted his head and stared into the distance as if pondering-- "I'm afraid I'm about to upset Tavish's entire apple cart."

"His apple cart?" she echoed.

"I'm a father," he whispered. "I've come to share my news."

"With my queen? What . . . Leslie is with ch—"

"No. Not her. Not yet." He sighed, and Siobhan suddenly missed the shadows that used to undulate next to him when he was the Dark King.

"Irial . . ."

He took her hand as if they were, in fact, simply old friends, and in a way, she supposed that was as fitting a label as any for their history. Then he told her, "I have learned that I am a father, and I have a great-grandchild, too."

"And that child is of interest to this court," Siobhan filled in.

"Clever woman," he said.

"You do make me nervous."

"Chaos, love. It's what I am." He lifted his glass. "To family!"

And with that, the once-Dark King downed an entire glass of Summer Wine.

AISLINN PAUSED in her perusal of the latest reports. There were advisors, merchants, and managers employed to handle the court's business—as there had been for centuries--but the Summer Queen had taken a keen interest in the business of providing for her court.

Learning to control the full weight of unfettered summer wasn't as easy as she'd hoped—especially as a former human. The Summer Court was volatile by design, and the weight of so much power was still hard to control after several years. She'd taken up courses, managing the accounts, and a number of other hobbies to try to practice focus.

She'd taken courses at the college and read books on a variety of marketing and investing plans. These may not be the normal purview of faery queens, but Aislinn Foy had been mortal first. She would and often did let summer's essence fill her, and she did frolic as a proper Summer Queen should when the time was right—but she would also be a decision-making party when it came to her court's financial and business interests. Eternity was a very long time, and the practicalities of providing for a court could be expensive.

"Aislinn?" Tavish suddenly stood there, drawing her attention to him with the power of something greater than magic.

He moved like moonlight sometimes, present suddenly and beautifully, and rather intense without realizing it. "My queen . . ."

"That look never seems to be a harbinger of joy, Tavish."

She stood and went to the faery who had been her guide and strength in her new role as queen. He'd become her family, as much as many of the faeries she counted on in her new life as a queen, but Tavish was more. He was the brother she had never had.

Embracing him, she asked, "What can I do to cheer you, brother? Summer isn't meant for such gloom."

Tavish had finally relented to her insistence on calling him "brother," but he only agreed to that if there were no witnesses. Hearing it—according to him—allowed her to let him know they were alone.

"Not gloom. Wishes of a bit of lightning to toss..."

Aislinn laughed and teased, "Shall I smite someone for you?"

"I would enjoy that," he said, lighter by a few degrees. "Alas, it would cause complications. You have a guest."

"With that expression, let me guess . . . Donia? Devlin? Irial?" She paused on the last name as Tavish nodded curtly.

"He is not our enemy, brother. Chaos is--"

"The self-same faery who once cursed this court." Tavish punched a section of wall. Here, without witnesses, he would reveal the side of himself that was more summerlike than anyone seemed to expect. Temper flared, and he glowed with a hot internal light.

Aislinn waited.

"Centuries, Ash. Centuries of futile searching, and he did not suffer. Our court. Our faeries. All of the mortals remade as faery. Keenan." He sighed. "You. So much pain, and for what?"

She reached out and squeezed his wrist. "I shall meet with

him without you at my side. Go, find an outlet for this. Summer may rage, but we are a court of joy, brother."

"As you command."

"As you need," she corrected. There was little else she could say or do.

Tavish wasn't wrong, but she couldn't refuse Irial's visit. He was, these days, an entity that was welcome in all courts. The last embodiment of Chaos was only with the Dark, and that had led to hunger for power. Chaos had become War, and in doing so, Death had been summoned.

Aislinn had no desire to see such bloodshed again. She would have peace. Summer was for joy, for pleasure, for languid days and drunken mornings. Violence lurked, and she could feel that impulse. It was why she invited other regents to her table, broke bread and shared drinks with them as the long-dead Summer King Miach had done. Unity and balance were what let the world thrive.

"I will meet with Irial," she said. "The past is a thing we must set aside."

Tavish's expression made quite clear that he did not agree—but this was why her court was benefitted by her relative youth. Barely in her twenties, Aislinn had only a heartbeat of time in their world. No centuries' old grudges to sway her. No near-eternity of suppressed rage.

Tavish dipped his head in a bow. His calm exterior seemed as if it reformed like a great wall around the storm she knew he felt inside. "Ash?"

"Yes?"

"May I ask that we have a revel? I have needs that are interfering with my duties." Tavish held her gaze. "If I do not address them, I fear that working with Siobhan will be impossible soon."

If he were anyone else or perhaps if they were any other

court, Aislinn would laugh, but this was the Summer Court. Pleasure was as much a joy as a duty.

"Of course! Seth will return soon and—"

"I would beg your leave that we do not wait that long." Tavish looked toward the room. "Seeing Irial embrace her did much to wear my last thread of control."

The Summer Queen nodded. Her advisor asked little for himself, so there was no chance she'd refuse. "You could speak to her, Tavish. I have no objection to my two advisors enjoying--"

"No. If she wasn't your advisor in opposition to me, perhaps . . ." Tavish frowned. "But this is the happiest she's been, Ash. I would not risk that to satisfy my own carnal interest in her."

Aislinn nodded. She already feared losing him to the High or Winter Court. If he could not find joy here, she would. There had to be a solution that meant keeping both of her advisors—and Tavish finding happiness. If not, she'd lose him.

AISLINN WATCHED the former Dark King walk into her aviary alone in surprise. Although Tavish hadn't mentioned anyone else, Aislinn had thought there must be someone else here with him. Leslie visited with Irial, typically, and though the two weren't as close as Aislinn would like, she wasn't sure what sort of thing would necessitate a visit from Irial alone. Dark Court business was a thing he absented himself from these days—at least ostensibly. No one who saw the way the former king watched Niall had any doubts of his allegiance.

Worry flooded Aislinn, and the weather around her reacted. A small storm cloud appeared as she asked, "Is Leslie well?"

"She is." Irial seemed unconcerned with the brief burst of rain that filled the room and drenched him. "As is Niall."

"Good." She waited, figuring out by now that there was no way to rush the fey when they were of a mind to stall.

"How are you?" Irial stared at her in a way that was wholly unfamiliar, as if he was studying her face for clues of . . . something. Odder still, he approached her, instead of keeping his usual distance.

Vines sprung up, lashing together in a fence of sorts between them.

"Close enough," she said.

Irial simply stood there, leaning into the fence, pausing to sniff a flower that sprouted near him. "Tell me of your mother. Your grandmother. What were they like when you were younger?"

"My . . .what?"

"Your family." Irial made a careless gesture in the air. "Tell me of them."

"Why?"

"Is it so hard to believe I'm curious?" His tone was light, and his smile was hard to resist.

Aislinn tried to resist the answering smile she felt threatening. "Without a reason? Yes."

"I do not know you well enough." He lifted a shoulder in a shrug. There was something irrepressible about Irial—to the point that Seth had grown oddly fond of him and Aislinn couldn't help but find Irial charming.

"You're being peculiar." She gestured and a chair woven of ivy and flowers appeared as she sat.

"May I?" Irial held up a cigarette.

"Around my plants? No." With a flick of her hand, another such seat lifted next to Irial.

"Nerves," he said.

Aislinn paused. Although faeries—especially Irial—lied by omission and misdirection, they could not lie outright. Further, Irial sounded sincere.

"Are you well?" she asked.

He sat without replying. After a moment, Irial leaned forward. "Shall I tell you the grand news, my dear?"

At Aislinn's will, a table rose between them. Fashioned of tree branches twisted into an infinite loop of Celtic knots, it provided the illusion of a barrier. She'd been working on it as a meditation piece.

"May I call you 'dear'?"

"Irial—"

"Was there an affectionate name you would have liked as a child?" he continued as if she hadn't spoken. "Or a pet? There is a beautiful lioness that I saw when I was in—"

"Irial!"

"Mmm?" He stared at her in a way that she would almost call besotted, but for the fact that she knew without a doubt that he had never shown any genuine interest in her romantically.

"What are you here to tell me?"

"Oh," he said, "I'm a father."

"Leslie is—"

"No. A hundred or so years ago, I met a lovely woman. We had children, Aislinn." He looked both joyous and forlorn in a matter of moments. "I've forgotten for years, by my own design, as my Thelma was fated to be . . . well, you." He gestured around the room. "This."

"Your children's mother was mortal."

"Yes." He stared at her. "Thelma was a mortal."

"And she would have been the Summer Queen?" Aislinn echoed, trying to wrap her mind around whatever Irial was sharing. "If she'd have . . . and then I'd have . . . I would have been mortal."

"No, my dear." Irial met her gaze. "You were never truly mortal. Elena's father was fey. You've always been part-fey, a halfling like Ani and Tish—and your grandmother."

Irial leaned back in his vine-wrought chair and watched her expectantly, as she pieced together his statements to the conclusion he was implying. When she burst out laughing, flowers popping into existence throughout the loft, and several of the birds came zipping into the room.

"Oh! You almost had me!" Aislinn rarely felt so light-hearted around him. "Your expression. . . You are a master at lying without actual lies, Irial."

Irial, however, frowned.

She giggled. "That was so convincing. The whole set-up, walking in as if you were drunk and . . ."

She stood and stepped toward him. Leaning down, she brushed a kiss on his cheek. If he could play a prank on her, he could tolerate a token of affection.

"Was this Leslie's idea? Seth's?" she asked. "I can't imagine Niall having this sort of prankster urge."

Irial caught her hand as she started to step back. "Aislinn, I am serious. Many years ago, I met a woman, a fierce rebellious beautiful mortal, and I knew she was the one who could free summer."

Aislinn stared at him.

"I made that curse," Irial continued. "Over nine hundred years ago, I bound Keenan. There was a beautiful mortal girl, and—at that time—I thought it was clever to hide that sunlight in a family of women. Your family."

Aislinn pulled free of his grasp and sat back down grace-lessly. No traces of her laughter remained. "No. Stop it. This isn't funny now--"

"Aislinn . . . I cannot lie outright. You know this." He paused, watched her intently as he added, "Centuries after my oh-so-clever curse, I met her. Thelma. Thelma Foy."

"You must be confused—"

"I am not. I see her in you now that I have my memories freed. Her courage and strength . . . She would be proud to see what you've achieved." Irial's expression was the same one he had when gazing at Niall or Leslie. He was as subtle as a brick through a window when it came to love. "I fell for Thelma, willing to damn the world if that was the cost."

"Foy is Grams maiden name, but . . ."

"She kept her mother's name. I had no name to give her." Irial met Aislinn's gaze. "I'd have married her, damned the world for her—and my daughter. After I'd lost Niall, I feared I'd never be loved again. Truly loved, not adored or admired or desired, but loved."

"Leslie and Niall love you." Aislinn stood and walked away from him, her back to him, wishing she could have Seth at her side.

"I don't deserve it, but I am grateful that they do," Irial said, tone still tender and open. "I would do anything for love. I learned that lesson when Niall left me. Had I known that I was cursing my own, I would never have cursed that long-ago mortal woman, Aislinn. I swear to you."

Aislinn nodded. She wasn't sure she could say the words she needed for the revelation he'd brought to her. What were the words? Did he want a pardon? Understanding?

"Thelma was desperate, you see, to avoid her fate." Irial's voice had grown softer still, tender as if she were a small child —and to him, she supposed she was. "I wanted to stay in Faerie, raise Elena there."

"So was my mother," Aislinn whispered. She glanced over her shoulder at him. "Desperate, I mean. She died to stay human."

Irial nodded. "I wish I could have known, could have saved her. I wish I could have raised Elena—and been there for Moira and for . . . you."

He walked closer and dropped to his knees before Aislinn. "I loved Elena when she was born, and I love her granddaughter, my great-granddaughter already. Instantly. Family is precious, has always been precious to the Dark Court. You are my family, Aislinn. Let me into your life."

Aislinn stared down at the faery who had cursed her, who had cursed her mother and grandmother and great-grandmother—the faery who had loved her great-grandmother.

"You're my . . ." Aislinn's words fled. She couldn't even say the words.

"Great-grandfather," Irial finished, sounding reverent. "And I want to rebuild our family."

"I can't." She shook her head and backed away. Grandfathers weren't to look your age, or be sleeping with your friend. They were old and smoked pipes. They told rambling stories, and they had not cursed you. "I just . . . I can't . . ."

SIOBHAN CRINGED at the sudden storm that flashed over the entire loft and—from the look of the torrential downpour outside—the surrounding area as well. Her queen had not summoned her, and as advisor to the Summer Queen, she'd feel a call if Aislinn needed her.

The loft, though it was rebuilt for the current inhabitants, was not designed for holding this much water. There was a grate that opened, and once that was done, the flood that currently rose over Siobhan's ankles would sluice down into the open park that was the site of their revels.

Lightning flashed inside the aviary, and the birds all flew out into wherever they nested at such times. The blur of vibrant feathers looked like magic in the air, as if a riot of blossoms had been launched into the park.

She realized that she was laughing in glee as she sloshed toward the valve to open the grate. There was something invigorating about a sudden deluge, not quite a waterfall, but near enough that a part of her wanted to let the water build so they could swim.

The water was more than knee-deep as Siobhan finally reached the valve.

"Can you turn it?" Tavish was there, at her side, soaked and gorgeous. "Siobhan?"

Logic said not to let instinct rule.

Logic said she wasn't interested in rejection.

She said nothing as she gripped the old-fashioned valve and cranked. The water sluiced out, sucked past her legs and sending her toppling into Tavish's arms. She could've resisted, but why not enjoy it?

She smiled at him as his arms stayed wrapped around her. For all the faeries she'd met in the time she was a part of this world, and for all that she, too, was completely fey now, there was something about Tavish's inhuman beauty that left her breathless.

The silver strands of hair that were usually kept tethered in a braid had come loose, and the overall effect was a softening of an otherwise austere face.

"It is hard to trust you, Siobhan, when you look at me with cunning smiles," Tavish said finally, breaking into her reverie.

"Perhaps, Tavish, there are good reasons for those 'cunning smiles.'"

"Tell me."

"I haven't seen you look like this in years."

"Bedraggled?"

"Aroused," she countered. "My years as a Summer Girl might be coated in softer things, but my memory is not gone."

He said nothing.

"Tell me no," she whispered.

He leaned down and kissed her until she wasn't sure she'd still stand if not for the tightening of his arms around her. Her lips parted to invite him to deepen the kiss, and her hands reached up to tangle in the metallic silver that was so rarely free.

But he stopped.

"No," he said finally. "You are her advisor, Siobhan. To pursue this, one of us would have to abandon that duty."

Siobhan blinked to try to push her lust back enough to answer him. "Ash said that?"

"No." Tavish rested his forehead against hers. "I have served this court since the last king's father was ruler. How could I leave my responsibility? How could I abandon her for . . ."

"A meaningless fuck?" Siobhan finished, stinging with his rejection and lack of regard for her. "I suppose I could ask Irial if there are others in his court not so opposed to my affections."

"Then I suppose you should await the end of his meeting with Aislinn, to advise her and speak to him," Tavish said. "I would rather not speak to him at all."

Tavish stepped away, striding out of the room before she could reply.

And Siobhan was grateful that the rain was still dripping on her face. It helped hide her tears. No man had ever wanted her —not the Summer King who stole her humanity or the Dark Kings who saw her only as a friend and sometimes lover. Was it so impossible to find one who wanted her wholly?

Perhaps she was not suited for the Summer Court.

Aislinn stared at the faery who watched her with such open and obvious affection. The room flooded, and if not for the bubble of sunlight she created around them, he'd have been drown. He'd not moved even as rain and thunder rolled through the loft.

"I can't do this," she repeated.

"Talk to me? We speak often, Aislinn." Irial stayed on the

floor, but his voice had a comforting tone she'd rarely heard. Oddly or not, it upset her to have him worry over her feelings.

"We cannot be family. You are partner to the Dark King."

"And your partner is child to the High Queen." Irial lifted a shoulder in a half-shrug. "My other partner is friends with the Summer Queen, who is friendly with the Shadow Court, as well."

Aislinn sighed. "I assume Sorcha knows?"

"She cursed me." Irial shrugged again, but the look of pain in his expression was enough to make the coldest heart soften. "Your great-grandmother and I wanted to keep our daughter safe."

"Grams. You forgot about Thelma to protect Grams." Her grandmother, the sweetest and fiercest person Aislinn had ever known, was half-fey. She'd hidden it or . . .

"Does Grams—"

"Elena knows," Irial said. "We are to meet, and she has already told me that if I keep trying to send guards or buy her things, she will ask you to set 'my faery arse on fire.' I believe there was an explanation about a magnifying lens and sunlight. I seem to be an insect in this example."

The embodiment of Chaos, the former king of the worst of the faeries, looked positively charmed by Grams threatening his life. It was disconcerting.

"Aislinn?"

She met his gaze.

"Elena has a brother," Irial said softly. "He's not as human as she is. Some fey children are more human, and others are more fey."

"Like Ani and Tish." Aislinn felt a twinge for Tish, who had died in the months when Bananach was rampaging.

"They were like children to me," Irial mused. "I didn't remember then that I had children, but I wanted a daughter. I dreamed sometimes of—" He shook his head. "I would have given Elena the world if I could, but the only way to protect her and Thelma was to leave. If I stayed, Keenan would've discovered her. Or Beira would've. How could I let him touch my beloved? Or my daughter? Or . . ."

When Aislinn said nothing, Irial took her hand tentatively. She looked at him.

"Or you." Inky tears slid down his cheeks. "I missed a century of having my daughter. I'll never meet Moira . . . please, Aislinn, at least consider letting me into your life."

"We're almost friends, so . . ." she started awkwardly. "You're already here. And you're Chaos. Upheaval"—she stood and walked toward the door—"which you more than deliver. Surely, that's enough."

"Aislinn . . ." His voice broke.

She shook her head, back to him. "I had no father. No grandfather. I have no idea what one even does with a father, and it's not as if you seem much like a grandfather."

"Faeries are different," he began.

Aislinn looked at him. "I cannot offer anything easily. You must know that, Irial. I have duties. I am a queen to a court that was cursed. By you. I am a faery because of your curse."

"No," he said, walking to stand at her side. "You are a faery because I fell in love with your ancestor. I surrendered her and my children knowing then that I would meet you. I saw it, Aislinn. I saw the future; Sorcha allowed it. I looked into the now, and I saw you. You were the reason I was able to give up Thelma. I knew that you would exist, and that you would break the curse."

Aislinn stared at him. It was all she could do without letting the emotional storm inside escape.

"I knew you would be a magnificent queen, and that because of you I would again meet the daughter I once held in my arms." Irial's voice broke. "I remember it all now, the love I had for Thelma. The loss. I was ready to let the world die if it meant being with her and my children."

"Do I know my . . . grand-uncle?"

Irial shook his head. "Elena tells me he left home when he was young, and that she hasn't heard from him in almost forty years."

"So, there is a faery that knows who you are, who I am," Aislinn said, not sure what that could mean. "He's related to two faery courts by blood, and we have no idea what he's doing."

Irial nodded. "He will visit you or me now that we know."

"He's your *son*." Aislinn shivered. "I cannot fathom what he must be like."

At that, Irial grinned. "Elena is my daughter, and she's a magnificent, kind, gentle creature. A lady like her mother."

Aislinn laughed. "Can I be there when you tell her she's gentle? And ladylike?"

While Aislinn loved her grandmother wholly, she was well aware that Grams was as gentle as a lion. She could be sweet, but threats to her loved ones were not tolerated. In a flash of clarity, Aislinn realized then that she understood that impulse —and that she was looking at the faery from whom they had inherited their ferocity.

She turned to Irial and kissed his cheek quickly. "I need time. To consult with my advisors and . . . I cannot promise anything."

Irial looked like he had received a lifetime of gifts all at once. "Anything for you, granddaughter. Anything I can do or slaughter or bring."

She wasn't ready for his intensity. So, she nodded and repeated, "What I need is time. Please?"

"As you wish." The former Dark King, her great-grandfather, bowed deeply and strode toward the door, sloshing through water and floating flower buds.

And Aislinn had no idea what to do with this knowledge—other than begin to try to locate Grams' brother and figure out what this all meant for her grandmother, who was apparently over a century old and had been hiding that detail.

SIOBHAN WATCHED A MARKEDLY LESS cheerful Irial exit the queen's chambers. He seemed lost in thoughts—which undoubtedly did not bode well. She waited until he was at the door before stepping to his side.

Irial met her eyes.

"Does my queen have need of me?" Siobhan asked.

"You're her advisor these days." Irial studied her. "She'll tell you. She must. Before word and whisper circulate, she'll need to figure out what her thoughts are."

"On?"

"The news that my great-grandfather has been found," Aislinn said as she stepped into the room, not drenched as Siobhan was. The Summer Queen appeared as beautiful and radiant as always. Her once-black hair was sun-kissed, and her skin had the perpetual tan of days lounging at beaches.

"I was always here," he said, staring at her covetously. "I missed so much. I want to grant your request for time, but Elena . . . insists that I gain your consent before spending time with me, Aislinn. Her loyalty to you is a beautiful thing, but I want to know my daughter."

"Will Grams die?"

"We all die eventually," he hedged.

"Irial . . ."

He sighed. "I have no idea. The obstinate streak in her—" He pressed his lips together in a most un-Irial way. "She won't answer a thing until you consent. Visiting her would alarm people, as if I am a threat to my own daughter, so I am left hoping your request for time is not--"

"I need time," Aislinn said. "Grams is her own person; she does what she wants. And if the other courts are alarmed by your visit to her, I will manage it. I do not object to your visiting your daughter."

Irial bowed deeply, and when he stood, he was smiling as widely as Siobhan had ever seen him do. "You are a gift, my dear."

And then he was gone, presumably off to see the queen's grandmother.

His daughter.

Siobhan and Aislinn exchanged a look, and then her queen said, "You can tell Tavish." She sighed. "Be gentle with him. . . and let him know that if his feelings toward me change, I . . . I accept it. I cannot do more today. Tomorrow we will deal with whatever this means. Update Tavish. I will speak to you in the morning."

Aislinn turned and left Siobhan to break the news to her co-advisor.

Siobhan tapped at Tavish's door. "Tavish?"

"Enter."

She stepped into the room, struck by the sheer number of plants in his space. One wall held a number of faery-made weapons. Cutlasses, rapiers, and daggers, fashioned in fey-friendly metals hung in cabinets with glass doors. A sitting area, complete with comfortable seats and a wet bar, filled the left of the room. Off to the right, behind a thick wall of foliage, was Tavish's bed. Wooden, simple, and overflowing with luxurious linens.

"Things looks different," she said mildly.

"We are settled finally." Unmistakable pride thickened his voice. "Should I have no creature comforts?"

"Not a criticism." She met his gaze. "It's welcoming, the kind of space that says a lot about the owner."

He shrugged. "I do not have many guests."

"Ours is a court of pleasure." She stepped closer. "I remember you having regular guests."

Tavish stiffened.

"I remember being your guest." Carefully, she touched his chest, resting the flat of her hand over his heart. "Fondly, Tavish. I remember those nights and days with joy."

"Niall and I had a duty to the Summer Girls," Tavish said, voice low enough that she wanted to move closer still.

"Was that all?"

He swallowed audibly. "No."

"Then why do you reject me?"

Tavish sighed. "Siobhan . . ."

"I have appetites still," she said, no longer hesitant to admit things that she'd have denied as a mortal.

"No advisors to enjoy. No Dark King," Tavish said, nodding. "Are there no guards you could enjoy? Or perhaps one of the solitary fey?"

And Siobhan felt an unusual burst of guilt. She shouldn't, not in the Summer Court, but the fact of his seeing intercourse as a task made her feel rejected. Had he only lain with her out of duty? Had it been an onerous duty?

"I suppose I shall need to see if Seth or Irial have any willing victims," she said, heat shimmering in her voice.

"You could speak to Ash if you have immediate needs."

Siobhan stepped back from him. "Perhaps. Unlike Keenan and his advisors"—she held his gaze—"Ash doesn't send me to faeries' beds for information."

"Did you dislike going there?" Tavish sounded confused, as if being sent to spy was a joyous act.

"I enjoyed the act. Here. And in their court. I will not disparage the joy I took in the Dark Kings' beds—either of them." She shook her head. Over the decades, she'd been sent to the Dark King, and while she'd enjoyed the acts of intimacy at the time, the reality that she had been used was depressing. Because Irial had longed for Niall, the Summer King would send her first to Niall and then to Irial.

"But...?"

"Pleasure doesn't erase the lack of choice," Siobhan said. "I was Keenan's spy, his discarded lover, and . . ." She stopped herself and met Tavish's gaze once more. "Is it so wrong to have wanted one of them to love me? To know what foods I liked best or what flowers or what color even. As a Summer Girl, I was bound to the will of the Summer King because of the curse, but . . . to go from words of love to being asked to bed the friends of the man I thought I loved. . . to learn he was faery, that I was no longer human . . ."

"Were you forced?"

Siobhan sighed. "There is no true answer there. To love Keenan? No. To become a faery? Yes, but that was a curse."

"By the Dark King," Tavish frowned and rose from the floor.

"No. Niall was kind. He refused me often."

"The other one?"

Siobhan laughed. "Irial? Never. He always offered drink or meal or conversation instead of intimacy." She paused, weighing how much to admit, before adding, "I sought him out because he had the thing I wanted. Love. It wasn't love for me, but if I had been with Niall, if his touch and scent were recent on my flesh, Irial treated me as if I mattered."

If not for the faith her queen had in her, if not for the fact that Niall and Irial had reconciled, she would have left the sunlight for the shadows when she was freed. They had their charms, and she was a woman who'd appreciated those charms.

Often. It had seemed like a fine plan at the time, but there was no place for her now.

Stiffly, Tavish said, "I have difficulty seeing any merit in Irial."

Siobhan sighed, stepped closer to Tavish, and prompted, "But do you understand what I sought?"

The look Tavish gave her was, perhaps, the most honest she'd seen him appear when dressed. "I spent nine centuries concentrating on my king's lovers. Bedding the ones who were not the queen, advising him on the next one, always the next one." He gave her a wry smile. "I've never been allowed the time to pursue a woman of my own interest, and my duty still prevents my desires. Unfortunately."

The guilt Siobhan felt over being a burden in her days as a Summer Girl twisted with heartbreak that he'd, apparently, found her so unappealing. Steeling herself so as not to reveal her crushed ego and wounded heart, she updated him on Irial's revelation.

"We shall speak with Ash tomorrow, then, about our court's plan."

"I'm worried," she admitted, voice barely a whisper. "The Winter Court will not respond well."

Tavish nodded. "Indeed." Then, he caught Siobhan's wrist. "Fresh berries with the dew still wet."

"What?"

"Your favorite food," he clarified. "You say it's fruit or berries, but the ones that make you happiest are those berries that are only just barely off the vine. And your color isn't one, but the way the skies look when the sun is about to rise. You said as much when we were in the southern continent."

Siobhan stared at him, mouth slightly agape.

"I've thought about what I wanted," Tavish said. "When you left to be in other beds, in other arms, when I was too old or too silent or too . . . me to have you. When I had to do my duties to my court and king." He cupped her face. "You were never a chore."

He brushed his lips over hers. Then, before she could react, he pulled back. "You were never truly mine, Siobhan, but that didn't change what I wanted. Duty merely prevents it."

Somehow, she found herself outside his room, alone and perplexed. She touched her lips. Tavish saw her. Not the girl she was when Keenan chose her. Not the woman who had been cursed. Not the advisor to the queen. Her.

And he was going to ignore his feelings—and hers—as if denial was romantic somehow.

Siobhan looked at the now-closed door. "You're a fool, Tavish."

~

BEFORE MEETING THE QUEEN, Siobhan had to see Tavish for a training session. This time, however, she was not opposed to being there in the makeshift gymnasium. She'd barely slept—not only worrying over Tavish's revelation but also over the news that the Dark King delivered to their court.

Despite everything, though, Tavish acted as if there were no major events on the court's horizon. He treated her no differently, either. If she had any doubts about her own memories, she would be alarmed.

This was the faery who advised the emotionally excessive Summer King for nine centuries, who advised his father before him. He was not easily unsettled, and if he was, he certainly didn't reveal it.

Siobhan made it her personal mission to touch him as often and as inconspicuously as possible all morning.

By the end of the session, he was looking at her with flashes of either desire or fury in his eyes.

"Meeting," she reminded him with a casual stroke of his upper back.

"Siobhan." Tavish pinned her with his gaze.

She licked her lips. "Are you warm? I'm becoming desperate with this heat."

One of the Wild Hunt visitors said his name then, drawing him into a discussion about the efficacy of wooden weapons as an alternative to faery-made metals since the access to Faerie was now limited.

"Sorry to interrupt," she said cheerily. "Would you mind terribly if I borrowed your shower? We need to meet the queen soon, and I'm sweaty."

Siobhan ran her fingertips over her cleavage, drawing many gazes in the gesture. Admittedly, she didn't usually act that way now, but years of being a Summer Girl had a few advantages.

"Fine." Tavish stared at her. "I'll stay here until you're done."

She laughed. "Silly man. I don't mind being naked around you."

He gave her a look that seemed almost angry, but she knew how he felt now. If he hadn't wanted her to find a solution, he ought not have revealed his feelings.

Quickly, she stretched up and kissed just under his ear, on the side of his neck. "You're the best," she said lightly.

His jaw clenched tighter.

"Off to get naked," she murmured cheerily.

The Dark Court guest flashed her a wicked smile and walked away as Siobhan laughed. Sometimes she wondered if Tavish had hidden how ruthless he could be or if the war had changed him.

"Siobhan?" Tavish said, voice barely level.

She paused. "Mmmm?"

"Do warn me if you'll have a guest with you," he said.

"Not to worry, I can handle it myself," she teased. When he said nothing, she added, "Do you want to watch?"

He closed his eyes.

"Siobhan, are you coming?" Mae, one of the other former Summer Girls, said in tone that implied that the question was a repetition.

Tavish opened his eyes and stared at them both.

Siobhan blushed at the look he was giving her. Perhaps she'd pushed him too far. Forcing her gaze to Mae, Siobhan asked, "Coming where?"

"Shopping." Mae smiled with the sort of genuine happiness she'd only recently developed. The Summer Girls had been dependent on the Summer King for their entire lives. For all practical purposes, he had been the sun: they bloomed or wilted because of him. The end of the curse benefitted many faeries, not just the former king.

Mae all but bounced in place as she waited for Siobhan's reply. "Everyone is coming."

"Next time, ok?" Siobhan hugged her. "I need—"

"You really do. I saw that look." Mae grabbed Siobhan in a fierce hug and whispered, "Ask Tavish to train longer. A bit of grappling would be good for you both."

Siobhan looked back at her co-advisor. "Trust me. I know."

#

Aislinn wasn't surprised to see Siobhan walk into the study early. Of all of the faeries in the court, Siobhan was the one most likely to treat Aislinn with the comfort of a friend, rather than insist on distance. The others weren't unkind, but the ease with which Siobhan talked to her was rare. Whereas most of the Summer Girls, guards, and court members occasionally forgot the deference that said that she was their queen, Siobhan occasionally remembered it.

"I'm bored," Siobhan complained.

"I thought the girls were going shopping," Aislinn said. "Perhaps after the meeting . . ."

Siobhan gave her a level look. "If new frocks were exciting, why didn't you go?"

"I like shopping." Aislinn frowned as she said it, though. She hadn't used to like it, but there were times when being the embodiment of Summer had meant changing who she was. "Evolution" was what Tavish called it. She wasn't so sure she liked evolving, but she liked who she was and loved her court so she didn't ponder that detail overmuch.

Siobhan flopped onto one of the overstuffed chairs, and then almost immediately stood and paced, and then sat again. Her foot tapped on the floor, and her hands seemed to move constantly, sweeping her hair up into a twist, fidgeting with her necklace.

"What?"

"If I quit, would you hate me?" Siobhan blurted out.

Aislinn smiled. "Tavish?"

"He's a fool," Siobhan said. "I could totally advise you and do . . . be . . . well, whatever it is."

"Date him?" Aislinn supplied helpfully.

"That. I guess." She sighed loudly. "I could love him, I think, although"—she let out a muffled scream of sorts—"that's fucking terrifying. The last man I loved stole my humanity."

"I am aware," Aislinn said. "We'll figure it out."

She looked up and saw the door open as Tavish stepped into the room. He looked between them and his expression grew wary. "Has the meeting begun without me?" he asked lightly.

"No," Aislinn said in the same tone. "Siobhan was considering her resignation. She is having difficulty working with you, I think."

"Why?" He looked at them both, and then settled his gaze on Siobhan. "Did I offend you?"

"No." Siobhan glanced at her queen and muttered, "Thanks, Ash."

Aislinn burst into peels of laughter. "My pleasure. You've both brought this to my table, and I happen to think my choice of advisors is inspired, so we need a new plan."

"Aislinn?" Tavish prompted.

"Kiss her, Tavish. Woo her. Seduce her." The Summer Queen gestured between them. "It's the season for love. Why are you trying to argue with your queen?"

"Respectfully, your majesty, I am not sure that"—he lowered his voice—"intimacy between your advisors is a wise plan."

"Noted." She clapped her hands together. "This is the Summer Court, and if you don't want me to lose an advisor, I suggest you stop being obstinate and romance one another."

Her advisors exchanged a look.

"Now," Aislinn continued, tone serious. "What shall we do about my dear old great-grandfather?"

Siobhan and Tavish exchanged a look, and for a moment, she wondered at his thoughts. Hidden behind dark eyes and stern looks, Tavish seemed like an odd fit for the summer, but she knew he was a writhing mass of passions, barely hidden some days. Talk of the Dark King rarely brought out his better side—and Aislinn knew that.

She was, however, young. She'd lived merely two decades, and of a handful of those years was as a faery. She was impulsivity embodied. In truth, knowing that the blood of the last Dark King flowed through her veins explained a few things. Aislinn had a courage that was more than human, more than fey. Add shadows to the Summer Court, and she was the result.

"I don't suppose we can murder him, and hide the evidence," Tavish said, voice light enough to make it sound like a joke.

"Bananach murdered him once already," Aislinn said cheerily. "Didn't take."

"Alas." Tavish downed a drink. "Perhaps we might speak to Niall first."

"And Donia," Siobhan added.

"I told Seth," the queen said. "Not who although I bet he already knows. He said he doesn't, but that's only true if it involves him." Aislinn scowled and muttered, "Future-seeing makes for confusing relationships."

Siobhan reached over and squeezed her hand, offering silent support. Then she asked, "How do you feel about it?"

Tavish had advised a cursed king and before him a frolicking king. Aislinn's age and gender were sometimes confusing to him, but Siobhan was relieved to see that the flinch gave way to kindness.

"He has redeeming traits," Tavish said, sitting taller in his seat. "He protects his court, Ash. Or did."

"I know." Aislinn scowled. "I just . . . I've never had a father or grandfather. I grew up with Grams. A house of women. Female friends—other than Seth but he was always more. What do you do with grandfathers or fathers?"

"He's probably not like others," Tavish offered.

A knock heralded a frowning guard. "Your Majesty?"

"There is a . . . cub. Well, two cubs," he said, as he stepped to the side. There, tumbling over themselves were a pair of small tigers. They were absolutely, without a doubt, the cutest, least appropriate thing Siobhan could imagine raising in the loft.

But the queen was already on the floor, snuggling a tiny predator.

"The note says—"

"We know who sent them," Tavish started.

Aislinn was giggling even as she said, "Utterly foolish man." Then she was growling at a baby tiger and asking it, "What in the world am I to do with you?"

"'Light and dark go well together. A little shadow doesn't undo the brightness,' it says." The guard looked at them, not sure what to do.

"Is it signed?" Siobhan asked.

"'Love from your . . . Pappy.'"

Aislinn scooped the tigers into her lap, and then set sun spots across the floor so they could pounce on them. "I always wanted a kitten," she mused.

There was no work that would distract her then, so Siobhan and Tavish excused themselves.

Outside the door, Tavish looked at her, "We will need to speak to Niall about this."

Siobhan nodded. "At least they're cubs."

Tavish sighed. "Nature thrives around her, so it's not a crisis. What if it's the start of a habit? Where would we put a menagerie?"

At that, Siobhan was assailed by visions of nonstop gifts from a doting former Dark King who had always, apparently, wanted children. "Call Niall."

Tavish paused before turning away. "May I woo you?"

"Yes," Siobhan answered. "A million times yes."

He touched her cheek. "I want to take our time, do things right. I've watched both of my kings destroy women they loved. I've watched Irial destroy Niall. I don't ever want to hurt you."

Siobhan thought she might legitimately swoon. They'd been intimate many times, danced, spoken, fought, but this was different. New.

"I'd like that," she said, feeling oddly shy and young. "I want to take care of you, too." She leaned up and kissed him softly before pulling back just enough to speak. "And then, I want to have my way with you."

Tavish closed his eyes briefly.

"Over and over," she added, "until neither of us can walk."

He swallowed audibly and rasped, "That . . . would be good, too."

And before she could reply, he kissed her until she had to lean on the wall for support. It would, in fact, be very, very good.

~

AISLINN KNEW who Urian was the moment he stepped into her court. Her great-grandfather's warning that he would come wasn't why. Urian looked like family.

Shadow-dark skin and what would've been a twin to her own dark hair before sunlight changed her. He stood with his father's arrogance, and something of a wicked glint in his eye. This was not a faery who had found his heart.

This was an angry faery.

"What shall I call you?" Urian didn't bow, didn't even lower his gaze. "Niece? Ash-Girl?"

Aislinn lifted a hand to stop the guards who started to move closer.

"Murderess?" he asked, voice lower.

Aislinn lifted her chin and stared back at him. "Queen."

He laughed. "Not *my* queen. I bow to no one."

Aislinn repressed a shiver of fear. She was strong enough to fight any faery in existence now—at least those in her world. That didn't mean she wanted to do so, and power didn't always overcome skill.

Urian looked around, smiled at Siobhan and winked at a guard. "I thought I should meet the woman who mattered so much that my niece died." He stared intently at Aislinn and said, "You are a strangely pretty little murderess."

"I didn't kill my mother," Aislinn started.

Urian brushed his hand to the side, shadows slid across the ground as if he was summoning them.

He shouldn't be able to manage that. The Dark belonged to Niall now, not this faery.

"No." It was one word, but it was enough. Her guards came in, a rush of vine and bark.

Urian smiled, cold and vicious. That was a look she remembered well from Bananach, madness tinged with fury.

"We are fine," she told her guard. She motioned for them to leave. Perhaps it was foolish, but she wanted to try talking to him. Tavish and Siobhan stayed, but no one else was near. Only them. If Tavish were anyone else in the court, Aislinn would feel unprotected. He was fierce—and Siobhan was brutal when provoked.

And Aislinn was the queen, a faery with the ferocity of summer inside her very skin. Her uncle was no threat to her.

"If you must, you may call me Aislinn."

"Aislinn," Urian echoed. "My sister's granddaughter. The last ashes of my family."

He might be family, but he wasn't the sort of person Grams was, not even the sort of person her mother had been—or that Irial was. At least not the Irial she'd met and known. Urian reminded her of the fey things that had been the stuff of nightmares for her growing up, vicious in ways she would never understand.

"Such an odd little mortal-turned-faery. You took my mother's crown, my niece's crown."

"Thelma didn't want it. She *ran* to avoid it," she reminded him. "My mother didn't either. She ran and died avoiding it."

"And you?"

"I fought to avoid it. This wasn't the life I wanted, but it's *mine* now. This court is *mine*."

"You like power, though. You've drawn the eye of the High Queen's son," Urian added. "

"I knew Seth before he was her son."

What makes you so interesting, Ashes?

"I don't know, Uncle. Why are *you* here?"

As Urian laughed, shadows skittered closer as if he was theirs somehow. It frightened her. A tiny part of her wanted to kick everyone here out and call the rest of her family, which was now both Grams and Irial as well as Seth, but Aislinn had doubts as to Urian's temper—and stability. He hadn't approached his father or his sister. He hadn't approached Seth, the faery who was de facto leader of the solitary.

"Seth," she said, latching on to that detail. "Is this about him? Some solitary fey thing?"

"Oh, it's about a lot of things, Ashes." Urian shook his head, as if he was sad, but it wasn't sorry glinting in his eyes. Rage and hunger simmered in him, so hot that she could have been looking into Bananach's eyes.

Without meaning to, a sword of sunlight formed in her grip, blinding bright and sizzling with heat.

Urian glanced at the sunlit blade. A smile that was identical to his father's curved his lips. "Do let them know I've come calling, Ashes."

Then he flung something glittering toward Siobhan.

"Siobhan!" Aislinn was halfway across the room before she finished the word, but Tavish was closer and almost as fast. He pushed Siobhan aside.

He was there, in front of his co-advisor. The blade that had been hurled at Siobhan stabbed Tavish's stomach. And then he was on the ground, blood pouring from his wound.

Her advisor. Her friend. Her brother-by-choice. Aislinn was livid. The sword that was in her hand a moment ago was there and raised. She met her uncle's eye and stalked toward him.

"Will you let him die, too?" Urian asked, taunting her with the sort of voice best suited for playground quarrels. "Or will you kill the son of the last Dark King? Whose life matters to you? What do you choose today? Death or life, Ashes?"

Her guards came in.

"No!" Aislinn called. "He is not yours to touch."

"Ash!" Siobhan called. "Tavish needs you."

"We aren't done," Aislinn said.

Urian merely grinned.

But when Aislinn turned toward her advisors, Urian walked to the door and left as quietly as he'd arrived.

～

"SUNLIGHT?" Tavish asked.

Aislinn flinched slightly, not so much that it was obvious to anyone who didn't know her. She knelt at his side. "There are complications."

"I know," Tavish assured her, voice shaky from obvious pain. "The side effects . . . are acceptable. Appealing, even."

The Summer Queen said nothing.

"Siobhan?" he asked.

"I'm fine, you fool." She knelt on the floor opposite the queen. "You, however, have a scratch."

He laughed. "My queen? Sister?"

"You will escort Tavish to his room as soon as I fix this." Aislinn nodded at the oozing wound. The edges were blackening as if ink had poured there, and the skin started to writhe.

"Poisoned," Tavish whispered. "If you could heal me soon . . ."

The Summer Queen pressed her lips together tightly, and she lifted his torn clothing so that the bloodied skin was visible.

"Are you sure?" Aislinn asked. "We can call a healer and—"

He looked at Siobhan as he answered Aislinn. "Yes."

Siobhan wasn't quite sure what she was missing, but her queen looked her in the eye and said, "That yes was to you, Siobhan. Remember that."

Then, the Summer Queen began to glow. Sunlight seemed

to radiate from her entire body, as if she had summoned the sun itself and somehow held it inside her small frame. The guards, the freed Summer Guards, assorted Summer Court faeries all started flowing into the room as if they were being called to their queen's side.

"Be well, brother, and be loved," Aislinn whispered, and then she brought her hands down on the wound, cupped them there at first, and then pressed down.

Tavish moaned, first in pain as she seared whatever poison had entered his body and then in a sort of agony as the skin sizzled and burnt. When the Summer Queen finally lifted her hand, a tattoo was there, a sun much like the blackened sun already on Tavish's throat.

"My queen," he whispered. Then he looked at Siobhan and murmured, "My beloved."

"Ash?"

"He's drunk on sunlight." Aislinn didn't sound much more sober. The room was erupting in flowers, and couples—or couples for the night—were kissing and caressing.

Tavish slid his hand over Siobhan's leg, at first caressing her calf but within moments his hand was above the knee and showing no sign of stopping.

Siobhan caught his hand in hers and asked, "What are you doing?"

"Seducing you . . . ?" Tavish smiled drunkenly.

Siobhan stifled her giggle. She hadn't ever seen him quite this drunk other than the week Aislinn became queen. That week, he'd kissed Siobhan until she thought her whole body might melt. The next day, he was as taciturn ever.

Siobhan vaguely heard Aislinn say, "Seth!"

And the queen's formerly-mortal lover stalked toward her. "Sorcha said you would need me, and I thought—"

"My uncle was here to murder someone," Aislinn said, sounding far too light-hearted. "But . . . can we . . ."

The queen and her lover were gone then, and Siobhan was left with her amorous, intoxicated co-advisor.

"What happens in the morning?" Siobhan prompted, catching and again holding tightly to Tavish's hand which had escaped her grasp.

"More sex!"

Siobhan started laughing. "That sounds wonderful, but I thought you wanted to think things through."

"Fuck it," he said cheerily. "Loved you for almost a damned decade. Had to watch others be where I wanted, but if you're mad enough to want me, I'm done arguing."

Siobhan helped him to his feet—and discovered that without restraint, his hands were everywhere.

"You have the perfect arse, Siobhan. Like a firm apple." Tavish had both hands on her bum, squeezing and caressing.

"I had no idea," she murmured, pushing him back slightly. Although she was sure he truly wanted her, feeling the obvious proof of his desire straining toward her, Siobhan also knew Tavish. Sober again, he'd be mortified that he was so amorous in public. He was a wonderful lover, but not as public about it as many in their court.

Siobhan started to steer him toward his room, trying to ignore the stares and even a smattering of applause and remarks of "it's about time" or "finally come to his senses, has he?"

"I shall compose a sonnet for each breast," Tavish declared, voice low enough that only she heard. "Two sonnets. One for the left, and one for the right. Perhaps a Rondeau on your apple cheeks, though."

"A what?"

"Lyric poem," he said, speaking in that exaggeratedly correct way of the truly drunken.

They'd made it to the edge of the room when Tavish looked

at her and said, "Let me love you, Siobhan. Let me be impulsive and enjoy this sunlit madness."

"If you try to walk away in the morning, I'll stab you myself this time," she warned.

"As you should," Tavish said before kissing her thoroughly.

In a moment, she realized his hands were unfastening her buttons, so she half led, half dragged him to his room where they made love stumbling and drunken and desperately until he sobered—and then did so again and again with more care and soft words.

THE NEXT MORNING, Tavish and Siobhan met the Dark Court's guests. Aislinn had left Seth resting in her chambers, so it was only the regents and their advisors—and the two tiny tiger cubs. They rolled and romped as if they'd always been a part of the Summer Court.

The current and former Dark Kings had arrived; their semi-human consort, Leslie, was not there. And as Siobhan looked around the jungle-like room, she realized with a near human awkwardness that she was currently sitting in a room with her two past lovers, her future lover, and her best friend.

Tavish looked uncomfortable, so she leaned over and kissed him speechless. He was still sore from the injury Urian had inflicted, but he was upright and therefore determined to be at the meeting.

"Well done!" Irial said. "That's one way to keep the old boy in the Summer Court."

"Irial!" Niall and Aislinn said simultaneously. The tigers pounced into Aislinn's lap, and she gently put them on the floor.

Tavish shrugged slightly. "He's not wrong."

When no one spoke, he added, "I'd still rather we murder

you than meet with you, but my queen, my friend"—he nodded toward Niall—"and my . . ."

"Lover," Siobhan filled in. "Beloved, I hope?"

He squeezed her hand and repeated, "and my beloved seem to think you have redeeming qualities."

"They are sometimes not evident, but they are present." Niall took a long drink of whatever libation he was consuming before adding, "The Dark Court appreciates your consideration and patience, Tavish."

Irial opened his mouth to reply, but a band of shadows covered it immediately. The former Dark King raised a brow and looked at Niall pointedly.

Tavish snorted as Niall ignored his own beloved.

"While Irial is not under the command of my court, I will give my word as Dark King that he has no ill will toward your court—or you." Niall looked briefly embarrassed. "And as both a man and king, I want you to know, Siobhan, that I had no idea at first of the way Keenan misused you."

Siobhan did not miss the key omission in that statement. Niall was, however, a creature who ruled the things of nightmares. He had become the Dark, and so he was—and previously had been—more shadowed than sunlit.

"You were good to me." Siobhan looked at Irial. "Both of you." Then she shrugged and added, "If Ash didn't need me, I'd thought to defect to your court."

"I thought as much," Irial said quietly, as the shadow-wrought gag vanished. He looked immeasurably pleased with himself as he noted, "That's why I provoked him."

"What?" Tavish asked.

He tapped his own chest. "Chaos, my dears. Cha-os. My lovely granddaughter needs you, and love"-- Irial looked around at them—"love makes madness seem rational. If you love our girl Siobhan--"

"Woman," Siobhan interjected. "Not a girl."

"And not yours," Tavish added. "My woman."

Aislinn laughed. "Well played, grandfather."

And at that, Irial preened. "Love. For it, we would do the impossible."

"Yes, but could we address the topic at hand?" Niall's tone was stern, but no one there could miss the look in his eyes as he glanced at the embodiment of Chaos. The Dark King was in agreement—and in love.

"And perhaps after that, discuss the topic of what gifts one can send the Summer Queen?" Siobhan added.

"She likes them," Irial said, pointing at the sleeping tigers curled into the Summer Queen's lap. "It was an excellent gift."

Tavish lifted his glass to the Dark King and then to the Summer Queen. "I do not envy either you."

Irial frowned, but after a moment, he sighed loudly and said, "Now, let us address the matter at hand. My lost son . . ."

End

*A*vailable now: *Cold Iron Heart*

How far would you go to escape fate?

In this prequel to the international bestselling WICKED LOVELY series, the Faery Courts collide a century before the mortals in *Wicked Lovely* are born.

Thelma Foy, a jeweler with the Second Sight in iron-bedecked 1890s New Orleans, wasn't expecting to be caught in a faery conflict. Tam can see through the glamours faeries wear to hide themselves from mortals, but if her secret were revealed, the fey would steal her eyes, her life, or her freedom. So, Tam doesn't respond when they trail thorn-crusted finger-tips through her hair at the French Market or when the Dark King sings along with her in the bayou.

But when the Dark King, Irial, rescues her, Tam must confront everything she thought she knew about faeries, men, and love.

Too soon, New Orleans is filling with faeries who are looking for her, and Irial is the only one who can keep her safe.

Unbeknownst to Tam, she is the prize in a centuries-old fight between Summer Court and Winter Court. To protect her, Irial must risk a war he can't win--or surrender the first mortal woman he's loved.

. . .

REVIEWS:

"Set against the lush backdrop of 1890s New Orleans, Marr's spellbinding prequel to the Wicked Lovely urban fantasy series invites readers back into the world of the fae. . . . The resulting conflict delivers all the magic, intrigue, and romance that Marr's fans expect. Readers will be pleased." -- Publisher's Weekly

"WHAT A DELIGHT TO discover how much I loved being back in the Wicked Lovely world, discovering details about beloved characters that made me want to race back for a series reread. This is Irial's story set in 1890s New Orleans, brimming with faerie court drama and steamy romance. Can we. and should we, outrun fate? And if so, are we prepared for the consequences? I could not put it down." --Angela Mann, Kepler's Books, Menlo Park CA

"SET 100 years before the events in Wicked Lovely, Cold Iron Heart finds Irial, the king of the Dark Court, in New Orleans and entranced by a mortal. Is his interest in Thelma Foy just a passing fascination, or could it change the course of her life and the world forever? Melissa Marr masterfully rises to challenge of writing a prequel by both expanding on the mythology of the original series while telling a story that exists wholly on its own. Fans of the series will inhale this delicious glimpse into Irial's past."-- John McDougall, Murder by the Book, Houston, TX.

ON THE AUDIO EDITION:

"In this prequel to the Wicked Lovely Novel series, narrators Kristin James and Tim Paige--both gifted with rich, easily distinguishable voices--immerse the listener in the elegant, fascinating, deadly, and intriguing world of the Summer and Winter Faery Courts. Lovely jeweler Thelma Foy, who has the second sight and can see faeries, catches the eye of the Dark King himself. Unbeknownst to Thelma, she is the key to ending the battle between the two courts. James has a lilting, lush, and whispery voice that perfectly captures Thelma. Paige has an affected mien that is equally perfect for the gorgeous and hedonistic king. This listen is wicked--wickedly enjoyable." --A.C.P. © AudioFile 2020

"I loved *The Wicked and The Dead*! A sassy, ass-kicking heroine, a deliciously mysterious fae hero, and a wonderful mix of action and romance. Add that to Melissa's usual great world-building, and I'm already looking forward to book 2!"
— Jeaniene Frost, *NYT* Bestselling Author

The Wicked & The Dead is AVAILABLE NOW!

In near-future New Orleans, *draugar*, again-walkers, are faster and stronger than most humans, but not venomous until they are a century old. Until then, they shamble and bite. Since not everyone wants to see their relatives end up that way, Geneviève Crowe makes her living beheading the dead.

But now, her magic has gone sideways, and the only person strong enough to help her is the one man who could tempt her to think about picket fences: Eli Stonecroft, a faery who chose to be a bar-owner in New Orleans rather than live in *Elphame*.

When human businessmen start turning up as *draugar*, the queen of the again-walkers and the wealthy son of one of the victims, both hire Geneviève to figure it out. She works to keep her magic in check, the dead from crawling out of their graves, and enough money for a future that might be a lot longer than she'd like. Neither her heart nor her life are safe now that she's juggling a faery, murder, and magic.

Available 2022
Pre-Order Now
Dark Sun: A Wicked Lovely Novel

When the bestselling WICKED LOVELY series ended, the Faery Courts were in order. In the years following, peace was still tenuous, but every court seemed devoted to balance.

But now, Urian—son of the former Dark King and the fated Summer Queen, Thelma Foy—has decided to claim his destiny.

Urian knew the secrets that protected his relatives--both the mortal and the faery ones--since childhood. After the Summer Queen claimed the throne that should have been his mother's and a lowly advisor claimed the throne that was his father's, Uri is done hiding. The Dark Summer Prince is ready to claim one—or both—of the thrones that should rightfully be his.

When Urian discovers Kyla, unaware of her ancestry, he finally has the ally—or general—he's needed. . . whether or not she agrees.

Far from the world of the fey, Kyla has spent her life aware that her bloodlines aren't as mortal as those around her. When one of the creatures she's been told to hide from discovers her in the desert, she decides to protect her human family by finding her place in the world of the faeries. She can't trust Uri, but she feels drawn to him in a way she never imagined.

Secrets are revealed. Peace is threatened. And neither family ties nor accidental love can keep the balance between the courts now.

PRAISE FOR THE WICKED LOVELY SERIES:

"Marr offers readers a fully imagined faery world that runs alongside an everyday world, which even non-fantasy (or faerie) lovers will want to delve into" *--Publisher's Weekly* (starred review)

"This is a magical novel... the first book in a trilogy that will guarantee to have you itching for the next installment." *Bliss*

"Fans of the fey world will devour this sequel to Wicked Lovely. Marr has created a world both harsh and lush, at once urban and natural." *--School Library Journal*

"Complex and involving." *-New York Times Book Review*

PRAISE FOR GRAVEMINDER:

"If anyone can put the goth in Southern Gothic, it's Melissa Marr. . . . She's also careful to ensure that the book's wider themes —how and if we accept the roles life assigns us, and what happens to us when we refuse them—matter to us as

much as the multiple cases of heebie-jeebies she doles out..."
—NPR.org

"Spooky enough to please but not too disturbing to read in bed."—*Washington Post*

"Dark and dreamy. . . . Rod Serling would have loved *Graveminder*. . . . Marr is not tapping into the latest horde of zombie novels, she's created a new kind of undead creature. . . . A creatively creepy gothic tale for grown-ups."—*USA Today*

"Plan ahead to read this one, because you won't be able to put it down! Haunting, captivating, brilliant!" —*Library Journal* (starred review)

"Marr serves up a quirky dark fantasy fashioned around themes of fate, free will—and zombies. . . . Well-drawn characters and their dramatic interactions keep the tale loose and lively." —*Publishers Weekly*

"The emotional dance between Rebekkah and Byron will captivate female readers. . . . Fantasy-horror fans will demand more." —*Kirkus Reviews*

"No one builds worlds like Melissa Marr." —Charlaine Harris, *New York Times* bestselling author of the Sookie Stackhouse series

"Welcome to the return of the great American gothic." —Del Howison, Bram Stoker Award-winning editor of *Dark Delicacies*

ABOUT THE AUTHOR

Melissa Marr is a former university literature instructor who writes fiction for adults, teens, and children. Her books have been translated into twenty-eight languages and have been bestsellers internationally (Germany, France, Sweden, Australia, et. al.) as well as domestically. She is best known for the Wicked Lovely series for teens, *Graveminder* for adults, and *Bunny Roo, I Love You*. In her free time, she practices medieval swordfighting, kayaks, hikes, and raises kids and chickens in the Arizona desert.

Visit her online:
http://www.melissamarrbooks.com

facebook.com/MelissaMarrBooks
twitter.com/melissa_marr
goodreads.com/melissa_marr